irises

irises

FRANCISCO X. STORK

ARTHUR A. LEVINE BOOKS

An Imprint of Scholastic Inc.

All rights reserved. Published by Arthur A. Levine Books, an imprint of
Scholastic Inc., *Publishers since 1920*. SCHOLASTIC and the LANTERN LOGO are
trademarks and/or registered trademarks of Scholastic Inc.

Library of Congress Cataloging-in-Publication Data
Stork, Francisco X.
Irises / by Francisco X. Stork. — 1st ed.
p. cm.
Summary: Kate, eighteen, and Mary, sixteen, must make some adult decisions
about the course their lives should take when their loving but old-fashioned
father dies suddenly, leaving them with their mother, who has been in a
persistent vegetative state since an accident four years earlier.
ISBN 978-0-545-15135-1 (hardcover : alk. paper) [1. Coma — Fiction. 2. Sisters —
Fiction. 3. Death — Fiction. 4. Identity — Fiction.] I. Title.
PZ7.S88442Ir 2012
[Fic] — dc23
2011023798

10 9 8 7 6 5 4 3 2 1   12 13 14 15 16
Printed in the U.S.A. 23
First edition, January 2012

FOR MY WIFE, JILL

PROLOGUE

K ate had finally agreed to pose under the willow tree. Mother came and stood behind Mary at her easel. She placed her hand on Mary's shoulder. "It's beautiful!"

"Let me see." Kate started to get up.

"No!" Mary and Mother shouted at the same time. They looked at each other and laughed.

Kate sat down again reluctantly. "I want to see."

"Be patient," Mother said.

"How much longer?"

"Soon," Mary said.

"I've been sitting here for hours." Kate shifted in the wooden chair. The late afternoon sun illuminated her face. A slight breeze shook the leaves of the tree.

Mother touched the back of Mary's head. "Kate looks like a saint. There's a halo around her."

"I tried to capture the light that surrounds her."

Mother bent to examine the painting. "The light seems to be coming from inside of her too."

"It *is* coming from inside of her. It's her inner light. Can you see it, Mama?" Mary stopped painting for a moment and looked at Kate.

"What light? Are you all done now?" Kate asked.

"Almost. I just need to touch up the lips. I'll finish the background later."

"Her hair looks blacker than it really is," Mother said.

"The black is dark now because it's wet. It'll be just right once the paint dries."

Mary continued painting in silence. Mother walked to the back fence and touched the bud of a white climbing rose. "Mary, these roses you planted are going to be so beautiful when they bloom."

They all heard the phone ring inside the house.

"That's probably for me." Kate made a move to stand up.

"Papa will get that," Mother said quickly. "Let your sister finish."

"Five more minutes, Kate, that's all. Do you know how long I've been wanting to do this?"

Mother stood next to Mary again. "If you only knew what I had to promise to get her to sit for you."

Kate said, "Shhh, Mama, that's our secret, remember?"

"What did you promise her?" Mary looked up at Mother.

"Should I tell?" Mother asked Kate.

"No."

"Yes," Mary countered.

"Keep on painting, Mary. I don't think you're going to be able to keep your sister in that chair for too much longer."

"Okay, but tell me what you promised her."

Mother looked at Kate. "I'm sorry, sweetie, I have to tell her. Kate and I are going to visit Aunt Julia in California."

"Just the two of you?" Mary asked.

"You'll need to stay with Papa and help him around the house. I promised Kate a special trip before she starts high school. In two years, when you graduate from middle school, we'll take a special trip as well."

"I just wish it didn't have to be Aunt Julia's," Kate said.

"You're going to like this trip," Mama said. "I have a surprise planned for you."

"I think I'm done," Mary said. "I put a touch of brown on the hair, just like you asked."

Mother stood back. "Wow!"

"Can I see?" Kate came to where Mary stood. Her eyes opened wide. "Is that really me?"

"Of course it's you."

"I look beautiful," Kate said, her voice full of discovery.

"I touched up your bad spots," Mary said, smiling.

"Can I see that brush for a second?" Kate took the brush from Mary's hand.

"What are you going to do? Don't touch my painting!" Kate swung the brush like a sword and tried to paint Mary's cheek. "Nooo!" Mary screamed and ran. Kate chased her.

"Kate!" Mother laughed. She ran after the girls. Kate cornered Mary by the chain-link fence and dabbed her sister's arms and face with paint. Mother tried to take the brush from Kate's hand and ended up with a brown splotch on her forehead.

The three of them burst out laughing.

Four Years Later

Kate and her father sat in the shade of the willow tree, side by side in two wooden chairs. It was unusually hot for an April day in El Paso. Father had taken off the black coat he always wore to church, and Kate had tied her hair back in a ponytail. Two glasses of lemonade stood on the small wooden table between the chairs.

"Kate." Her father's voice was unusually soft, almost a whisper. "I noticed that you were not paying attention to Reverend Soto's sermon."

"I'm sorry, Papa," she said, looking down at her feet.

"A part of me, the vain part, would like to think that your lack of attention was due to the fact that it wasn't me delivering the sermon." He stopped as if waiting for her to realize that this was an attempt at humor. But if it was, she didn't notice it. He went on, "But I've noticed the same lack of interest the past few months, long before Reverend Soto came to the church. I've hesitated to bring it up."

For a moment, Kate thought of telling her father what was occupying her mind, but she decided against it. "I have been a little distracted, thinking about school. It's nothing you should worry about, Papa." She looked up and saw a single gray cloud in the otherwise light blue sky.

After a while, her father spoke again. "It used to be that I could look out into the congregation and find you attentive to every word of the Gospel and every word of the sermon."

Kate tried to think of a funny reply, something that would make her father smile, that would lighten the conversation. Her father was so solemn, and she loved him for that, but there were times when she wished she had a father like her best friend, Bonnie, did — a father who cracked jokes, who could understand the ways of an eighteen-year-old.

"Is something the matter?" he asked.

She sneaked a look at her watch. She wished Mary would come out and tell her that the meat loaf was burning. "Oh, Papa, you worry too much. It's just that I have so much to think about these days. I'm taking some very hard courses."

"Yes. But if that were all, I wouldn't be talking to you now, the way I am. I believe there is more to it than that."

"Like what?" She didn't mean to sound as if the question scared her.

"How is your soul?" He looked at her softly.

"Pardon me?"

"The state of your soul, your faith. How is it doing these days?"

"It's fine," she said quickly, aware that quite possibly, she had just lied to her father. She saw the sadness in his face, his disappointment at her unwillingness to share with him what-ever was in her mind. "I have to finish cooking dinner," she said kindly.

He closed his eyes, then opened them again as he spoke. "I have tried my best to raise you and Mary. After your mother . . . entered her current condition, after the accident, I tried to get you to be self-sufficient. I have endeavored to make you strong. I wanted to fortify your heart against sorrow. I believe I suc-ceeded, but I might have been overzealous. You and Mary are strong in different ways, but strong nevertheless. I wonder sometimes if I wasn't too extreme in my efforts and now you are too strong. You can withstand any blows that life hits you with, but . . . at what cost?"

Kate stared at the chain-link fence, where beautiful white and red climbing roses bloomed. It was strange to hear her father talk like this — not just the words but the tone. She had never heard him confess to any faults, and now he spoke wearily, as if he had suddenly discovered that human speech was exhausting. "You've done all right," she said, trying to cheer him.

"I've never worried about Mary. She will find a way to keep her faith. You're the one I worry about."

"I know," she said. Mary had spent the whole sermon draw-ing on the small pad of blank paper she always carried in her purse, and yet Kate understood why her father was not wor-ried about her sister's faith or her interest in the sermon. Faith was in Mary's blood.

She started to get up, but her father touched her arm. *One more moment, please*, he seemed to say. She sat down again.

"I want to tell you something today." He was having trouble breathing, and there were drops of sweat on his forehead despite the shade.

"Are you all right, Papa?"

He waved her question away. "I want to tell you this. I have tried to do my best as a father. I should have been more of a mother as well. Maybe I should have been more lenient, more understanding of young people, of young girls. If I was strict, it was because I was afraid that, without rules, you would not be able to care for yourselves when the time came." He coughed and put his hand on his chest.

"Would you like to go inside now?" she asked, concerned.

"Yes, I believe I will go inside and lie down for a while. I don't really feel like dinner today."

"Maybe you will later. I'll make a plate and save it for you."

"Okay, but let me finish telling you what I want to tell you." He looked at her and spoke slowly, deliberately, as if he wanted his words to be remembered. "You are the oldest in the family. If something ever happens to me, you will need to put the family first. You'll think it's not fair for such a burden to be placed on you, but that burden will fall on you nevertheless." He waited for her to look into his eyes. When she did, he said, "Without love, the burden will be too heavy for you to bear." Then, as if remembering something he had read or heard a long time ago, he said, "Love makes everything that is heavy light."

He paused and then tapped her forearm. "All right, I'm ready to go now."

2

Mary saw her father enter the house and shuffle toward his bedroom, his legs trembling as if they were about to crumble.

"Is Papa okay?" Mary asked Kate when they sat down for lunch.

"He's just tired," Kate said.

The girls started to eat in silence.

"Simon's going to pick me up in half an hour," Kate announced. "I'll be back around four."

"But you said you would take care of Mama while Papa goes on his visits. Renata and I are going to the museum. They have that new Georgia O'Keeffe exhibit I want to see."

Kate lifted her eyes from her plate.

"I had to beg Papa forever to let me go. You know how he feels about painting. He even called Renata's mother to make sure she was okay with taking us."

A small, vertical wrinkle appeared in the middle of Kate's forehead. She nodded to acknowledge that what Mary said was true. "I'm sorry. I'd forgotten I have a calculus test tomorrow. I really need to study with Simon. Can you go next week? I can get Simon to take you."

"Why can't you and Simon study here?" Mary asked.

"I can't study here." Kate's eyes darted toward their parents' bedroom. "I'm sorry."

"I'll see if Renata can go next week," Mary said reluctantly.

"Thank you," Kate said. Mary saw a shadow of guilt cross her face. "Look, I totally forgot about your museum, and I promised Simon I would study with him."

"It's okay." Mary tried not to sound hurt.

They did the dishes together, although usually when Kate cooked, Mary did them alone. It occurred to Mary that maybe Kate wanted to talk about whatever was churning in her head, for something surely was. But they washed the dishes quietly until Mary spoke. "Do you think Papa likes Reverend Soto?"

"Why do you ask?"

"I think Papa might be worried that the church hired Reverend Soto to replace him. Do you like him?"

"Reverend Soto?"

"You like him, I know you do. I've seen the way you look at him."

This brought a smile to Kate's lips. "He's young for a minister, don't you think?"

"How old do you think he is?" Mary asked.

"Twenty-two," Kate said.

"You seem very certain."

"I heard the church ladies talk this morning. They're all in love with him. They think he's movie-star good-looking."

"He's sorta, kinda cute, but not movie-star good-looking," Mary said. "Do *you* think he's cute?"

"I think he's good-looking."

"Simon is more."

"Mmm. In a different way. Reverend Soto has an air of mystery about him," Kate said with a grin.

Mary was happy that the conversation had put Kate in a better mood. "What I don't understand is why he's here," she said. "Papa doesn't seem to want to say too much about it."

"Reverend Soto is here for a couple of months until he finds a more permanent position. It's kind of like an internship, to build up actual experience. I think his family is close to Mr. Lucas, who convinced the deacons to take him on."

"How can he be a minister when he's barely twenty-two?"

"Father says he's super smart. He went to school summers and has his Master of Divinity. That's all you need to be a minister in the Church of God."

"But don't you think Papa's worried, really?"

"Father needs all the help he can get. He's got nothing to fear from Reverend Soto." Kate looked out the kitchen window. "The roses you planted are beautiful," she said.

Mary remembered that she was going to miss the exhibit she had wanted to see for so long. She especially wanted to study Georgia O'Keeffe's flowers, the way she made the petals seem so delicate, so full of light and life. Who knew if she could get Renata's mother to take them next week? Who knew if Papa would give her permission again?

"Kate, I really want to see that exhibit."

Kate looked at her as if she didn't know what the word *exhibit* meant. Then she seemed to remember. "Oh. Sure."

"If for some reason Renata's mom can't take me, you and Simon will need to take me. It's really important to me. Going to that exhibit is like you wanting to get an A on your test. It's no different."

"Let's not start that discussion again," Kate said.

"It's just that you never take my art seriously. Papa doesn't either. There's no difference between me wanting to be a painter and you wanting to be a doctor."

"I think your art is important. So does Father. It's just that there are other things we need to take care of first," Kate said softly. She looked like she was about to say more, but she was interrupted by the honk of Simon's car.

From the front door, Mary watched Kate get into the red Impala. The car coughed a puff of white exhaust and then sped away. One moment Kate was drying the dishes and a moment later she was out the door. It was almost as if Kate felt there was not enough air inside the house.

Mary needed to call Renata to tell her about the change in plans. Then she would check on Mama and make sure she was okay, and after that, she would go to her room and work on her painting. Three months ago, she had decided to copy as many of Van Gogh's paintings as she could in order to learn his techniques. Today she was working on his *Irises*. It was a painting she had been struggling with for a long time.

"But she said she would take care of your mother so we could go to the museum," Renata complained over the phone.

"My mom is all set to take us. She's looking for the car keys right now."

"Kate had to go to Simon's to study for a test. We can go next week, can't we?"

"I can't next week. My mother's forcing me to go to my aunt Luisa's birthday party. I can't believe how much you let Kate push you around."

"I know," Mary admitted. It was hard to argue with Renata, especially over the phone. "Can you come over later this afternoon?"

"I don't know. I'll call you. Bye."

The best thing about Renata, Mary thought, was that as much as she liked to pretend she was angry, it was always just pretend.

The only telephone in the house was on a TV tray in the hall between Mary and Kate's room and their father's office. The girls liked to joke that their father placed the phone there so he could monitor their conversations, and since there was no place to sit, the conversations tended to be short. Mary returned the receiver to its cradle and walked to her parents' bedroom.

Mama lay calmly on one of the two single beds, her unfocused eyes barely open. Papa was on the bed next to hers, on his back with his shoes still on. Mary sensed something unusual as soon as she saw him. She stopped as if she had heard a noise in the dark. The sounds of labored breathing that her father made when he was asleep were not there.

She walked over to her father's bed, sat on the edge, and put her hand on his silent chest. The realization that he was dead sent a shuddering shock through her body. She restrained a sob and, after a few moments, she closed her father's eyes and combed his white hair with her fingers. A soft radiance glowed from his body. She watched the light slowly dim and then disappear. Then she let herself cry.

Simon's telephone number was inside the address book Kate kept in the middle drawer of her desk. Simon's mother answered first, and then Kate came to the phone.

"What do you mean Father's dead?" Kate shouted into the phone.

"I went to check on Mama after you left and he had died."

"Oh, oh my —" Kate stopped herself. "Did you call 9-1-1?"

"No."

"Do it now! Never mind, I'll do it! I'll be right over."

Mary hung up the phone. She examined Kate's words carefully, the way she examined an object she was about to paint. Why didn't it occur to her to call 911 right away? Why hadn't she panicked when she saw that her father was not breathing? There, by his side, she felt that his soul needed time to leave his body quietly. She was sure she had acted the way Papa would have wanted. But would Kate understand?

3

Kate arrived as the paramedics were trying to resuscitate her father's body. She held Mary's hand while one of them jolted her father a few inches off the bed with the shock of the defibrillator. After a few more tries, the paramedic shook her head and began to pack the equipment. "His body is still warm," she told them. "We might have saved him if you'd called us earlier."

Kate glanced quickly at Mary and released her hand. She walked to her father and touched his forehead with the tips of her fingers. A wave of sorrow settled in her throat but did not materialize in tears. Surely, the tears would come later when there was no one looking.

Kate left the room to call Dr. Rulfo and the funeral director. She glanced again at Mary, who was now holding their mother's hand. Why hadn't Mary called 911? Why had she let Father die? She was immediately glad that she had not asked Mary those questions. She could feel some weird chemistry taking place in herself, transforming sadness into blame.

"Simon!" she said when she saw him in the hall. She hugged him, and he wrapped his strong arms around her.

"I'm so sorry, Kate," he said, stroking her hair.

"Can you get me a glass of water?" she asked him. He left her to go to the kitchen. When he returned, she took the glass and went to her room to look for Dr. Rulfo's phone number. Her address book was not in her desk drawer where she had left it, and it occurred to her that Mary probably took it when she called Simon's house. She was amazed at how well her mind was functioning.

It took Dr. Rulfo only ten minutes to get there. Dr. Rulfo had been the family doctor forever. After the accident, when the hospital notified Father that they would terminate Mother's life support unless he was able to find another health provider for her, it was Dr. Rulfo who accepted responsibility for her at Father's request and arranged for her to be taken care of at home. He visited Mother every week.

Dr. Rulfo examined Father's body. "Your father's heart simply stopped beating," he told Kate when he came out of the room. "I don't think an autopsy needs to be performed. I'll talk to the medical examiner." Dr. Rulfo suddenly stopped and his eyes moistened. Kate reached out and touched his arm.

"You were always good to him," Kate said to Dr. Rulfo.

"I'm going to miss him," said Dr. Rulfo.

Mr. Lopez, the funeral director, and his assistant were outside waiting for Dr. Rulfo to sign the death certificate. As soon as the doctor left, Mr. Lopez sat down with Kate and Simon. There were decisions to be made. Burial or cremation? Wake? Open or closed casket? When would the church service take place? In a way, it was good to have things to think about. Kate could feel grief and uncontrollable thoughts waiting for her, ready to invade as soon as there were no more details to arrange.

When they finished discussing the arrangements, Mr. Lopez asked Kate and Simon if they wanted to go in and say good-bye before he removed the body. Simon deferred to Kate, and Kate nodded. She realized for the first time since Dr. Rulfo arrived that Mary had been in the room with their father all this time. Mary may have been the one to find Father dead, Kate thought, but at least she had been the last one to speak to him.

She stood up, disturbed by her own thinking. What was happening to her? It was crazy to feel competitive with Mary over their father's death. She rubbed her forehead with the back of her hand and tried to wipe the thoughts away as she walked to the bedroom. Mary was sitting next to Mother, still holding her hand.

"Can I have a few moments alone with Father?" There was kindness in Kate's voice. Mary smiled and slowly left the room, closing the door behind her.

Kate stood next to her father. Not more than three hours ago they had been talking in the backyard, or rather, he had been talking and she had been barely listening. She remembered how she had looked at her watch, and she felt a burst of tears in her chest ready to explode. She took her father's hand gently to her lips and kissed it. The image of her father delivering the children's sermon that morning came to her. The children had been captivated by his simple words.

Then after a while the uncontrollable thoughts continued their attack. *Now you are free*, they said to her. *You can leave El Paso. You can go to Stanford.*

Kate ordered them to go away. She focused again on the conversation with her father. *I wanted to fortify your heart against sorrow. I believe I succeeded, but I might have been over-zealous.* That's what Father had said. Was her heart so fortified now that she couldn't cry?

She walked over to Mother's bed and sat on the edge, just as she had found Mary sitting when she entered the room. She took her mother's hand and remembered.

It was the summer before her freshman year. She and Mother were visiting Aunt Julia in San Jose, California — the trip Mother had promised her. Kate had been the best student in her class for the past three years, and this trip was a reward for all her hard work.

One morning, Mother woke her up earlier than usual.

"Come on, lazybones," she said, shaking Kate awake.

"Where are we going?"

"It's a surprise!"

Aunt Julia had already left for work. They caught a bus to downtown San Jose. Then they climbed on the Caltrain, got off in Palo Alto, and took a shuttle to Stanford University.

"Why are we going to Stanford?" Kate kept asking as the small white bus made its way through the palm-lined streets.

"You'll see," her mother answered.

When she stepped off the shuttle, Kate was awestruck. Stanford had everything El Paso lacked. It was green and colorful, not dry and brown. She loved to study, and here was a place brimming with an atmosphere of learning, of curiosity. She saw the aged red roofs of the buildings, the students speeding to class on their bicycles, and she felt at once a sense of belonging. This was the place she had always dreamed about.

"You want to be a doctor, don't you?" Mother said.

"Yes," Kate answered.

"Well, here's where you're going to study to be one."

"Here? At Stanford? This is one of the best universities in the whole country. How do you know about it?"

Her mother smiled. "When we were growing up in San Jose, your grandfather worked here as a gardener. He loved Stanford. On Sundays, he and Grandma would sometimes bring your aunt Julia and me to spend the day here, even though he'd spent the whole week working here already. It was his dream for Julia and me to come here someday. We would be the first ever in the family to go to college. But Julia wasn't interested in college, and I married your father right after high school. Besides, I don't even know if I could have gotten in. You have to be real smart to get into Stanford. Smart like you."

"But it's so expensive. . . ."

"You'll need to work extra hard to get a scholarship."

"Papa's never going to let me come here. He'll want me to go to UTEP."

The smile on Mother's face disappeared. She grabbed Kate by her shoulders and turned her so that they were facing each other. "You are *so* smart," her mother told her, looking deep into her eyes. "That kind of intelligence is a gift that you have to develop. If you want to come to Stanford, then we'll figure out how. God wants you to be as smart as you can, to hold nothing back, to be the best doctor you can be so you can help others. This is the kind of place where you can be the very, very best. You have to promise me you'll work very hard in the next four years so you can come here if you want to. Do you promise?"

Kate touched her mother's hand. "I promise."

"Do you think you'd like to come here?"

Kate laughed, excited. "Yes, yes, yes!"

"You must keep this a secret between us until the time is right. Okay?"

"Okay."

"Promise me you won't tell anyone. Not even Mary."

"I promise."

"Good. See, now you have a dream that will carry you through. No one can keep you from your dream unless you let them."

"Why would I let them?"

Mother was quiet for a second, and then she said softly, "Because you love them."

"Is that why you didn't try to come to Stanford? Because of your love for Papa?"

The only answer was a silent smile.

Mother moaned and Kate snapped out of her reverie. For a moment it almost seemed as if Mother had squeezed her hand, encouraging her not to forget the promise she'd made. She let go of her mother's hand quickly and stood up. Such things were impossible.

But she stood for a moment looking down at Mother. Despite what had happened to her mother, Kate had followed through on her promise. She had the best grades and the best SAT scores of any senior at Riverside High School. Ms. Pauli, her counselor, had told her she could go to any university she wanted. Kate knew her father had expected her to attend the University of Texas at El Paso, but she had also applied to Stanford without telling him. She thought the best strategy was to wait and see if she was accepted and if she got a scholarship, and then present her case.

And now he would never know. She watched her father's face and she was surprised by the gentleness of his features. She had held him up to be stern and unmoving so many times in the past. Had she gotten it all wrong? Had she misinterpreted his love? She walked over to his side again, lifted his hand, kissed it again, and held it to her cheek, and then finally the tears came.

4

Reverend Soto came the next morning. He wore black pants, a black jacket, a black shirt, and a white collar. Mary shook his hand and was struck by the sorrowful expression in his eyes.

"I am so sorry," he said. "I tried to come yesterday, but I was out of town visiting my mother and I didn't get the message until very late. How are you holding up?"

"We're okay," Kate said.

"Your father was an amazing man. He was the soul of this church, of this community."

"Thank you," Kate said softly.

The ladies from the church who had come with breakfast went into the kitchen. Kate and Mary sat side by side on the sofa, and Reverend Soto sank down in the armchair in front of them. Mary lifted her eyes and studied him carefully. He had a deep, quiet, soothing kind of voice today. It wasn't his intense, energetic sermon voice. Today he sought to calm and console.

"Okay," Reverend Soto said. He took a black notepad and a silver pen from his coat pocket. "Let's go over some details for this coming week. I understand from Mr. Lopez that you want to have visiting hours at the funeral home on one evening only."

"Yes," Kate answered without hesitation. "Tomorrow."

"And you want to have the funeral and the church service the day after tomorrow?"

"We would like to." The ladies of the church had objected that the rushed schedule did not give people enough time, but Kate was firm in her decision, and although she had not been asked for her opinion, Mary agreed. She felt that Papa would not have liked to have his body exhibited longer than necessary.

Reverend Soto wrapped his hands around his right knee. "Are you sure you don't want to have two evenings of visiting hours? You want to make sure that all of the church people —"

"They can all go tomorrow." Kate cut him off. "Many of them have come to see us today already." She nodded toward the kitchen. "Everyone knows about it by now. It's not that big a church."

"What about family from out of town? Don't they need time to get here?"

"There's no one coming," Kate replied.

Mary spoke up. "Our aunt Julia lives in California, but she won't be able to make it to the funeral. We called her and she's coming in a few days to be with us."

"It must be hard for you not to have any family. Will you be okay financially?" Reverend Soto asked.

Kate changed the subject. "Are you going to say the eulogy at the funeral?"

"Yes," Reverend Soto answered. "The deacons have asked me to conduct all the services."

"But you didn't know him. You didn't know Papa," Mary said suddenly, her voice rising up a notch.

"Mary!" Kate exclaimed.

"It's okay," Reverend Soto said.

Mary couldn't believe she'd been so rude, but decided she might as well continue. "Why can't Father Hogan speak at the service? He was Papa's best friend." It was nothing personal, she told herself. She was only expressing what her father would have wished.

"Well . . ." Reverend Soto tried to move to the edge of the armchair, but the hole created by its broken springs pulled him down. "It's just that Father Hogan is not of our church. St. John's is a Catholic church."

"Why does that matter?" Mary saw the questioning look that Kate was giving her but kept going. "Papa would want Father Hogan to speak, I'm sure of it."

Reverend Soto smiled nervously. He glanced toward Kate for support.

"Mary, Reverend Soto is now the minister. It's up to him to say the eulogy."

He seemed to be thinking. Then he suggested, "What if I go back to the deacons and ask them if Father Hogan can take part in the service? I'm sure that will be all right."

"Thank you," Mary said. "I'm sorry, I didn't mean to —"

"It's okay." He stopped her. "You don't need to explain. I'm sure your father would want Father Hogan to say a few words."

Mrs. Mendoza came out of the kitchen with a cup of coffee for Reverend Soto. "Can I get you girls anything?" Mary and Kate shook their heads.

Reverend Soto lifted the cup to his lips, sipped, and then placed it back on its saucer. He wiped his mouth with a paper napkin. "I know it must feel wrong to have a stranger speak about your father. But what I want to tell you is that in the month that I've been here, I got to know your father a little. I got to see what kind of person he was. I think I know him as a pastor. But what I wanted to do today is have you share with me some of your memories of him so I can know him as a father, as a person."

Mary leaned back on the sofa. She felt her mind go blank. What memories of Papa would she choose to share with the congregation? It was strange to force herself to search for a memory of him. It seemed more appropriate for memories to appear of their own accord than to be willed into existence. She turned to look at Kate and saw in her face a similar struggle.

"He was a good father," Kate said, after a long silence.

"Can you give me an example?" Reverend Soto urged. "Something I can use in my eulogy?"

Kate thought. "He let me volunteer at the hospital every Saturday for a few hours. It was hard for him because I could have been helping here at home or working at the Red

Sombrero, making more money for us. But he knew how important it was to have an extracurricular activity." She talked as if she were speaking to herself, remembering.

Reverend Soto didn't quite understand.

"For college," Mary explained.

"Ahh. That's good," he said. "What about you?" he asked, turning to Mary.

"I can't think of anything right now." She was thinking of how difficult it had been to get Papa to let her stay an extra hour after school to work on her painting. Most of her memories of Papa were of him saying no to the things that she and Kate wanted to do. She tried to think of times when she remembered him laughing or even smiling, but she couldn't.

"I understand. But if a memory comes to mind before the service, will you give me a call?" he asked them.

"Yes," Kate said. She smiled at Reverend Soto. Mary remembered that yesterday, while they were washing the dishes, Kate had said he was good-looking. Reverend Soto had carefully combed, wavy black hair, and an ample forehead that made him look intelligent. His dark, thick eyebrows gave him an intense look. *Cute* was not the right word for him. He was attractive, good-looking, handsome — very. He was much better-looking than Simon, if the truth be known.

He and Kate looked at each other for a few seconds more. "Would it be possible to see your mother?" he asked her.

"Why?" Mary asked. She couldn't help the tone of alarm in her voice.

"I would like to pray for her," he answered calmly.

"It's okay," Kate said to Mary. "Father would have liked him to pray for Mother."

Mary wasn't sure. Papa might have felt as she felt, as if something very private were about to be exposed. Reverend Soto was here to offer condolences, to plan the service. How did seeing Mama fit into all that? But she stood up reluctantly and followed Kate and Reverend Soto. For some inexplicable reason, she felt as if she needed to protect Mama.

Reverend Soto stood on one side of the bed. Mary saw him stare at the feeding tube that connected the dangling plastic bag of liquid food to Mama's stomach. But his face did not have the look she had seen many times when people first encountered Mama — a look of slight terror, as if a corpse had suddenly opened its eyes.

"How long has she been this way?" Reverend Soto asked.

"Almost two years," Kate answered.

Reverend Soto shook his head. Mary couldn't tell exactly what the gesture meant. There was compassion in his expression, but there was also something else.

"And she's been staying with you all this time?"

"She was in a coma for a couple of weeks after the accident. Then she entered the state she's in. It's called a persistent vegetative state." Kate sounded tired. Mary wondered why she was being so polite.

"A persistent vegetative state," he repeated, as if to himself.

"You're familiar with the condition," Kate said.

"Yes," Reverend Soto said. It sounded as if he wished he weren't. "Is there any hope of regaining consciousness?"

"No," said Kate, her head down.

"You don't know that," Mary said to her, raising her voice. "You're not God."

Kate turned, a shocked look on her face. Before she could say anything, Reverend Soto spoke. "I'm sorry, I didn't mean to offend. What's your mother's name?" he quickly asked Kate.

"Catalina."

"Ahh. You're named after her," he said, smiling.

Kate nodded. Reverend Soto lifted his hands and held them over Mama. "Let us pray," he said. His voice got deeper and more solemn. "Lord, we pray for the soul of Reverend Romero and for the soul of Catalina. We pray for Kate and Mary, that you be with them these hard days. Let your Holy Spirit come to console them and guide them in the difficult decisions that await them. Amen."

An awkward silence followed. Then Mary whispered, "Mama's not dead."

"Pardon?" Reverend Soto asked.

"You prayed for Mama's soul like she was dead, like her soul was with Papa's. Her soul is here, with her, with us, right now."

"Mary, what's come over you?" Kate asked.

Mary searched for an answer, but she couldn't find one.

5

Kate and Mary had always shared a bedroom. When they were babies, they slept in adjacent cribs. Later they slept in the same bed. Now they each had a single bed, separated by a nightstand, with a lamp that Kate used to read late into the night. The night after the burial, they lay next to each other in the dark, awake but silent, each enveloped in her own memories and thoughts.

Kate replayed the events of the past few days. They had stood in a receiving line at the funeral home for four hours shaking hands and hearing the same condolences: "I'm sorry for your loss. If there is anything I can do for you, anything at all, please let me know." She smiled to herself now and shook her head. She wondered if any of them had really meant it. Maybe it was the way they said it — like they were trying too hard to sound sincere. What would they say in a month if she called them up and told them they didn't have any money to pay for their mother's care? How would they take care of

Mother? Of themselves? These questions circled tirelessly in her mind.

Then there was Simon. Simon had taken it upon himself to stand next to her in the receiving line, a gesture that bothered her because it expressed that their relationship was more serious than it really was. He had been her boyfriend for a year and a half. Did that give him the right to stand next to her? Maybe it did.

Thank goodness for Bonnie. Every once in a while she would come up to Kate in the receiving line and whisper a comment that would make Kate smile. Other than that, the only good thing about the whole experience had been Reverend Soto. His eulogy had been fiery, the opposite of the mousy eulogies she had always heard. She remembered his voice and the way he looked at her when he spoke. She didn't think the portrait of Father he painted was totally accurate, but it was an inspiring portrait nevertheless. Reverend Soto had described Father as a warm, loving man. Father was a loving man, she agreed, but his love was solid, lasting, hard, and not necessarily warm. It was unfortunate, especially for Mary's sake, that Father Hogan was in Mexico with his church's youth group and was not able to speak.

She knew Mary was awake, but thought she'd ask anyway. "Mary, are you awake?"

"Yes."

"What are you thinking about?"

"I was just thinking about Mama and wondering whether she can tell that Papa died."

Kate was silent for a few moments. "Mary . . . don't do that to yourself. She's not capable of understanding."

"She'll miss him, though, somehow," Mary said. "Do you really think it was all right not to allow any of the people who came to the house to see her? They wanted to pay their respects."

"We made the right decision. It would have seemed like some kind of show, like putting her on display. People would feel sorry for us more than they already do." One of the ladies who came to the house had said, "It's so sad that Catalina is not able to take care of you now that you're all alone." She spoke with such pity in her voice that it made Kate's stomach turn.

"What if Mama knows what's going on deep down?" Mary said.

"Do you really believe that?"

Mary was silent.

Kate continued, "She's not aware of anything. You're creating false hopes for yourself. Her mind is gone and won't ever come back." Her voice was full of tenderness.

There was a long pause, and Kate feared her words might have hurt Mary. But it was important that Mary realize the truth once and for all, especially now that Father was dead. It was just the two of them, and there was no room for illusions.

"I saw Papa's soul leave him. That's why I didn't call 9-1-1," Mary whispered.

"His soul?"

"It was like a beautiful, strange light with a warm glow. When I went to the bedroom to check up on Mama and I saw that he wasn't breathing, I sat next to him on the bed and saw this light, his soul, slowly disappear."

"How do you know it was his soul?" Kate asked.

Mary paused. "I used to see a light coming from inside of people. I saw this light all the time when I painted, and I saw it again when Papa died. I think the light came from his soul. What else could it be?"

"Oh." Kate kept herself from responding. What could she say? Mary was so different from her. She belonged to Father's world, the world of spirits and invisible things. *How is your soul?* Father had asked the afternoon he died. Kate felt that *soul* was just another word for the mental processing that went on inside our heads, for consciousness, and consciousness expired when the body ceased to function — or even before, as with Mother.

She could pinpoint the exact moment when she stopped believing in soul as an entity separate from consciousness. It happened a month or so after Father brought Mother home. Kate was rubbing Mother's legs with alcohol when all of a sudden her mother began to make whimpering noises, as if she were having a bad nightmare.

"Mama, are you okay?" Kate asked instinctively, forgetting her mother's condition. She shook her gently, but the more she shook, the more the whimpering increased until it began to sound like a baby crying. Kate climbed onto the bed and hugged her mother tightly, and her tears came convulsively, in rhythm with the noises her mother was making. She stayed like that, her arms around her mother, long after Mother had returned to her silence.

That was when she stopped believing in a soul, or in another world where souls go after the death of the body, or in a being that is spirit and creates all souls. There could not be a soul trapped inside her mother's body. The sounds her mother made that day, the sounds of anguish, could not be made by a being that still felt pain, a being that at some level was able to understand her own pitiful condition. It would be cruel to have it otherwise.

"Kate," Mary continued, "I know you may not agree with what I did. But I wanted you to know why I didn't call 9-1-1. I was certain he had died and I wanted to let his soul leave his body peacefully."

"You should have called 9-1-1," Kate said.

"But —"

"You could have saved his life."

"His life was gone, Kate." Mary's words came out with force.

"Let's drop it. What's done is done."

Another silence. Then Mary spoke again, changing the subject. "Mrs. Guerney took good care of Mama while we were at the funeral. Thank goodness for Talita and Mrs. Guerney. They're saints."

"Yes, thank goodness for Talita and Mrs. Guerney," Kate agreed. Talita was the nurse who came over for a couple of hours each day to replace the bag and clean the tube that provided Mother's nutrition and hydration. Mrs. Guerney came when Father went out on church business. The rest of the

time, it was Mary and Kate's job to take care of Mother —
putting ointment on her lips, moving her arms and legs gently
so they wouldn't atrophy, changing her diaper. Mary also kept
her company, listening to the radio, talking to her, waiting
for her to wake up one day. Sometimes it seemed as if all their
free time was given over to Mother. Kate's mind came back to
the same questions again: How would they pay for her care
without Father?

"We're on our own now, Mary."

It took a few moments for Mary to respond. "We
have Mama."

Kate sighed. Sometimes it was impossible to talk to Mary.
"Mother is someone we need to take care of. I mean, we need
to take care of ourselves now."

"There's Aunt Julia."

"I don't think we can count on her for any help."

"She's Mama's only sister."

"She didn't even come to the funeral," Kate said.

"She couldn't leave her beauty shop at such short notice.
We did rush things."

"No, we did the right thing. It was too painful to be sitting
around . . . waiting."

"Anyway, you need to be nice to her when she gets here
tomorrow. I know you don't like her."

"I'll try," Kate said grudgingly. But it was going to be hard.
Kate thought Aunt Julia was very bossy.

"We'll be all right, won't we?" There was apprehension in
Mary's voice, as if the possibility that they might not be all
right had just dawned on her.

Kate suddenly remembered that her father had life insurance. She knew about it because one day, a few weeks before, he'd asked her to come to his study. He opened a desk drawer, showed her a folder marked *Personal Documents*, and told her that was where he kept the insurance and tax records and other important papers. She had a fleeting notion to get up and look for the insurance policy, but she decided to wait until morning. She wondered whether the life insurance would be enough. "Yes. We'll be all right."

"At least we have each other," Mary said.

"Yes," Kate answered. She closed her eyes and sighed.

6

What color was a sigh? How would she paint it? It would be impossible to find the right color for it. Purple? Indigo? Indigo with tinges of light blue, maybe. Kate's sigh reminded Mary of Van Gogh's irises, the ones she had been trying to paint.

When Mary was a child, Mama would save her drawings and paintings and show them to Papa when he came home. Mama framed one especially beautiful drawing, a picture of a bald eagle flying on a blue-sky background, with rays of golden light illuminating its flight. Papa kept the picture on his desk until the day Mama came home from the hospital. Then he put it away somewhere. Mary never knew where.

Removing the picture from his desk marked the beginning of Papa's change in attitude toward Mary's paintings. It was as if Mama's accident meant they could no longer waste time on impractical things. He thought that people who painted were weak, unable to survive in the harsh world, and he was afraid for her.

Something else happened to her painting then. Making art had always come naturally to Mary. It was simply something she did without thinking. Through painting she could see the light that dwelled in all things, in all people. Those who saw her paintings were amazed. They could not believe that some- one her age could paint like that. Even then, people offered to buy her work.

But after Mama's accident, the very act of painting was not the same as before. Painting became a duty rather than a joy. The light was no longer seen. She continued painting because the sense of loss was less when she painted, but she knew in her heart that something was missing. Her painting now took place in darkness. The feeling behind the paint- ing was gone.

Nevertheless, people admired her work. When Mary was a freshman, her art teacher, Mr. Gomez, came to the house to convince Papa to let her stay after school for extra studio time. Mary had never heard anyone speak to Papa the way Mr. Gomez spoke to him that day. "You don't understand," he said. "She has an extraordinary gift. She needs to learn a little tech- nique, but not much. She's already more original than people who have their stuff hanging in galleries."

"She needs to look after her mother after school," Papa answered.

She knew that when Papa spoke that way, there was no moving him. But somehow Mr. Gomez convinced him. He reminded Papa how he had entered one of Mary's paintings — one she had done before her mother's accident — in a citywide competition, and it had won first prize and a five-hundred-dollar award. Perhaps it was the money that convinced Papa. They were always in need of extra cash.

Mary waited to make sure that Kate was asleep. As hard as Papa's death was for Mary, she knew it had been harder for Kate. In the midst of all her sorrow, Kate was worried about how they were going to live without him. Mary worried too. After a long, long time, Kate finally stopped tossing and turning. Mary got up softly, put her slippers on, and slipped out of the room. When Papa was alive, the girls kept the door to their room closed, but this past week they had kept it open so they could hear Mama. Mary glanced in and saw that Mama had her eyes closed and was breathing softly.

Then she walked to Papa's office, closed the door, and turned on the lamp on his desk. Papa had a brass lamp with a cream-colored shade that cast a soft glow over the room. One of Mary's earliest paintings, the one that won the five-hundred-dollar award, was a watercolor still life of Papa's study. It showed the huge oak desk with its three drawers on each side. The wall in front of the desk was blank, because Papa didn't want to have any distractions while he was writing his sermons. On top of the desk she had painted an open Bible, a few white sheets of paper, an old-fashioned fountain pen, and a bottle of ink. She invented the fountain pen and the bottle of ink because she thought it would give the scene a quiet, peaceful mood. She depicted a room where thinking and writing were done slowly. In reality, Papa used a pencil and an old Olivetti typewriter.

Mary looked for the crayon drawing of the bald eagle. She wanted to know that Papa had not thrown it away. She wanted to believe that deep down Papa valued her painting, even if she no longer did. The drawing was not in her parents' bedroom, because she had searched for it before when she was taking care of Mama. Now she opened all the drawers in the desk, starting from the bottom. She lifted out the folders and papers in the drawers and looked carefully. There was a gray file cabinet where he kept all his old sermons and she looked inside it, but she couldn't find any of the paintings or drawings she had given Papa over the years — not just the drawing of the eagle, but the pictures she had given him for his birthday or Father's Day.

Mary sat on the floor and put her hands over her eyes. Papa had thrown away the drawing of the eagle. He had thrown away all the paintings and drawings she had ever given him, and she felt a terrible and dark loneliness.

7

Aunt Julia arrived the following morning. She came into the house, gave Mary and Kate each a hug, dropped her turquoise suitcase, and plumped herself down on the sofa, breathing heavily, her hair disheveled. She was thinner and paler than the last time Kate had seen her. Kate expected her to make some excuse as to why she hadn't attended the funeral services, but Aunt Julia was silent on the subject. Instead, after telling them how the taxi from the airport had not been air-conditioned, she looked directly at Kate and asked: "So what are you girls going to do?"

"We're going to be okay," Kate said. Aunt Julia had not been in the house more than five minutes and Kate could already feel her blood rising.

"Who's going to take care of Catalina while you girls go to school? I can't stay here forever. I have to go home soon."

She has to take care of her cats, Kate thought.

"Aunt Julia, would you like to go in and see Mama?" Mary said.

Aunt Julia ignored her. "Did your father leave you any money?"

"I have to find out," Kate said coolly. "There's an insurance policy."

"How much?"

"I don't know. I haven't had a chance to look."

"That's something you need to check quickly. You'll need to file a claim and send a death certificate. When my Phil died, it took a couple of months to get a check from the insurance company. They'll do whatever they can to keep from paying." Aunt Julia seemed to think they were little children who did not know the ways of the world. "Do you still have a nurse come every day?"

"Yes," Mary answered. "Talita. She loves Mama."

"How much does she charge?"

"I don't know," Kate responded. She made a mental note to find out how much Talita would charge to stay with Mother for the hours she and Mary were in school. For the time being, Aunt Julia would have to do.

"I don't know either," Mary said.

Aunt Julia looked at them for a moment before taking out a tissue and coughing into it. "Well, those are things you girls need to know." Kate thought that Aunt Julia looked like a dried-up prune. All her freshness and juice were gone. "What about the house? How long can you stay here?"

Kate didn't answer, so Mary said tentatively, "I'm sure we can stay here for a while."

"They told you that?"

"No, but Papa was the minister for nineteen years. They're not going to just kick us out." Mary's bold response made Kate smile.

"Pssh!" Aunt Julia said.

"We haven't had a chance to look into a lot of things." Kate stared briefly at Aunt Julia in case she had any notions of running their lives.

"I'm just trying to help," Aunt Julia said.

Kate grinned. She could not believe how Aunt Julia had started asking questions the minute she walked in. She thought of Reverend Soto. Maybe she could talk to him about the house, confirm with him that they could stay as long as they wanted.

"Aunt Julia, do you want me to take your suitcase to Mama's room?" Mary asked.

Aunt Julia shook her head quickly as if the very notion frightened her. "Poor Catalina," she said. "I wanted to come to visit her more often, but I couldn't. I . . . haven't been all that well. And then, to be honest with you, there was Manuel. I just couldn't face the fact that he was driving the car when they had the accident. If he hadn't been so careless, she wouldn't be like this."

"It was an accident," Mary said meekly.

"It wasn't an accident, really. Manuel went through that red light. It was in the police report. I could never get past that. Every time I saw him, that's all I could think about."

There was a long, awkward silence. Finally, Mary spoke. "Papa thought about that accident a lot too. He blamed himself a thousand times more than anyone else could blame him."

"How long will you be staying?" Kate inquired before Aunt Julia could say anything else. She had heard Aunt Julia's explanations before about why she couldn't come see her own sister, and she didn't buy any of them. The truth, as far as Kate was concerned, was that Aunt Julia was a selfish woman comfortable in her little world. She had married in her fifties to a man twenty years older, who had died a few years after they were married. She lived with her two cats in a house that was all paid for.

"We'll see." Aunt Julia pressed down on the sofa with her hands. "I think I'll sleep out here," she told Mary.

"You'll be more comfortable in Papa's bed," Mary said. "Mama hardly makes any noise at night."

"I'll be fine out here," Aunt Julia insisted.

Kate wasn't sure whether Aunt Julia was more repulsed by the thought of sleeping next to her own sister or by the fact that she would be sleeping in the same bed that her father had slept in. But she knew that however long Aunt Julia stayed, it was going to seem like an eternity.

After lunch, Aunt Julia fell asleep on the sofa. Mary and Kate washed the lunch dishes. During the years, they had gotten used to working side by side over the sink.

"I found the insurance policy this morning," Kate said. "It was in Father's desk drawer."

"Oh? But you told Aunt Julia you hadn't."

"I didn't want her to know." Mary looked at Kate. "I'm not sure what her intentions are here," Kate explained. "I don't trust her that much. Suppose she wants to get her hands on the money. . . ." She concentrated on a smudge on one of the glasses.

"She's not as bad as you make her out to be. She doesn't seem well."

"Mmm. Anyway, the policy is for one hundred thousand dollars."

"Wow! That's a lot of money. Isn't that a lot of money?"

Kate shook her head. "It has to last us until we get jobs and start making it on our own. That's a long time. In the meantime, we'll need to hire someone to take care of Mother for seven hours a day, at least until school is out."

"Seven hours a day," Mary repeated thoughtfully.

"That would be from eight o'clock when we go to school until three."

"But you work until eight and I don't get out of school until four."

Kate looked away from Mary. "You'll have to give up your hour of art studio after school."

Mary was silent. She dipped a dish into the plastic tub of soapy water, rubbed it with a sponge, and then dipped it into the hot, clean water.

"It's only one hour," Mary said.

"I'm sorry."

"Maybe I can go in a few hours on Saturdays."

"I need to keep my volunteer job at the hospital," Kate said. "I can't just stop going. People are depending on me."

"It's not fair," Mary said, shaking her head.

"You could paint at home."

Mary started to say something and then abruptly stopped. For the first time ever, Kate saw a flicker of resentment in her sister, as if Kate could not possibly understand the sacrifice she was asking Mary to make. "Can I at least stay in art studio for a few more days? There's something I'd like to finish."

"Okay," Kate said quickly. "We might as well take advantage of Aunt Julia while she's here. But only for a few more days. It's a long time to leave Mother alone with Aunt Julia."

"Talita will still be coming,"

"Still. You need to get home from school as soon as you can."

Mary stopped. She held a dish in midair. "Kate, will we need to hire someone seven hours a day when you go to UTEP? Evangelina's older sister goes to UTEP and she only has classes in the morning. Some days she doesn't even have any."

"We'll see," Kate said. Mary's question gave her a pang. Things would have been so much easier now if she had told Mary about Stanford from the very beginning. But it was *her* secret, hers and Mother's. The visit to Stanford, the promise that she made her mother was something all her own. Besides, she hadn't gotten into Stanford yet. Why worry Mary over something that might not happen? And then there were all the financial questions. Even if she got a scholarship, how would they pay for all that needed to be paid?

Kate carefully folded the dishcloth she'd been using and left the kitchen.

8

At school the following Monday, Mary wanted to eat her lunch alone in the art studio, but Renata insisted that she sit in the cafeteria. Renata was quiet at first, unsure whether to crack her usual jokes, but then a boy at another table stuck two French fries up his nose, and Mary and Renata laughed.

"I never expected you to come back to school so soon," Renata said.

"Kate wanted us to. I think she was going crazy being in the same house with Aunt Julia."

"Are you sure you're ready for this?" Renata asked, looking in the direction of the boy with the French fries. He had offered the same two French fries to the girl next to him and she was screaming. Mary smiled and shook her head. It amazed her how she could feel so much sorrow and laugh at something silly at the same time.

"Kate's probably right . . . for once," Renata said. "You want to come to my house after your studio?"

"I can't. I have to go home and take care of Mama." Mary looked at her peanut butter and grape jelly sandwich and put it back in the paper bag.

"You don't feel like eating?" Renata asked.

"No. Not right now. You want it?"

"Thanks. Mom made me the usual. Every week I ask her to buy something other than bologna, and what do I get?" She opened up the two slices of white bread and showed Mary the slice of bologna smeared with mustard. "Why, I ask you, *why* does she treat me like this? This is the kind of stuff they feed people in prison." She closed the sandwich and took a bite out of it. "Oh, well, a girl has to eat. And you do too. Here, have some chips."

"No, thanks."

Then Renata scrunched her forehead. "You have to go home and take care of your mother right after school?"

"Yes."

"What about studio?"

Mary folded the top of the paper bag. "I won't be able to do it anymore. With Papa gone, there's no one home."

"And Kate, what's she doing?"

"She has to go to work after school."

"How much does she make an hour, all of five bucks? There's no one at the Red Sombrero at that time. She can stay home with your mother and let you paint."

"We need the money," Mary said. There were times when Mary enjoyed Renata ranting about Kate, her righteous anger on Mary's behalf. But today was different. Even though she agreed with what Renata was saying, she did not want to feel any resentment toward Kate.

Renata waited a few seconds. "Are you guys going to be okay moneywise?"

"Papa had an insurance policy," Mary said.

"I don't want you to worry about anything. You're my sister, right?"

"Yes."

"I mean you got a sister, but I'm your *soul* sister. And you know Mom, she's already beating the drums, making sure those stingy deacons at the church do what's right for you. She's talking to friends who know about programs that can help you guys, taking care of your mom and everything. Okay?"

Mary felt a warm, watery lump in her throat, and her eyelids trembled. "Okay," she said.

Renata reached over, found her hand, and held it tight in hers. "I know, I know," she said. "I have this effect on people."

Mary took a deep breath. She had to look away from Renata or she would come undone.

"Hey." Renata shook her hand and waited for Mary to look at her. "I need to talk to you about something." She handed Mary a napkin and Mary blew her nose.

"What?"

"I've had some inquiries. A couple of very cute guys have very discreetly asked me if they could send you flowers."

"Sure," Mary said.

"Well, let's think about this more carefully. If I tell them you said yes, that they can send you flowers, they might get their hopes up that maybe you'll go out with them."

"Oh." Boys had been asking Mary out for years, but she never went out with anyone. A girl named Angie asked her once if she liked girls instead of boys, and Mary said no, she liked boys, and even named some of the cute ones. She just didn't feel like going out with them. Later, Renata told her that Angie was jealous because a boy she liked had said Mary was the most beautiful girl in school. People made comments like that all the time, but Mary tried very hard to ignore them. It was difficult enough to paint without being full of yourself. Mary thought that if there was anyone beautiful in her family, it was Kate . . . and Mama when she was young.

Renata continued, "I'm not saying they're not being sincere when they send you flowers, but in my vast experience with the male species, there's always an ulterior motive when they do something nice for you. I know, you have your painting, blah, blah, blah. But suppose, miracle of miracles, there's a guy somewhere in this universe who's actually nice and not intimidated by strong women like us." Renata stopped to grin. "Just suppose there is — don't you want to give that guy a chance?"

"Rennie, Papa just died!"

"They don't mean to be disrespectful, but you've been telling boys that your father won't let you go out until you're eighteen, so now they're wondering if the rules are gonna change."

"Tell them the rules haven't changed," Mary said, pretending to be very stern. Renata and Mary had known each other since the sixth grade, when her family started coming to the Church of God, and ever since then, Renata had considered it her primary duty in life to get Mary to be more or less like other girls.

"Okay, but they're not going to go away. They're not the usual bunch, either. I'm getting quote unquote 'expressions of concern' from extremely cute, non-jerky juniors and seniors."

"I have to go to class," Mary said, getting up.

"I'm not through with you yet," Renata yelled at Mary as she walked away. "I'll call you tonight."

Mary made it through her afternoon classes as she always did — not paying much attention to what the teachers were saying. Usually she daydreamed about how to solve whatever problems she was having with her painting, but that day she was thinking about Kate and Aunt Julia. Yesterday evening they'd gotten into an argument. Aunt Julia thought that since Papa was dead and Mama was incapacitated, it was up to her to decide what was best for them. Kate told her that she was eighteen, and as Mary's closest kin, she was responsible for her. Mary didn't understand why Kate couldn't just let Aunt Julia say whatever she wanted. She seemed to get weaker after every disagreement.

After her classes were over, Mary went to the art studio as she usually did. She felt a weight descend upon her at the thought that this would be her last week going there.

The art studio was the size of two regular classrooms joined together. There were easels for painting and tables for sculptures and silk screens. Mr. Gomez's office was in a small room down the hall. Mr. Gomez wasn't there, so she went on to the studio.

She walked to the corner of the room where she kept her easel and painting materials. The easel held the painting of the two irises she had been working on. The actual irises she had used for models now stood wilted in a crystal vase of murky water. Their purple was not the same purple as the irises in her painting. Her petals were opaque. They lacked the inner radiance of Van Gogh's flowers or of the real flowers. There was an invisible strength in those fragile-looking irises that had eluded her. Would she ever be able to paint like she used to?

A sound startled her. She turned quickly and saw a boy standing behind her.

"You Mary?" he asked.

She didn't recognize his face. Maybe he was new in school. He wore a long-sleeved blue shirt and jeans that looked worn out with use.

"I am Mary. What can I do for you?" she answered.

He looked at her as if he had never heard someone her age speak like that before. Kids at school were always making fun of her, in good and bad ways, for the formal way she spoke. But Papa never allowed slang at home, and his rule had unconsciously carried over into school.

"What is it?" she asked coldly. She had found that with certain types of boys, cold was the only way to be.

"Gomez told me to come here and ask for you."

"*Mr.* Gomez asked you that?"

"Yeah."

"Why?"

"What?"

"Why did Mr. Gomez ask you to see me?" She said this with such force that he actually turned his face away from her.

"I don't know," he said. "I was doing time in detention and Gomez asked me to come see you."

"I still don't understand," she said.

He reached into the back pocket of his pants and took out a piece of paper. When he handed it to her, she noticed a small tattoo of a four-pointed star on the skin between his thumb and index finger. She knew a tattoo like that was the mark of a gang member. A shiver of fear ran through her body. But there was a timid look on his face, as if he were afraid of what she would say. She unfolded the paper and saw a drawing of a circle with strange animal and human figures inside it. It reminded her of the Aztec calendar.

"You did that?" she asked. He didn't seem like the type who could do a drawing as precise as that.

"I was bored," he said.

She examined the drawing more carefully, and she began to understand why Mr. Gomez told him to come see her. Every so often, Mr. Gomez was asked to take on a troublesome student, the theory being that even art was more productive than detention, where students just sat and did nothing. Mr. Gomez encouraged this arrangement because the usefulness of the art studio was an argument he could use when the school board threatened to terminate the art program for budget reasons, as they did every year.

It took Mary only a few moments to recognize the flare of imagination, the natural inspiration she once had. The precision of the lines reflected a subtle and ordered sense of beauty. The drawing had captured an invisible source of light. She wanted to tell the boy that his drawing was good, because it was, but instead she walked over to a cabinet and pulled out a pad of paper and a charcoal pencil. Then she went to a desk and placed the paper and the pencil on top. "Here," she said.

"Here what?" She could tell he wasn't used to getting directions.

She went over to the windowsill and grabbed a white plastic horse the students called Hi-Yo. She put Hi-Yo on a stool in front of his desk. "Draw this," she told him.

He sat on the desk, crossed his arms, and stared at the horse. Maybe she should tell him to draw whatever he wanted. After all, he was not going to come back to the art studio unless he was sent there again. But she wasn't in the mood for confrontations. Everything still seemed so unreal, so petty after Papa's death. She felt a wave of sadness come over her as she turned back to her painting.

"I heard about you," she heard him say as she walked away.

She didn't turn around. When she got to her easel, she began to study her irises again. It seemed to her that the colors she had used were lifeless, like the colors of a corpse.

"I heard you were the hot girl who thinks she's too good for everyone."

She kept looking at the painting. She didn't say anything. Maybe she should have, but what was there to say? She tried to mix the acrylic paint on the palette, but she couldn't concentrate. Why pretend that she wanted to paint when she didn't? Why didn't she just admit that she had stopped *liking* to paint since Mama's accident? It was a show she had been putting on. A show for whose benefit? What was the point of creating colorful forms when Papa didn't want them, when Mama would never see them? Papa was right to throw away all her paintings when Mama became ill. What did painting irises have to do with the sadness of the world?

9

A unt Julia insisted that Simon come for supper. Kate couldn't quite figure out why she was so excited about his visit, and then it dawned on her that Aunt Julia had found out from Mary that Simon's family owned two restaurants. Kate herself worked in one of those restaurants after school. She could almost hear the little wheels in Aunt Julia's head go *click, click, click* whenever Simon's name was mentioned.

Aunt Julia made her famous pot roast and mashed potatoes in honor of Simon's visit. After the roast was in the oven, she showered, washed her hair, put on her best dress, and overly perfumed herself. It was almost as if Simon was coming to see *her*. When she heard the knock on the door, she smoothed down her dress and sat as straight as a rod on the sofa. She stayed seated when Kate introduced them and floated her hand out to Simon like a queen. Kate couldn't help but notice a look of surprise on her face. Perhaps she was expecting some- one more striking. Simon wasn't tall, but he was solidly built, and he had a rugged-looking face with lively eyes that focused on you and made you feel important. You had to look at him a couple of times before you realized that he was good-looking in his own unassuming way.

"So, Simon," Aunt Julia said when everyone was seated in the living room, "Kate tells me your family owns two restaurants."

Ah, good old Aunt Julia, Kate thought. *Nothing like getting straight to the point.*

"Yes, ma'am," Simon answered shyly, as if afraid to boast. "We had one for a long time and then last year we started a second one over by the airport."

"That's wonderful." Aunt Julia beamed, casting a meaningful glance at Kate.

"I should check on dinner," Kate said.

"The pot roast is all set," said Aunt Julia.

"I'm going to make the salad."

"I'll make it," Mary said as she stepped into the living room. "Hi, Simon." She waved.

"Hey, Mary!" Simon waved back. Kate shot Mary a look, but Mary either didn't catch the hidden meaning or decided to ignore it.

Simon was usually nervous whenever he came over, which Kate had always attributed to the dignified presence of her father. Now he was sitting on the sofa next to Aunt Julia and was still visibly jittery.

"Maybe I should check on Mother," Kate suggested.

"She's all right. You should stay here with your young man." Aunt Julia smiled at Simon.

"Simon's been here many times before. He feels at home," Kate said.

"I'm okay," said Simon, trying to defuse the tension. "I've been here many times before." He gave Kate a quick smile, as if apologizing for repeating what she had said. She decided she should stay in the room. There was no telling what Aunt Julia might say next.

"How long have you been engaged?" Aunt Julia asked.

"Aunt Julia!" Kate exclaimed. "We're not engaged!"

"Oh, I'm sorry, I thought you were," Aunt Julia said coyly. Kate could see her stratagem. She was planting seeds in Simon's mind, letting him know that she would approve of an engagement, as if it were up to her to approve.

Simon was blushing proudly. He seemed glad that their relationship had been mistaken for an engagement.

"If you're not engaged, then what are you?" Aunt Julia was looking at Simon, waiting for him to answer.

"Aunt Julia, you're embarrassing Simon," Kate said.

"No, no. I'm not embarrassed. It's just that, I don't know, I guess maybe we can say that we're pre-engaged," he said.

"Oh," Aunt Julia said. It was clear that *pre-engaged* did not mean anything to her.

Kate glared at Simon.

"So when are you —" Aunt Julia started to ask, but Kate cut her off.

"Let's go have supper." She stood up and waited for the others to follow. Aunt Julia ignored her.

"What do you plan to do after graduation?"

"Aunt Julia, don't interrogate Simon so much," Kate tried to joke. She sat back down again.

"I'm not interrogating him. I'm curious, that's all. Since he's *pre-engaged* to you, I should know. I'm the only relative you've got."

"That's all right," Simon said to Kate. He turned back to Aunt Julia. "I plan to manage one of my father's restaurants, the one by the airport. I'll work with him for a few months so he can show me the ropes, and then he'll turn the whole restaurant over to me. He and my mother have been running a restaurant for twenty-five years. They want to retire. My brother, Raul, will manage the other restaurant as soon as he graduates from high school. He's one year younger than me."

Aunt Julia made a face that conveyed she was impressed. "Managing a restaurant at such a young age!"

"I've been working in the restaurants ever since I can remember. I know the business. And I'll have a few months with my dad before I take over completely."

Aunt Julia was going to ask another question when Mary came in. "I think the pot roast is getting overdone. It looks dry."

Fortunately, Aunt Julia did not carry out any further interrogations during supper. Kate noticed that Mary's presence mellowed Aunt Julia. It was as if Mary saw a softer side to her, and she responded to that.

After they were finished with supper, Aunt Julia insisted that Kate and Simon go out to the backyard and enjoy the cool evening air while she rested and Mary did the dishes. She had gone back to her usual tired self.

Kate and Simon sat next to each other in silence. The night was gleaming with stars, and Kate focused her gaze on them. Whenever she glanced at Simon, she felt as if he was mustering enough courage to speak. She wanted to ask him about the "pre-engagement" comment. It was presumptuous of him to say that to Aunt Julia before discussing it with Kate. On the other hand, she did not want to talk about their relationship. She liked Simon and felt closer to him than she had ever felt to any other boy, but they had never discussed what would happen after high school, and she had never told him about the application to Stanford. She knew that Simon assumed she would stay in El Paso and their relationship would continue. Now here he was, searching for words to ask her what she didn't want to hear.

"Is everything okay?" he finally said.

"Okay? Like how?"

"Between us."

"Sure."

She could hear him inhale deeply. "Maybe it's time to make things more formal."

"Things?" She turned to look at him.

"Between you and me."

"More than pre-engaged?" There was a faint note of sarcasm in her voice, but Simon didn't pick it up.

"I know we've only been going out for a year and a half, but we've known each other since we were kids, since my family started going to your father's church. I'm one hundred percent sure about you. I've felt that way for ages. And . . ."

"Go on." Might as well have it all out. Simon put his left

hand in his pocket, and for a second she thought he was going to take out a ring. Kate's mind raced, trying to think what she would say if he did.

"Well, this is a good time to make a decision about us."

She was relieved when he took his hand out of his pocket again and it was empty. She wondered why Simon would not just out-and-out propose to her, why he preferred to talk about decisions, formal or otherwise. He must be testing and prodding to see whether his proposal would be accepted. There was a part of her that wanted to make it easier for him by telling him to go ahead and just ask, and another part that wanted to make it as hard as possible so that she wouldn't have to give any answers.

She said softly, "Are you sure this is a good time to be talking about this?" It was the gentlest way to put him off, at least for a while.

But Simon seemed determined to carry through with what he had to say. He took a deep breath and then said, "I want to be there for you. You need someone now more than ever."

She turned toward him, expecting to see affection or caring in his face, but what she saw instead was responsibility. The strong was offering to protect the weak.

"Are you worried about me financially?" she asked.

"That's not all. But I'll take care of you, all of you. I'll make good money with my own restaurant."

Kate rubbed her feet on the ground. The week before, she had sat with her father on these same chairs and he'd told her that the burden of taking care of the family would fall on her. She knew by the way her father treated Simon that he wanted her to marry him, probably the sooner the better. Marrying Simon would have eased the family's burden even when Father was alive; how much more would it do that now? *Love makes everything that is heavy light*, her father had said. But did she love Simon?

"I guess I need to know if you'd be willing to let me take care of you. I'm not that good with words. It's not just taking care of you, you know what I mean, providing for you. I care for you. I . . . I love you. I never said that before. I never said it to anyone, but you know I've always felt that."

She reached over, squeezed his hand, and then looked away. "Thank you," she said.

She felt the weight of silence. She knew he was waiting for her to say she loved him, but she couldn't bring herself to speak the words.

He went on, disappointment in his voice, "I know I'm not the most exciting guy out there, but I'm dependable and respectful and I would never do anything to hurt you."

"Simon, I know all that. I just don't know if I can give you the kind of assurances you want right now."

"I've been patient," he said. He sounded impatient when he said it.

"Patient?"

"You're always studying. When we get together, it's to do homework or research. We never do anything fun. We hardly even make out."

"We make out all the time."

"Once a week, maybe, and you always put a stop to it after a short while. You know what I mean," he said. He didn't sound like he was complaining; he sounded like he was marshaling his evidence to show she was not affectionate.

"I didn't know that bothered you."

"It doesn't *bother* me. But I'm a guy. I'm trying to tell you I never asked anything from you."

"I don't get it," Kate said. "What exactly are you asking for now? I thought you were talking about making a more formal commitment, like an engagement. Now it sounds like you're saying we haven't been intimate enough."

"No, that's not what I meant. I meant that we've been in the same place for a long time. I know your father let me go out with you because he trusted me, and I never wanted to let him down. I just think that now we should move on to the next step. I don't even know if it's engagement. It may be going straight to marriage."

"We would go from being boyfriend and girlfriend, skipping pre-engagement and engagement, straight to marriage." She couldn't help poking fun at him. "First you tell my aunt we're pre-engaged without even talking to me, and now you want to get married without actually proposing."

"Oh, man. I really botched this up. Can I start over again?"

Kate looked at the neighbors' house. Mr. and Mrs. Domínguez had lived in that house for thirty-five years. Their children had grown up and gotten married, and now a rusty swing set stood in the backyard, used now and then by the grandchildren. Kate thought of the Domínguezes' living room. It was carpeted with a thick, burgundy carpet. A wine-colored sofa and armchair surrounded a giant TV screen. An armoire full of porcelain angels that Mrs. Domínguez collected at yard sales stood in the corner. Every time Kate visited the Domínguezes, she imagined what it would be like to spend her life in that living room. Was she wrong in thinking there was more to life than that? Why did she fear she would end up in that living room forever if she married Simon?

Simon was dependable, respectful, hardworking. He didn't drink or belong to a gang. She had been his first serious girlfriend even though many other girls had been after him. They were comfortable around each other and never once did Kate feel discontented with what they had. She knew Simon would have sex with her if she let him, but she never felt strongly enough about him to have sex. What she wanted most of all was a more meaningful life, a life where she was useful to others, a life that in her mind could only be obtained someplace other than El Paso.

If she had to decide whether to marry him at that moment, her answer would be no. No, she didn't want to move on to the next step, as Simon put it. But something inside of her kept her from outright turning him down — a fear almost, as if her father were standing next to her, reminding her of her responsibilities. And Simon was such a good guy. He had been her steady partner. They studied and worked and joked together. He did not deserve to be hurt simply because she was indecisive.

"You don't have to start over," she said to him. "I know what you're saying. I think I'm still in shock from Father's death. Give me time. Give me a little more time."

Simon intertwined his fingers with Kate's. "Sure. I didn't mean to rush you or anything. I just didn't want you to worry.

You can still go to UTEP. You can still be a doctor. I'd support you in that like I always have. I'm just saying that things will be a lot easier for all of you if we're together. It's what's best for all."

Kate nodded to tell him that she understood what he was saying, not that she was in agreement. She doubted that Simon would get the distinction, but she didn't feel like making it clearer. She looked up at the night sky again, and it seemed that there were not as many stars as she had thought.

10

Mary knew something was wrong as soon as Kate and Simon came into the house. Simon's expression was deadly serious. He quickly shook hands with Aunt Julia and then excused himself, saying he had to go to the restaurant to help close it for the night. Kate was silent, but she too looked as if she would never smile again.

Aunt Julia must have sensed that something important had taken place, because as soon as Simon was out the door, she perked up enough to start with her questions.

"Well, did he propose?" she asked. "He looked like he wanted to propose. What is this 'pre-engagement'? Who's ever heard of that? He's an extremely responsible boy, the kind who would make a great husband. He has everything a girl like you could want. Well?"

Kate shook her head and didn't answer. Aunt Julia got more and more agitated. She began to shift around on the couch. "I hope you don't think you're too young to be married. Your mother was eighteen. Of course no one in the family thought it was a good idea, but that wasn't because of her age, it was because no one liked your father. Eighteen years is fine if the man and woman are mature enough. Simon seems very mature. He knows what he wants."

"I know he's mature," Kate said with control in her voice.

"Well, then, what's there to think about?"

"I don't know," Kate said.

Aunt Julia finally found a comfortable spot on the sofa. "Look, with your father gone and Catalina the way she is, you don't have the luxury of waiting around. You need to consider how you'll survive. A bird in the hand, as they say . . ."

Kate began to massage her temples with her fingers, and Mary saw that as her signal to speak up. "Aunt Julia, Kate will never marry Simon simply because we need to survive. If she marries Simon, it's because she loves him."

Aunt Julia looked surprised, as if she hadn't expected Mary to take Kate's side.

"Well," she said in a hurt tone, "it looks like you two girls don't need my advice."

"Everything is happening so fast," Kate said. "I can't even think straight. I need time to think about what's best. We all do."

"I'm trying to help you think things through," Aunt Julia insisted. "You have an insurance policy you don't even know for how much. You have a boyfriend who wants to marry you right now, and don't tell me he doesn't, because I know when a man is ready to get married, and that boy has marriage written all over his face. I don't see that you have many options here."

"The insurance policy is for one hundred thousand dollars," Kate said quietly. "That's going to get us through for a while."

Aunt Julia appeared to be calculating whether the new information changed anything she had been saying. "A hundred thousand dollars is not a lot of money," she said at last. "Not when you have to take care of Catalina, pay rent, and buy food. You'll need to start working full-time as soon as you finish high school." She sounded tired again.

"Kate doesn't have to marry Simon right away if she doesn't want to. She's going to college." Mary smiled at Kate. Kate looked away, and Mary realized that Aunt Julia had never once asked if Kate loved Simon. She spoke about what a good catch he was, but not what Kate felt for him. Maybe Aunt Julia just assumed they loved each other, as Mary did. Now Kate's silence made Mary wonder whether that was true.

"College?" Aunt Julia said, shaking her head. "You might as well forget about that."

It is rarely cold in April in El Paso, but that night it was chilly. Kate and Mary both wore their flannel pajamas to bed. Kate slipped under the covers, said good night, and turned her back to Mary. Usually she stayed up reading until long after Mary had fallen asleep. Mary could hear Aunt Julia taking her pills in the bathroom. She turned off the light and waited until she heard Aunt Julia settle in on the sofa bed.

"Kate, Kate," Mary whispered.

"I'm asleep," Kate said.

"I want to ask you a question."

"What is it?" She still had her back to Mary, but she didn't sound annoyed.

Mary took a deep breath. "Do you love Simon?"

Silence filled the room. Kate turned on her back and gripped the edges of her blanket. "We're a weird pair, aren't we?" she said.

"Why do you say that?"

"Look at us. Look at how we dress. Aunt Julia has cooler outfits than we do. We talk like old ladies. We've never even used lipstick. One time I plucked my eyebrows, and Father scolded me because it was vanity. Here you are, sixteen years old, and you haven't had a single boyfriend. You haven't even kissed anybody, because if you had, you would have told me."

"I don't tell you everything," Mary giggled.

"We're probably the only two students in the whole high school who don't have cell phones. We barely have a computer. And how hard was it to convince Father about that? Remember how upset he was when we first got it? He literally thought the devil was going to sneak in the house through the Internet cable."

"He was okay with you dating Simon," Mary reminded her. "That was huge."

"Huge? That was a miracle bigger than the virgin birth. But . . ."

"But what?"

"Nothing."

"I know what you're going to say." Mary actually had no idea what Kate was about to say, but she didn't want her to stop talking.

"What was I going to say?"

Mary said the first thing that came to her mind. "You were going to say that Simon was the kind of boy Papa wanted for you."

"Okay, Miss Woman of the World, what kind of boy is that?"

"Loyal. Well-behaved. Serious. Protective."

"You make him sound like the perfect dog."

They laughed.

"He's super nice," Mary added when they finished laughing.

"Shhh, you're going to wake up Aunt Julia," Kate said.

"So, do you love him?"

Kate pulled the covers over her head. "Aarrghh!" Slowly, her face crawled out. "I think Simon proposed to me tonight."

"You think?"

"I know he did. It's just that he did it in his typical Simon way, like getting married was the obvious, most practical thing to do. He sounded like Aunt Julia."

"Is that why you looked so sad when you came in? You didn't look like the man of your dreams had just proposed to you."

"The man of my dreams," Kate repeated.

Mary propped herself up on her elbow. Sisters were supposed to talk about their boyfriends and how they feel about them, and they had never talked about Simon. Did Kate love him? Mary had always assumed that what Kate and Simon had was their own way of loving each other. But here was Kate all gloomy over the fact that he had proposed. "You have to tell me exactly what he said and what you said," she pleaded.

"He thought marrying him was 'best for all.'"

"And what did you say?"

"I told him I needed time."

"You gave him some hope, then?"

"I didn't close the door entirely, I don't think."

"But when was he thinking of marrying you?"

"Right away."

"I guess you could still go to college, right? You could be married and still go to UTEP."

When Kate spoke, her words came slowly and without emotion. "He says he's okay with my going to UTEP. It was the funniest thing. I couldn't bring myself to say no to him. Before Father died, I would have told him straight off that I wasn't ready to make a decision like marriage. But now . . ."

"But what's changed? You should follow your heart. You shouldn't marry Simon if that's not what you want."

"I don't think it's as easy as all that now. He's such a good person. And he's offering me so much. He offers all he has, really. Shouldn't that be enough?"

"Kate, do you love Simon?"

"I don't know."

"You have to know. You've been with him for more than a year and known him since you were eight years old. How do you feel about him?"

"I feel peaceful. I feel comfortable when he's around. . . . But I'm not sure I feel the kinds of things people feel when they're in love." She spoke as if she realized for the first time that she was missing out on something.

"Oh." Mary's mind went blank and she couldn't think of anything else to say or ask.

"Maybe something's wrong with me." Mary heard Kate's voice quiver. She stretched her arm out of the bed, and Kate grabbed her hand. "Maybe what Simon and I have is love. Maybe love doesn't need to have the kind of feelings that people talk about. Have you ever been in love?"

"I don't think I've been in love with a person, but I always imagined love to be like what I felt for painting once. When I lost myself in painting, I felt like I was part of whatever it was I painted, how it felt to be a flower or a rock. Like a light in me recognized a light coming from what I was painting, and the two lights got all tangled up so I couldn't tell them apart. I had to work hard at keeping the lights together, but at the beginning the lights joined together naturally."

Kate pulled her hand away from Mary. "I've never felt that way about anything . . . or anyone."

Mary took a deep breath. "To be honest, I haven't felt that kind of love for painting since . . ."

"Since?"

"Since Mama had her accident," Mary said quietly.

"Why?"

"I don't know. I just don't feel like painting. The spark is gone."

"But you've kept on painting."

"Yes. But it's different. The lights I used to see in and around everything are not there anymore. It's like something I have to do rather than something I want to do. I don't enjoy it anymore."

"Like what I feel for Simon," Kate said thoughtfully.

"But you want to be a doctor, and that's a kind of love also." Mary wanted to change the subject.

Kate shook her head. Then she said, "You want to know why Simon's proposal made me sad?"

"Why?"

"I think Simon loves me. He's attracted to me and wants to take care of me and I don't doubt that he'd be by my side forever. That's just the way he is. I knew all that back when we first started dating, but I've never felt the way he does. Today I felt like I used him and strung him along because having a boyfriend meant I could get out of the house and do things that Father wouldn't let me do otherwise."

Mary wondered if Kate and Simon had ever made love. She didn't think it was right to make love to someone before marriage, and she couldn't imagine Kate making love to Simon, after what she had just said, but she wanted to ask, even if it was none of her business. "Kate . . ." Mary started to say.

Kate seemed to have read her mind. "Today he complained — I guess you can call it complaining — about not being intimate, you know, physical. We've never made love because I never felt *that* kind of love for him." Mary felt relieved. "It's a mess," Kate continued. "I don't know what I've been doing or what I'm going to do. Do I love Simon enough to marry him and hope the rest comes later? Is what we have a form of love? If it is, then isn't marrying him the best thing? The 'best for all,' as he put it? And even if it isn't love, there's no doubt that marrying him *is* the best thing for all of us . . . in a way. We'd be taken care of."

"You need to stick with your plan," Mary said, trying to sound comforting. "You need to go to UTEP and be a doctor. With the one hundred thousand dollars from the insurance, we can get Talita or someone to take care of Mama while I'm in school. I don't see anything wrong with you going out with Simon these past two years. It wasn't like you led him on. You never made any promises or told him things you didn't feel, did you? He knows about your plans?"

"Yes."

"What does he say about you going to UTEP?"

There was silence.

"Kate, are you all right? What's the matter?"

"Nothing, I was just thinking. About . . . UTEP."

"What?"

"Nothing. I need to go to sleep now, Mary. It's been a long day."

"Is there something you want to tell me? Tell me."

"No, there's nothing else. Good night."

Mary paused, took a deep breath. "Okay. Good night."

Mary shifted in the bed and lay her head on the pillow. Why did Kate pull back all of a sudden? It had happened so many times. Just as they began to get close, Kate retreated. It was as if Kate was afraid to be her sister, the way sisters are meant to be. Mary raised her hand and touched her cheek. She remembered the time in their backyard when Kate had dabbed her face with paint.

11

K
ate lay awake, thinking about Mary's questions. Did she love Simon? How would she ever know? What did it feel like to love someone? What should she do about college, about marriage, about Mary?

She hugged herself, wishing it was Mother's arms around her. *I need you*, she said softly to herself.

Kate stayed home from school the following morning and filled out the paperwork for the insurance company. When she studied the insurance policy, she was surprised to see that she was listed as the sole beneficiary. Her father had taken out the policy ten years before, so it was strange but fortunate that he had not listed Mother as well, because there might have been problems collecting the benefits, given that she was incapacitated. And Mary? Kate wasn't sure, but she suspected that if Father had listed both Mary and her as beneficiaries, they would have had to wait until Mary turned eighteen to receive any of the money.

After she put the documents in the mail, she called the insurance company to ask how long it would take to process the claim. The lady at the other end of the line was obviously accustomed to hearing the question. She couldn't predict, but it wouldn't be long; it could be as short as a week, no more than a month. There would be a small investigation and then the check would be issued.

"What sort of investigation?" Kate asked.

"Nothing unusual," the insurance lady said in a sympathetic voice. "We look into the cause of death. It's nothing to worry about. Was an autopsy performed?"

"No."

"Your father died suddenly?"

"Yes."

"We'll need to get his medical records."

"I need to send those to you?"

"We'll get them directly from his primary physician. The policy usually provides for a release of the records. We'll check. If we need a consent form, I'll mail it to you or you can come get it. We're right here on Mesa."

"Is the check mailed?" Kate asked.

"We may have someone deliver it in person or ask you to come get it. For your own security, we want to make sure that the right person gets the check, and we'll ask you to sign some documents saying you received it."

There weren't too many other details to take care of. She found her father's savings account book in the top drawer of his desk. Father didn't use a regular bank. He deposited his monthly paycheck from the church with the Ysleta Credit Union, and then he took out in cash what he was going to need for the month. He paid his bills with money orders that he bought at the post office.

There was four thousand dollars in the savings account. Kate hoped that was enough to keep them going until the insurance money came in. She had found out that the home care organization that employed Talita charged fifty dollars a day. If the insurance money didn't come in quickly, she didn't know what they would do.

Fortunately, there weren't any debts other than what was owed to the funeral home, and she thought the church would pay for that. It worried Kate that none of the deacons had so far mentioned that they would take care of those expenses. Her friend Bonnie had said that a special collection had been taken up for them, but she hadn't heard anything more about it. Father had also mentioned a retirement account. She reminded herself to talk to the deacons about that. At school she was great with numbers, but these kinds of figures were confusing and worrisome and they clouded the mind with questions. How, for example, did Father manage to pay fifty dollars a day for home care for Mother? His small monthly paycheck must have gone directly to Talita.

She couldn't help feeling that it was unfair. She was eighteen years old. Her classmates at school were worried about the prom and trying to have as much fun as possible during their last semester in high school. She had to worry about money and make decisions about marriage. In the next few days, Kate threw herself into her schoolwork, or tried to, as a way to forget the many thoughts that whirled in her mind. It was good that advanced calculus, astronomy, and Honors English demanded all of her attention, even if she couldn't fully give it to them.

She and Simon sat together for lunch as they always did, but there were more and more silences between them. She could tell that his pride had been bruised. She felt bad about the sad way he had walked out of the house, and part of her wanted to reach out to him and give him hope, but she thought that to do so might make it worse in the long run. For the first time, she wished that she and Simon could talk to each other freely. They would talk about Mother, about how important it was to go to the best school she could get into, about all the things they each dreamed of for their lives. She wondered if Simon was capable of this type of communication. Another time, she might have tried. But she was too tired to do so now.

And there was also this strange feeling she suddenly had toward Mary — a sense of regret. She wasn't sure whether the regret came from disclosing too much, or from not telling her about Stanford, or from what she had discovered about herself as she talked with Mary. Was something wrong with her because she didn't feel passion for Simon? Why couldn't she feel the kind of feelings Mary felt toward painting? Mary was wrong when she said that Kate's desire to be a doctor was love. Love had a softness and a receptiveness to it. Her desire to be a doctor was strong, willful. It would not bend.

It was all very strange. Kate had never been the type to dwell on how or what she felt, and here she was wondering about things like love. She longed for the insurance money to come, for the acceptance letter from Stanford to arrive. She wanted to clearly and definitively say yes or no to Simon, to make decisions, to have a plan and go for it. The problem was that nothing was settled and everything was in the air. She'd get back to being herself when all the pieces stopped moving.

Kate wanted to ask Bonnie for advice about Simon's proposal, but she knew that if she did this, the news would be all over school in a flash, and Simon would be hurt. It was one thing to be turned down privately and another for the world to know. So as much as she wanted to talk about it, she didn't tell Bonnie.

"You know what you need?" Bonnie said to her one day after school. She was giving Kate a ride to her job at the Red Sombrero.

"What?" Kate turned down the radio.

"You need to go shopping."

"Yeah, right." Kate chuckled to herself. She could just see herself spending a ton of money on new clothes.

"I'm serious. I know your dad died and everything, but you got to keep on living, and you can't go on living the way you lived when he was alive. You need to catch up with the times, girl." Bonnie took one of her hands from the steering wheel and poked Kate in the thigh. "We need to get you some decent clothes. You have a great body. You need to show it."

"Maybe," Kate said.

"What do you say we go this Saturday? I can pick you up and we'll go to the mall and hit every store. It will be soooo much fun. I'd love to upgrade and accessorize you. You'll be transformed, like Cinderella."

Kate laughed. How good it felt to laugh. "Am I that bad?"

A car full of boys pulled up next to them and started making catcalls. Bonnie flipped them the finger. "Idiots," she said. She sped away. "You're not *bad* bad. You're just, I don't know, frumpy."

"Frumpy? Oh, great."

"You know what I mean. It's not your fault. That's just how it is at your house . . . was."

"It was Father," Kate said, immediately regretting it.

"That's the way he was. What he believed and all." Bonnie hesitated. "I always thought you had problems with all that strict stuff."

"I thought I did too." The car was making a right turn and Kate could hear the tick of the signal blinker. She knew Bonnie wanted her to say more.

"You don't anymore?" Bonnie's look was full of curiosity. "I'm sorry if I offended you. I always thought . . ."

"Don't be silly. You didn't offend me," Kate said quickly. "Of course I didn't agree with him. My father had good intentions and I loved him, but we didn't need to have all those restrictions on how my sister and I dressed, what we listened to on the radio, who we went out with."

Bonnie seemed relieved. She pulled into the Red Sombrero's

parking lot and stopped the car. "I can't believe he didn't even let you drive. Are you going to get your license now?"

Kate shrugged.

"No?" Bonnie asked. She turned off the motor. Kate thought that was a nice gesture. It meant that Bonnie was okay with talking a little longer.

"I'd like to, but I don't know when or how I would study for it. I was thinking the other day how incredible it is that we don't even own a car. My father didn't believe in owning one after the accident. We couldn't even have a horse and carriage like the Amish," Kate joked. Bonnie had a questioning look on her face, and Kate realized that Bonnie didn't know who the Amish were. "Whenever Father had to go visit someone at the hospital, he took a cab or he got a ride from someone at church. Mary's spent most of her life on the Ysleta bus. I'm lucky to get rides from Simon or you."

"Unbelievable," Bonnie said, shaking her head in dismay. "I honestly don't know how you do it."

"Sometimes I don't know, either." Kate stared at the restaurant's front doors. The thought of stepping in there and smiling at strangers filled her with nausea. "Well, off to work." She opened the car door.

"What time shall I pick you up on Saturday?" Bonnie was grinning.

"What?"

"Shopping!"

"I guess I could call the hospital and tell them I'd be there at two. We could go in the morning. But . . ." Kate stopped. She didn't want to tell Bonnie about her financial concerns.

"Okay, I'm going to pick you up at your house at ten. We'll shop, have Japanese at the food court, and then shop some more. Bring your credit card." Bonnie started the engine. Kate stepped out, closed the door, and waved.

Credit card, she said to herself. *Yeah, right.*

12

It was Mary's last day of art studio. She was not looking forward to saying good-bye to Mr. Gomez. Even though she would still see him around school and she could still drop by anytime, things would be different now that she would no longer paint under his supervision and guidance.

Mr. Gomez was in his office, typing on his computer. His desk was cluttered with open art history books, school forms, and advertisements for art supplies. Mary stood at the entrance and looked for a few seconds at her painting on the wall, a yellow lotus floating on a dark green pond. She remembered how happy he'd been when she had first given it to him. She knocked on the door.

"Mary!" he said, turning around. He stood up and shook her hand. Mr. Gomez was a short, pudgy, balding man with dark-rimmed glasses and a large nose. He did not look like anyone's idea of an artist. If it weren't for his hands, which were always spotted with different colors, no one could ever tell he painted. "Come, sit down." He picked up a stack of student notebooks from the only other chair in his office and plunked them on his desk.

"I came to pick up my paintings," she told him as she sat down. "I can only stay a few minutes."

He made a funny clicking noise with his tongue. "You don't know how upset I've been since you told me you couldn't come after school anymore. I've been dreading the day you come to pick up your things. It's like now it's really final. There has to be a way to get you to stay. Is there someone I can talk to? This aunt of yours, what about her? If I could convince your father, I can convince anyone."

Mary thought that the extra hour of painting probably wouldn't make much of a difference, given how she was feeling about painting. "It's not possible," she said. "It wasn't a decision that Aunt Julia made. It's something that my sister and I decided. I need to go home and take care of Mama."

Mr. Gomez nodded, but the furrows on his forehead said that he wasn't happy about it. "Well, I guess one way of looking at it is that you really don't need what little guidance I give you. You can paint on your own now, you always could, and you can always ask for my help, in the unlikely case you need it." He smiled.

"Mr. Gomez, I don't know how to thank you."

"*Por favor!* I've learned more from you than you have from me. What you have is a gift, a *don*, as we say in Spanish: a way of seeing and feeling that I've never encountered in a young artist before."

It always embarrassed Mary to hear Mr. Gomez praise her painting that way. There was something about taking credit for her paintings that didn't seem right. A finished painting surprised her most of all. Who did *that*? Did *she* do that? It was as if some other painter had used her eyes and hands as instruments. After Mama's accident, getting complimented for seeing and feeling was particularly hard, since she knew it wasn't true anymore. "You shouldn't sell yourself short," Mary said.

"But I am short," he said, winking.

"You know what I mean. You taught me all I know about painting."

"Okay, I will grant you that. I taught you all you *know*. But your painting is so much more than knowing."

"Knowing is good," Mary said. She thought about how she had studied every single painting that Vincent van Gogh had ever painted, all that she had learned about the substances he used to mix his colors, his brushstrokes, even how he framed his paintings.

"Yeah, I suppose," he said sadly.

She stood up. "I'll come by to say hi whenever I can."

"You better," he said, perking up again. "But even if you forget about me, I won't forget you." He pointed at her painting of the lotus. "Oh, by the way, I've asked Marcos to help you." Mary was about to ask who Marcos was when the phone rang. Mr. Gomez answered it and then immediately put his hand over the receiver. "He's a good boy," he whispered. Then he turned back to the phone.

When she entered the studio, she saw the same boy who had told her how unapproachable she was. He was bent down over a desk, drawing, and did not see her. Was he Marcos? Who Mr. Gomez said was a good boy? This was the person who was supposed to help her? Help her with what?

There was no way to get to her corner of the studio without passing him. She needed to pack her supplies into a plastic bag and grab the painting of the irises she had been working on. She would take home the paintings stored in the back room little by little. If she hurried, she could be out of the room in about five minutes. She took a deep breath, straightened herself up, and walked directly toward her painting.

She went past him without looking at him or acknowledging him in any manner. She reached her easel and began to pack up her supplies. Then she heard the chair of his desk screech and knew he was standing up. In a few moments she felt him standing next to her. She moved away.

"I'm not going to hurt you," he said.

She ignored him and continued putting brushes into a plastic bag.

"I want to show you something."

He held out a piece of paper. She looked at it without taking it from his hand. It was a picture of Hi-Yo the horse.

"I finished it the other day after you left."

She squinted. It was not an extremely accurate drawing, but he had captured in a mysterious way the horse's elegance. "It's okay," she said, looking away.

"Okay? I thought it was pretty good. The head was the hardest, and at first I got the front legs shorter than the back ones, but I finally got them right, don't you think? I couldn't get out all the eraser smudges."

She took the drawing from his hand. Maybe if she commented on it, he would leave her alone. "You finished this the other day?" she asked.

"Yeah. What do you think?"

The curve of the horse's back was perfect. She could tell it was drawn in one single movement. "How long did it take you?"

"I don't know, about five minutes. Another hour to fix the damn legs."

She tried to hold back a smile, but couldn't. Then her eyes caught sight of the tattoo on his hand and she reminded herself to be careful. "Do you like to draw?" she asked.

He leaned back and sat on the edge of the desk he had been using. "I guess," he said. "I'm always doing it. Mostly in boring classes and on walls."

He was trying to be funny, but she didn't laugh. Once, someone had sprayed the side of their church with graffiti, and she remembered how hard Papa took it. "Were you sent here from detention again?"

"Nah," he said. "Mr. Gomez grabbed me during lunch and told me to come. I thought he wanted me to do some more drawings, but then he asked me if I had a car and I told him yeah, and he wants me to give you a ride, to help you take all your paintings and stuff."

Mary looked at him quickly. She had anticipated that picking up her supplies and leaving the art studio would be full of sadness, and now here she was occupied with this boy. She realized she was still holding on to the drawing of Hi-Yo. "The drawing is okay," she said. "You drew the way a horse is supposed to look pretty accurately . . . except for the legs. But if you want to really draw well, you need to stop drawing what you think something looks like and draw what you see." He looked as if he hadn't understood a single word she said. "Do you know what I'm saying?"

"No, not really."

She walked over to the shelf and grabbed Hi-Yo and then went back and stood next to him, holding the drawing and the horse in front of them. "Look carefully at the horse and look at your drawing. See any differences?"

He leaned forward and peered closely at both. "Yeah!" he exclaimed. "This horse has a line on the jaw that my drawing doesn't."

"Among other things," she said. "The head of your horse is thin and his nostrils are round. This horse's face is rounder and his nostrils are kind of oval."

"I even got the tail all wrong."

"It's not wrong," she said. She gave him back the drawing and placed Hi-Yo on his desk. "It's just that if you want to learn how to draw and paint, you need to learn how to see first."

She saw a funny smile come over his face. He walked over to the painting she had been working on. "I've seen that type of flower before, and your painting doesn't look like them."

"Once you learn to see, you'll be able to feel how things really are. I'm trying to draw the flowers I feel." She paused. "I didn't get it right, but that's what I was trying to do. I was trying to paint the colors I felt."

He thought about it for a few moments. "First you see and then you feel."

"Yeah," she said, smiling at the expression of discovery on his face. "What's out there, what you try to paint, is both the thing you see and the thing you feel." She felt dishonest saying that. When was the last time she felt what she painted? She remembered the time she painted Kate in their backyard. *You are a wonderful artist*, Mama had once said to her. *You can see inside a person's soul.*

"What is it?" Marcos asked.

"Nothing," she said, coming back to the present. "For the time being you should try to draw the real horse and not the image of a horse that you carry in your head. You understand?"

"Ahh, yeah, I think I do," he said.

The way he said it made her feel bad. He was right. She had just spoken to him as if he were incapable of understanding her. "Sorry," she said. "I didn't mean to speak to you that way." It struck her that even though he was in a gang, she wasn't afraid of him.

"Where's all your stuff?" he asked, changing the subject. "I could start loading it in my car."

She paused and took a deep breath while she looked at him. If she were painting him, what would she feel? Would she feel trust? She had looked into his eyes the last time she saw him, but hadn't noticed their color. Now she looked again and saw that they were hazel. His eyes, the nose, the mouth, the fore-head, the eyebrows, all these had a symmetry and a balance to them. There was nothing uncomfortable about the way he was looking at her. He was just sitting, waiting for her answer to his question.

She went to the back of the room and took out all of the paintings she had stored there.

They walked to the parking lot in back of the school, their arms full of paintings and plastic bags. His car was a ratty-looking black station wagon that looked like a miniature hearse. It had clearly been in an accident at some point, since the right side was caved in and smeared with the white paint of the other car. A sheet of clear plastic stretched across the space where one of the windows used to be. He walked to the side of the car that wasn't smashed in and opened the door from the inside. He put the paintings he was carrying in the backseat and then crawled in and opened the back hatch.

"That's the only way it opens," he said, sticking his head out the back end of the car. "Why don't you arrange the paintings so they don't get bent and I'll go get the other load?" Before she could say anything, he had climbed out of the station wagon and was hurrying back to the art studio.

They filled the car with ten paintings of various sizes. The framed paintings took up the most room, but they managed to fit them all in, even with all her supplies. They got in the car, and Marcos started it and drove out of the lot. Mary thought how strange it had been to hide her paintings from Papa as if they were sinful in some way. She had kept all her artwork at school except a few supplies in her dresser and an easel and some paintings under her bed. Now she'd be able to have these things at home as well. As she rode in the car with the window open and the air rushing by her face, she couldn't help but feel a sense of lightness and freedom.

She reached behind her head to put a seat belt on, but there was none. "I need to put one in," he said apologetically.

"Isn't it against the law not to have one?" she asked.

"Probably. I have them on the driver's side and in the back." He pulled his. "When I take my *jefita* and my sisters shopping, they go in the back and I drive like their *chofer*."

He has a mother, and sisters, and he takes them shopping. The thought made her smile. She looked at his hand gripping the steering wheel, the tiny star between the thumb and forefinger. "Are you in a gang?"

He looked at her quickly and then turned away, his eyes fixed on the road. He seemed to be deciding whether to tell the truth or lie. "Yeah," he finally said.

"Oh." She didn't mean to sound as if she was personally disappointed.

They drove in silence for a while and then he said, "You can ask me questions about it if you want."

"Questions about what?"

"About being in a gang. You looked like you wanted to know more about it."

"I don't care." She crossed her arms and looked out her window. Then, "Why?"

He placed both hands on top of the steering wheel and stared straight ahead. "Sometimes you don't have a choice."

She shook her head. "You always have a choice."

"It would have been hard for me and my family if I didn't join. My family still needs me." They stopped at a red light and she could tell that he was having trouble speaking. "I've always been good at drawing, and the Calle Cuatro guys, it's this gang, they told me I had to join or else."

"Or else?" The light turned green and the car lurched forward. She held on to the dashboard.

"Sorry," he said. "The clutch isn't working that well either. Or else my life and my family's life would be hell. So I joined a gang for protection. I didn't join the Calle Cuatros, because they were bad, bad people. I joined a small gang around my house called the V Tiguas."

She couldn't help giggling. The names of the gangs made her think of comic books and little boys playing games.

"I know. It seems like a silly name."

"I know where Tigua is, but what does the *V* stand for?"

"It stands for *barrio*. It means that our territory is Tigua."

"*Barrio* is spelled with a *B* and not a *V*," she said. She sounded like a teacher, she realized, and smiled. She wasn't exactly the best speller herself. "What do you do exactly? Besides spray the sides of buildings?"

"Mainly we protect ourselves and our people. We're Little League, really. Strictly self-defense." He took out a red bandanna from his khakis and wiped his forehead.

"Do you have guns and get into fights and kill people?"

He let out a long stream of air that almost turned into a whistle. "We protect ourselves. Mostly we try to act tough and we stay together in a group, always. Sometimes there's fights and stuff, but we don't go looking for it." He was staring at her when a car suddenly stopped in front of them. He slammed on the brakes.

"Gosh! Do you even have a license?" she asked when they started moving again.

"Believe it or not, I do. I got it this summer."

"You're seventeen."

"Yeah. And you're sixteen."

"How do you know?"

"I know. But *you* haven't even asked what my name is." They stopped at a red light. The light turned green, but he didn't move, apparently waiting for Mary to speak. But she felt shy all of a sudden, and turned to look out the window.

"My name is Marcos," he said after someone honked at him.

They drove in silence the rest of the way to her house. She didn't feel the need to speak further. He helped her take the paintings and other things to the wooden shed in the backyard. Papa had used it to store a lawn mower, a few old hoses, cans of paint, and Mama's garden tools, which they still kept. Later she would organize the things in the shed so there would be room for all her artwork.

They walked back to his car. She knew she should say "Thank you," but her body was filled with a strange mixture of chills and heat, and all she could do was smile and nod.

"Good-bye, Mary," he said. He turned around to leave and then stopped, as if remembering something. "I wish I could get out."

"What?"

"Of the gang. I wish I could get out."

"Maybe getting out is like a painting," she said. "First you see and feel every detail of what you want to paint, then you proceed very carefully, sketching with a pencil first before you put down the paints." She stopped herself. What did she know about being in a gang? Where were all these words coming from anyway?

"You mean, like I first need to imagine what's it's like being out, then imagine how to get out."

"Yes. Something like that."

"Got it. Oh, I forgot to tell you I was sorry."

"Sorry about what?"

"Last time I saw you over at the studio, I said stuff to you. Then I found out your old man had died the week before. That stunk on my part. Sorry about that. I mean, even if your old man hadn't died, I shouldn't have said what I said."

"What did you say? I forgot." She was pretending not to remember.

"I said that you were that hot girl who thought she was too good for everyone."

"I don't know about the 'hot girl' part," she said, "but what did you mean by 'too good for everyone'?"

"As in you don't let any guys get close to you."

"If that's what you meant, then you were right."

She wasn't joking, but he smiled anyway.

13

K ate had expected Aunt Julia to object to the trip to the mall on Saturday morning, but Aunt Julia thought it was a wonderful idea. She even volunteered to lend Kate money, to be paid back when the insurance check arrived. Kate told her she would take whatever money was needed from their father's savings account, which was also in her name. She waited for Aunt Julia to ask how much was in the savings account, but for once, she didn't seem to be interested in money matters. Instead, she said, "It's okay to go to the mall with your friend, but you need to take Mary with you."

"Mary is in the backyard painting. She's happy."

"She spends too much time by herself. It's not right for someone her age to be so solitary. She's either painting by her-self or keeping Catalina company. It's not normal."

"She's always been that way."

"She's been that way because your father was so . . . I don't even know what the right word is. He was abusive in his own way."

"That's not true." Kate thought her objection did not sound convincing.

"Well, I'm not going to argue with you. But I've seen the way he was with Catalina before you were even born, and I know how he was with you when you were too little to notice anything."

"He was strict, but he wasn't abusive," Kate said calmly.

"There's such a thing as being too strict," Aunt Julia said with finality.

Kate stood up and went to the television to turn the volume down. "Bonnie's coming in fifteen minutes," she said.

"I'm going to tell Mary to get ready," Aunt Julia said, also standing up.

"Fine, but you shouldn't make her go if she doesn't want to."

"Oh, she'll want to, all right."

Kate went into her room to change. The clothes in her closet seemed so meager. A few dresses for school and church, some skirts and blouses, a few of which were hand-me-downs from her mother. She turned and saw herself in the full-length mirror that hung on the back of the closet door. She pulled her T-shirt off over her head and looked at her body. Bonnie was right. She had a body full of beauty. There was no need to hide it any longer.

She was tightening her sandals when Mary came into the room, carrying the wooden box that held all her tubes of paint. She placed the box against the wall by the bed. Kate could tell Mary was upset.

"You don't have to go if you don't want to," Kate said to her.

"It's not that. I couldn't concentrate. I just stood there staring at the canvas."

"Why don't you stay? I don't know why Aunt Julia wants you to go."

"We probably shouldn't rile her up. She's been so easy to live with lately, and she's been very helpful staying with us as long as she has."

"You never have trouble concentrating when you're painting. Are you worried about something?"

"I don't know what it is," Mary said thoughtfully. "It's strange. It's been hard for me to paint since . . . I was trying this technique where you paint over wet paint. It has to be done very carefully, otherwise you end up with a mess, and guess what. I ended up with a mess. Oh, well. I'll try again some other day."

Kate could tell that Mary was not telling the truth. What was it Mary had said that night when they talked about Simon? Something about her painting not being the same since Mother's accident. She wished for a second that she had paid more attention, but there was no time right now to pursue the subject. "Bonnie's coming any minute. You better get ready if you want to go."

"Can't I go like this?"

"In overalls that have paint all over them?"

Mary laughed and went to the closet.

Kate said, "You know, now that Father's not here, you could wear shorts when you paint outside."

Mary didn't seem to hear her. "Gosh," she said, reaching for the flowered skirt she always seemed to wear, "I don't think

I've ever been to a mall. Can you believe it? This will be the first time ever."

Kate observed Mary getting dressed. It made her sad to think that Mary's sole shopping experiences had been at Walmarts and other discount stores, and when she went, it was Father who had the final say as to what she bought. That would have been true for Kate as well if she hadn't had Simon and Bonnie to take her places. She couldn't buy clothes at the mall because her father would ask where they came from, but at least she had *visited* malls.

"What's the matter?" Kate asked when she saw a gloomy shadow appear on Mary's face.

"I feel funny," Mary responded.

"Why?"

"It's like I'm going against Papa's wishes, like I'm doing something wrong."

"You think it's a sin to go to the mall?"

"No, not a sin, exactly. It's just that — it's just that Papa believed we shouldn't be concerned so much with how we look or what we have. It's hard to all of a sudden stop seeing life the way he did, the way he brought us up."

"There's nothing wrong with going to the mall," Kate said with certainty. She stood up and zipped the back of Mary's skirt. She took her sister by the shoulders and walked her to the mirror. "What do you see?" Mary blushed. "Look," Kate insisted. She had noticed a long time ago that Mary looked in the mirror only to the extent that it was absolutely necessary. She put her hand under Mary's chin and gently lifted her face. "Look at that face, those eyes, those eyelashes. You're gorgeous. You recognize beauty everywhere except in your-self. What's wrong with getting some shiny jewelry or colorful clothes to brighten up that beauty? Let your light shine before all men, especially all the good-looking men, and all that."

Mary slapped Kate's hand jokingly. "Kate, now you're mak-ing fun of scripture. If Papa could only hear you!"

"Yeah, if he could only hear me," Kate said dryly. "I'm going to check the mailbox. I'll meet you out front."

Kate slid into Bonnie's front seat even before Bonnie had the chance to honk. Mary and Aunt Julia came out. "Be careful," Aunt Julia said as Mary was getting into the backseat.

"Hi, Mary." Bonnie located Mary's face in the rearview mirror.

"I hope it's okay that I come. Aunt Julia insisted."

"Sure it's okay." Bonnie pulled out onto the main road, leaving a cloud of dust behind. "Which mall do you want to go to?"

"We need to stop at the credit union first," Kate said.

Mary asked, "Kate, do we have enough money to go shopping?"

"We have enough," Kate said.

"Kate," Bonnie said, "what is that smile on your face? What happened? You can't hide anything from me and you know it."

Kate's smile got even bigger. She opened her canvas hand-bag, took out a thick white envelope, and waved it in the air.

The car swerved off the paved road for a second. "Oh my God!" Bonnie screamed. "Is that what I think it is?"

"Don't crash! Don't crash!" Kate yelled.

"Where?"

"Stanford!"

"Ohhhh! That's so awesome! That's where you've always wanted to go. Your first choice! Wait, wait, I have to give you a hug." Bonnie maneuvered the car to the side of the road. The driver in the car behind them honked angrily. The two girls got out and they hugged and held hands and jumped in unison.

Mary opened the door and stepped out, a bewildered, lost look on her face. "What about Stanford?" she asked.

Kate stopped her celebration with Bonnie to face Mary. She wished for a moment that Mary weren't there. "I was accepted to Stanford. I'm getting a full scholarship."

Before Mary could say anything, Bonnie was screaming again, "Get outta here! A full scholarship? Oh my God! Oh my God! Get in the car, girl, we are going to celebrate!"

Bonnie ran around the back of the car to return to the driver's seat. Kate and Mary stood alone by the side of the road.

"Be happy for me, okay?" Kate said.

"I'm happy for you," Mary said. Then, tentatively, "Is that the Stanford near San Jose, where Aunt Julia lives?"

"Yes." Kate took a deep breath. "Mary, I need to tell you something. Remember the time when Mama and I went to visit Aunt Julia by ourselves?"

"Yes."

"Mama took me to visit Stanford. She made me promise that I would do all I could to go there. It was her dream when she was my age, and then she dreamed I would go there in her place. It became both our dream." She took Mary's hand. "I've been working for this, dreaming of it, for years, Mary. We'll work everything out, all right?"

"All right," Mary said. Then she gave Kate a long hug. When they separated, Kate saw that Mary had quietly begun to cry.

14

Mary sat in the backseat of Bonnie's car and tried to look happy. Kate and Bonnie kept talking about Stanford. She had always expected Kate to go to college, but it never occurred to her that she would leave El Paso. The only reason she could think of why Kate didn't tell her about Stanford was that she needed to keep it from Papa, and that meant, in Kate's mind, keeping it a secret from Mary too. But Kate was wrong. She would have kept her secret well.

Every once in a while, Kate turned around to see how Mary was reacting to it all. Whenever she did this, Mary immediately smiled.

"Please be happy for me," Kate said to Mary again, one of those times.

"I'm happy if it makes you happy," Mary said.

"Here's the credit union," Bonnie said before Kate could say anything else.

While Kate went into the credit union, Bonnie and Mary stayed in the car with the air conditioner running. "That's so awesome about Kate. Dang!" Bonnie said. She banged her hands on the steering wheel for emphasis. "I can't wait to tell everyone in school. A full scholarship too! You know what that means? That means she doesn't have to pay a cent, not for tuition or room and board or anything. Plane fare, maybe books, that's about it."

"Plane fare," Mary repeated to herself. She was looking out the window. Cars were driving up to the automated tellers on the side of the building. People stuck their arms out and completed their business in a matter of minutes.

"I wonder what Simon is going to say when she tells him?" Bonnie fiddled with the radio. She began to bob her head to the music when she found the right station.

"Simon doesn't know?"

"What?" Bonnie turned the volume down.

"Simon doesn't know about Stanford?"

Bonnie shook her head. "I'm the only one she told," she said, sounding guilty. "I think she was afraid that people would get worried about her leaving and all, you know."

Mary nodded. She wondered how she was going to live first without Papa and now without Kate.

Kate came out of the credit union, waving an envelope and beaming. "Let's go shopping!" she said as she opened the door to the car. Mary hadn't seen her so buoyant and carefree in a long time.

"How much did you get?" Bonnie asked. "Not that it's any of my business. I just want to know what we're working with, you know what I'm saying?"

"One thousand," Kate answered.

"Kate!" Mary couldn't help sounding like Papa.

"It's not just for shopping," Kate said. "We need it to pay bills and buy groceries. I don't want to come to the credit union every day and go through the hassle of proving to them that I'm on the account." She said this in a way that Mary hadn't heard before, like money matters were something for Kate alone to decide.

They drove on to the mall. Bonnie chattered so fast that Mary caught only a word or two. Kate seemed to agree with whatever Bonnie was saying, but Mary got the impression that her mind was someplace else. Mary closed her eyes. When she got to talk to Kate alone, she would not worry her with concerns about how she and Mama would get along without her. It was obvious that one of Kate's dreams had just been fulfilled. She only wished Kate had shared her dream with her as she had shared it with Bonnie.

The mall was bustling with people. Some of them walked purposefully, as if they knew just what they wanted to get or were looking for a particular store. Others ambled aimlessly through the corridors, swept away by the frenzy of sights and sounds. Mary had been in large stores before, but the proximity and variety of the stores in the mall overwhelmed her. Colors darted at her from everywhere, and there was hardly any time to recognize them. There were clothes in racks in different patterns and shapes. She could not find a place to rest her eyes.

Bonnie and Kate decided to go into a store that had mannequins dressed in black. Outside the front of the store stood a fountain surrounded by granite benches.

"I'll wait for you here," Mary told Kate.

"You need to get some things as well," Kate said.

"I will," Mary responded. She didn't think she needed any new clothes, but she didn't want to disappoint Kate. "I'm going to wait until we get to the big stores."

Kate opened up her purse, took out two fifty-dollar bills, and offered them to Mary. "The big stores are at each end of the mall. Want to meet here in an hour?"

"Kate, this is way too much money," Mary said, staring at the bills in her hand.

Kate grabbed Mary's hand and closed her fingers around the money. "Don't be silly. Look at you. You've had that dress for two years now and it's so worn out, you can almost see through it. You can buy old-fashioned-looking things if you want, but at least they'll be new. Trust me, one hundred dollars is not going to get you much."

"Okay. I'll meet you here in an hour," Mary said. Kate smiled and started to walk to the store. "Kate," Mary called after her.

She stopped and came back to Mary.

"I'm happy for you about Stanford, I really am."

"Thank you," Kate said. "Now don't be so serious all the time, and go spend some money."

Mary walked around the noisy halls of the mall in a daze. It wasn't just the noise and the visual images that flashed before her. Her head was filled with memories of her childhood, of Kate, and imagining life without her, all intermingled. She came upon the food court, found an empty table, and sat down.

Across from where she was sitting, she saw a store that specialized in arts and crafts. She remembered the day Mama took her and Kate into a similar store. First they got a chemistry set for Kate, then they bought a palette of watercolor paints and a pad of thick paper, not the flimsy kind that Mary had been using up to then. The palette had twelve colors, two rows of six, and the tint of the colors was high quality. Mary remembered how Mama looked at all the brushes. She picked up one after another and ran her finger across the bristles. "This one feels so nice," she said. "Why is it so much more expensive than the others?"

"That one is made from ox hair, Mama."

She was shocked. "Ox hair? Ox, like a *hueye*?"

Mary grabbed the brush from Mama's hand and tried to tickle her arm with it, but Mama brushed it away, a look of disgust in her face. "I hope they gave the ox a bath before they cut the hair of the poor thing."

Mary put the brush back and picked up another one. "Look at this one, Mama."

"Oooo. That's so soft."

"This one is even more expensive than the ox hair."

"Don't tell me it's made from some poor old lady's hair, because I'll be very upset."

"No, silly, this is a sable brush. They're the best kind of brushes you can have."

"A sable? I thought those animals were extinct," Mama said.

A little girl at the table next to Mary dropped her ice-cream cone on the floor and began to cry. Mary snapped back to the present. At that moment she felt her mother next to her, her warmth and intelligence vibrant as always. She smiled at Mama's confusion about saber-toothed tigers. Mama was so proud of Kate and her. Mama loved Kate's intelligence and she loved Mary's talent for painting.

Mary walked into Sears and bought a blouse and a pair of jeans, which she tried on to make sure they were loose and comfortable. Everything she bought was on sale, so she spent forty-five dollars all told. The bag that she carried out of Sears looked big and bulky. Kate would be happy with her. Then she went into the arts and crafts store and looked at the tubes of oil paint. She picked up the yellow and thought of the portrait of Kate she had painted once, the rich yellow background she had given it. She placed the tube of paint back on the shelf and walked back to sit by the fountain.

Fifteen minutes later, Kate and Bonnie appeared, their arms full of packages. Mary's bag looked very small in comparison. "Is that all you bought?" Kate asked.

"There's a lot in there. It's just folded really well." Mary smiled, knowing that Kate would see through her.

"Oh, you're impossible," Kate said. "Come on, you're coming with us."

"You guys go," Bonnie said. "I'm going back in there to buy that cute pink blouse we saw." She pointed at the store with the mannequins in black.

"I'm all set, really," Mary objected.

"You should get her some makeup too," Bonnie suggested.

"She doesn't need makeup," Kate said reproachfully.

"Something subtle," Bonnie said as she turned to go into the store. "The kind a guy never even knows is there."

"I don't want any makeup," Mary said.

"Don't listen to her," Kate told Mary. "Let's start with shoes. You definitely need shoes."

"I can get those for myself," Mary protested.

"We have to get you new dress shoes," Kate said. "The ones you have are old-maidish. You're sixteen!"

"I only wear those to church. No one there cares," Mary protested.

"How much of the money did you spend?" Kate asked.

"About fifty dollars."

"We'll buy dress shoes with what's left over. It will be fun."

"Kate, we should save the money. We're going to need it, don't you think?" Mary tried not to sound worried.

Kate shook her head. She seemed tired of reminders that they should be responsible. Mary suddenly understood that Kate needed to be, at least for a short while, as carefree as that day when they walked out of the arts and crafts store holding Mama's hands, she with her paints and brushes and Kate with her chemistry set, all three of them connected by a single happiness.

15

Kate woke up to the sound of Mary getting ready for church. Kate had decided to go this Sunday morning for Mary's sake. It was the first time they would be back in church since Father died, and it was not fair to let Mary bear the brunt of people's questions and curiosity about their future. Besides, it would be nice to see Reverend Soto again.

There was no pressure from Aunt Julia to attend church. One of her long-standing grievances against Father was that, according to her, Father had forced her sister to become a Protestant. As far as she was concerned, *no* church was a thousand times better than a *Protestant* church. But she'd begrudgingly agreed to watch Mother so Kate and Mary could go.

Usually, Simon came over half an hour before services and the three of them walked the two blocks together. In the year and a half that he had been dating Kate, Simon had never missed a Sunday. It was one of the reasons Father trusted him so much. But today, Mary and Kate waited outside the house for ten minutes, and when Simon didn't show up, Kate told Mary that they should go ahead by themselves. Kate thought it was Simon's way of reminding her yet again that their relationship had changed since the night he had "proposed."

The sign in front of the church announced that Reverend Soto was now conducting the Sunday services. Kate felt surprised that she was not upset that Father's name had been removed from the sign so quickly.

She was wearing a light green sleeveless dress she'd bought at the mall the day before. It was nothing she would have worn if Father were alive, but when she put it on that morning, she felt as if she could finally breathe a full measure of air. She didn't think the dress was much different from what other women at the church wore, but she could still feel their eyes following her as she and Mary walked to their usual pew, the third row on the right-hand side. Mary took out her pad of paper and a pencil as soon as they sat down. Kate folded her arms and hugged herself. She cast a sideways glance at Mary, who had already begun her doodling.

"Why do you do that?" Kate whispered.

"What?" Mary continued drawing without lifting her eyes.

"You start drawing as soon as you come in."

"It helps me," Mary said.

"Helps you what?"

"It just helps me."

Kate considered Mary's answer and then looked away. It was one of those Mary-like statements that she had learned to accept. "But can you actually doodle and listen to what the preacher says? Did you ever listen to Father's sermons?"

Mary's answer came quickly, as if she had expected the question for a long time and was glad it had finally been asked. "Drawing helps me listen," she said quietly. "Sometimes I even draw what I hear."

Kate wanted to ask what she meant by that, but at that moment, Simon came down the middle aisle and sat next to her. He squeezed her hand. "Hello," he said. "I'm sorry I'm late. I had car trouble."

"Oh no!" Kate exclaimed a notch louder than she intended. Father had always urged people to use the time before the service to quiet their minds in silence. "What is it? Do you know?" she said in a softer tone. She couldn't help noticing Simon was wearing the same shiny black suit and purple tie he had worn to Father's funeral.

"I don't know," Simon said, shrugging his shoulders. "It's probably the battery. It started when I jumped it. I haven't done too well in the luck department lately." He looked at Kate meaningfully and she understood that he was still sore.

Wait until he hears about Stanford, she said to herself.

Mrs. Alvarado began to play a lively piece on the organ with blaring sounds meant to resemble trumpets. That was the cue that the minister was approximately five minutes away from entering. Only the very daring would continue to speak after Mrs. Alvarado sounded the general warning. Kate glanced back quickly and saw that the church was nearly full, fuller than it had ever been for Father, it seemed.

She had always enjoyed watching Mrs. Alvarado play the organ. Now the music stopped momentarily and Kate watched with affection as Mrs. Alvarado went through her ritual. First she pulled each finger of her hand until it cracked. Then she opened her black purse and fished out a wadded tissue with which she wiped the moist space between her upper lip and her nose. Finally, she straightened her back and placed her hands over the organ keys in a ready-to-strike position.

Mrs. Alvarado began to play a somber piece, and the members of the choir walked down the aisle two by two in their maroon robes. The size of the choir varied from Sunday to Sunday. Today the choir had fifteen members, a high number, with thirteen women and two men.

When all of the choir had found their places behind the organ, the back door opened and Reverend Soto entered the church. It seemed to Kate that he walked as if he owned the place. He swooped to the front of the altar with his white cassock billowing like a sail, made the smallest of bows before the golden cross, and then strode up the steps and sat down in back of the lectern.

They all stood up to sing the first hymn. Simon held the hymnal for Kate, but Kate only mouthed the words. She was watching Reverend Soto. The only times she had talked with him were when he came to the house after Father died, when he prayed for Mama, and again after the funeral services. Now she was able to take a longer look at him. He was strong-looking and walked with self-assurance. There was a maturity about him, an aura of power and wisdom that she liked.

Suddenly, as if he sensed he was being examined from afar, he lifted his eyes from the page and caught her looking at him. He smiled, and she looked down immediately, embarrassed.

The service moved forward to the sermon. Reverend Soto stepped up to the lectern and began.

"Jesus said, 'If you continue in my word, you are truly my disciples, and you will know the truth, and the truth will make you free.'" Reverend Soto paused and scanned the congregation. There was silence. "Now, what we have to ask ourselves is what Jesus meant by truth and why it will set us free. I'll tell you what Jesus meant by truth. If you 'continue in my word,' Jesus said, 'you will know the truth.' To continue in His word is to obey His word. And what is Jesus's word? It is love. Truth, then, is a response to His call of love."

Someone in back of the church said "Amen." Kate saw Simon turn to see who it was. Reverend Soto continued, his voice softer now. "Elsewhere He says, 'If any man wishes to come after me, let him deny himself, and day by day let him take up his cross and follow me.' Love is the denial of self. We must choose what is best for others first, regardless of whether it hurts us or not, regardless of whether it hurts them or not. For the truth of love may at times even require us to hurt the people we love. We need to be awakened, sometimes through pain, to recognize the true nature of love."

Kate moved closer to Simon. On her other side, Mary was drawing pointed geometric figures. She had said that sometimes she drew what she heard. Now Kate saw that maybe she had been telling the truth. When Father preached, Mary made circles within circles and designs the shape of petals, but the triangles and pointed shapes she was drawing now seemed to go hand in hand with the intense voice of Reverend Soto. He was certainly a more dynamic speaker than Father.

"Now hear this: We don't want to be awakened. We prefer to doze on with our weak love. This sentiment we call love is not love. It's something else: obligation; duty; security; good, nice feelings. But Jesus calls for a love that engages our whole being, our mind and heart and body. This love I'm talking about is so great that it can't possibly come from us."

Kate lost track of the sermon for a few moments. He had looked at her at the precise moment that he said the word *love*, and while it was surely a coincidence, something about this sent a shiver through her. Now he was talking about the nature of freedom and duty, and how they too related to love. "Love is not just what we are *obligated* to do. It is not just what we *have* to do. Love is also what we *want* to do. It is what we have to do and what we want to do with all the power of our being."

Kate tried to make sense of what he was saying, but it was hard for her to concentrate. As Reverend Soto preached, a few more people here and there in the congregation were saying "Amen," pronouncing the word the Spanish way: *Ahhh-men*. A kind of electricity filled the air, or it traveled through her veins, she wasn't sure which.

"To be free, we must first recognize our own poverty, our own dependence. To receive His love, we must first see and feel our need for His love. And when His love is offered, it is up to us to obey. How do we know what He wants from us? He shows us His will in feelings, in images, in our peace, in our discomfort, in our restlessness, in the words of our friends and enemies, in signs only we can interpret. Where our heart is touched, there is His will. He uses the needs of others to show us what we must do."

A part of Kate wanted to move to the rhythm of Reverend Soto's voice, while another part wanted to hold still, to hold the feeling in. She saw the people around her rapt, afraid to miss a single word from his lips. Some had their eyes closed. Some were nodding at his questions, and some were standing and raising their arms to heaven.

"Ultimately, to be free, to accept the truth that will set us free, is to let the Spirit of God act through us. 'If any man must follow me, let him deny himself and day by day take up his cross.' That is the test of love, isn't it? Am I denying myself? Am I putting others first? Am I taking up my daily cross? Am I giving myself away, day by day? To love is to be willing to sacrifice. That's the truth! The truth of love, the truth of sacrifice, will set you free."

Kate remained very still. She saw Reverend Soto's eyes fall on her again, and for a moment she felt as if he had spoken directly to her, as if the whole sermon had been meant for her, urging acceptance of a truth that was unlike any truth she had ever heard. She could feel Simon next to her, indecisive as to whether he should stand or remain seated, watching to see what she would do. Mary had begun to draw a chain of circles.

Then the rhythm of Reverend Soto's voice became slower and a hush descended on the church. He spoke in a soft tone, almost a whisper. "I will make you this promise: For however long I am with you, I will always tell you the truth. Truth is what I'm here for. I know some of you think I'm too young and inexperienced. 'What does he know of truth?' you ask. But truth does not have anything to do with age or experience. It is God's truth that I convey, not mine. That's where my confidence and strength come from. I am but a vehicle for God's truth."

Reverend Soto paused and waited for total silence. Then he went on, looking directly at Kate and Mary. "I want to acknowledge here before his daughters all the good that Reverend Romero did for this church. We are all indebted to him for his life, the same he gave to this church. We are grateful for his kindness. He was a sweet man, a saintly man. I ask that you not judge me by the standards he set. I'm not here to be sweet or saintly. I'm here to tell you the truth, and the truth is harsh sometimes."

Someone in the back yelled "Amen," and then Reverend Soto sat down while the usher took up the collection. When the service was over, he walked down the aisle and smiled at Kate as he passed her.

They waited for Mrs. Alvarado's music to end and then they stood. Kate saw in Mary's face an unusual expression of anger. She was sure that Mary was upset about what Reverend Soto had said about Father. Had not Father also told the congregation the truth? Mary wadded the piece of paper she had been drawing on and dropped it on the pew.

"That was some sermon, huh?" Simon said as they filed into the aisle.

"Yeah, some sermon," Kate responded absentmindedly. She felt disoriented, confused. If the sermon was directed at her, what was he trying to tell her?

"I'm going out the back way," Mary said. "I'll meet you at home."

"Okay." Kate wished she too could skip the greeting. Already she saw people coming to talk to her.

Mr. Cisneros was the first to approach her. He was in his late seventies, and whenever possible, he had driven Father to his pastoral visits so he wouldn't have to take a cab. Father called him his right-hand man. He gave Kate a hug and shook Simon's hand. "We haven't seen you since the funeral. We were worried," he said loudly. Mr. Cisneros was totally deaf in one ear and had a hearing aid in the other.

"Thank you," Kate said. "How have you been, Mr. Cisneros?" She called him Mr. Cisneros despite years of his insisting that she call him Manny.

"Oh, not the same since your father died. I don't have nothing to do. I used to feel useful when he was around."

"I'm sure Reverend Soto can find something for you to do."

"Pssh," Mr. Cisneros said, as if swatting a fly from his face. "Everyone here seems to be gaga over him. I like my ministers to be a little older. I think I'm going to go back to being a Catholic. These Holy Rollers are too much for me." People in front of them turned around to look at them. Everyone in the church probably heard Mr. Cisneros's statement. Simon laughed outright. Kate smiled and put her index finger to her lips.

"Oh, who cares who hears me?" Mr. Cisneros winked first at Kate and then at Simon. "If you want me to take you any- place, you or Mary, you let me know — I mean, if this young man is not available. It'll give me something to do." Mr. Cisneros winked again and exited through the back door.

All the longtime members of the church came to greet Kate and Simon. The line moved slowly. The greetings were, as Kate suspected, laced with curiosity. "What are you girls going to do now? Will you go live with your aunt? How will you be able to take care of Catalina?"

"We're going to be okay," Kate answered. She tried to avoid answering the questions directly. She was aware that many of the questioners automatically thought that Kate would marry Simon and Simon would take care of them. *People* like *Simon*, Kate thought. It was funny that she had never valued that before. People saw them as perfect for each other.

Mrs. Alvarado closed up the organ, came up the side aisle, and crossed over to talk to them. She expressed her hope that Kate would once again join the choir like old times. "Now more than ever," Mrs. Alvarado went on, "you need to sing. In singing you can express your sorrow."

"I'll think about it. I promise you," Kate told her. She remembered how hard it had been to get out of the choir in the first place.

"Simon." Mrs. Alvarado grabbed Simon's arm. "Convince her to come back to choir. You've heard her sing. And you should come, too! We have hardly any men, as you can see."

"I sing like a frog," Simon said, laughing.

"Well, then you'll sing bass." Then, turning to Kate, she exclaimed, "God, what a sermon! We're all hoping that Reverend Soto can stay with us. He's something else, isn't he?"

Kate nodded.

With that, Mrs. Alvarado said good-bye. Reverend Soto was two couples away.

"What's bass?" Simon asked.

"Someone whose voice sounds like a frog," Kate quipped.

Being tall and thin, Reverend Soto hunched over as he shook people's hands. He straightened up as soon as Kate stepped in front of him. She felt his penetrating gaze travel to the pit of her stomach. He took her hand in his two hands and it seemed to her his hands were unusually warm.

Kate's mind went blank. She thought about telling him what a great sermon he gave but she wasn't sure how she felt about the sermon. He was still holding on to her hand, and a current of electricity ran through her again. It was Reverend Soto who spoke first.

"Kate," he said. "Welcome. I'm glad you came." His voice was softer and more personal than the voice he used in his sermon. Then he let go of her hand and cordially shook Simon's before turning back to her. "I would like to come to your house for a visit," he said. "It would be good to talk. I haven't had a chance to talk to you and your sister since the funeral."

"Okay," she said tentatively.

"How about next Wednesday evening, say, seven P.M.?"

"I work," Kate said.

"You can get off early," Simon said to Kate. Then to Reverend Soto, he said, "She works at one of my restaurants."

"Thank you," Reverend Soto said to Simon. "Then I'll see you at seven," he said to Kate.

Kate could feel the people behind her growing impatient. She had taken more time than was permissible under the rules of church courtesy. "I'll see you then," she said. She moved on, still thinking about that touch, that look.

Outside on the steps of the church, Simon asked, "It's okay if I said you could get off early, wasn't it? I just blurted it out. I didn't even think that maybe you didn't want to talk to him. I guess you have to talk to him since he's the pastor."

Oh, Simon, she thought. *How can you be so dense?*

16

Mary snuck out the back of the church before anyone could see her. She always liked going to church. Despite what Kate thought, she paid attention to everything that happened during the service. The drawing that she did only deepened her concentration for what was taking place, and she felt close to Papa whenever she listened to his sermons.

But now she was angry. Anger was an emotion she wasn't used to feeling but that had begun to creep up more frequently. It had popped up sometimes when she thought about Kate going off to Stanford and leaving her alone with Mama, and it almost exploded today at the end of Reverend Soto's sermon. Reverend Soto said that Papa was a sweet and saintly man, but he said it as if Papa's sweetness kept him from telling the truth or speaking about the evil and suffering that existed in the world. Besides, he had spoken without any knowledge of Papa. *Sweet* was not a word she would ever use for him. Papa was kind, and that was different.

Mary got home to find Aunt Julia waiting impatiently for her. She wanted to leave for Mass early so she could get a good seat. She called a cab and then went into the bathroom to freshen up. It would have been easier for her to keep all her cosmetics and other beauty aids on Mama's dresser in the bedroom, but she preferred to store her things in the small wall cabinet in the bathroom. Mary had tried to understand what made her so afraid of being around Mama. The only thing she could think of was that Mama reminded Aunt Julia of death, and that was scary for some people.

Mary looked out the front window and watched Aunt Julia hurry to the cab and climb in the back. Lately, Aunt Julia seemed restless, as if she were itching to go back home as soon as possible. Mary hoped the insurance money would make Aunt Julia want to stay with her and Mother, since Kate was planning to go away. *Aunt Julia's not so bad*, she thought. But she wasn't sure she truly believed that.

Mary went into Mama's room and propped her head up with pillows. She did that a few times a day to change the position of her spine. Then she turned on the overhead light as well as the lamp next to the bed. The curtains were closed, so only the pale light from the lightbulbs fell on Mama's face. She reminded Mary of someone in a painting by El Greco, someone whose face glowed with light and shadow all at once. She wondered if she had captured that glow in the portrait of Mama she had done. At that moment, Mama had her eyes open, but they did not focus on Mary or anything else. In her portrait, Mama's eyes were focused on a distant point, as if she were contemplating angels hovering above her.

She heard a knock at the door and hurried to the front room. The front door was closed, so Kate must have gotten locked out. Mary opened the door and jumped back a step when she saw Mr. Lucas and Mr. Acevedo in their black Sunday suits. The kids at church called Mr. Lucas the Scarecrow because he looked like a brown version of the character in *The Wizard of Oz*. Mr. Acevedo was known as Humpty Dumpty behind his back on account of his round shape.

It was Mr. Lucas who spoke first. "Hello, Mary. May we come in?"

Mary looked at him and then at Mr. Acevedo. There was not even a hint of a smile on their faces. They had seemed happier at Papa's funeral than they did now.

"Sure," Mary said, opening the door.

She pointed toward the sofa and asked if they could excuse her for a second. She went to Mama's room and removed the pillows from behind her head, because there was more danger of her falling or choking when she was propped up. She returned to the living room and smiled. Mr. Lucas and Mr. Acevedo smiled back with forced, tight expressions. Mary knew right then that they were coming to deliver bad news.

"Is your sister here?" Mr. Acevedo asked.

"She was still at church when I left. She should be here soon."

"Oh." Mr. Acevedo glanced at Mr. Lucas. It was obvious that they had not anticipated Kate's absence and now they were lost. In the meantime, Mary was getting nervous that Kate had gone over to Simon's house. There was no reason for her to come home and prepare Sunday dinner the way she used to when Papa was alive.

"I guess we can wait a few minutes until she gets back," Mr. Lucas said.

"Would you like some lemonade?" she asked. Kate had made some the day before.

"Sure, sure," Mr. Lucas answered, apparently on behalf of both men.

She walked into the kitchen and went about preparing the drinks as slowly as she could, taking the tall plastic glasses from the pantry, cracking the ice cube containers over the counter, and filling the glasses with lemonade. The only time she had prayed that morning was in the few moments in church before Reverend Soto began to speak, but she prayed again at that moment for Kate to come home as soon as possible. She waited in the kitchen a couple more minutes, listening for the front door to open, but all she could hear was the raspy noise of Mr. Lucas's breathing.

She returned to the living room and handed them the lemonade. Mr. Lucas took a sip, smiled, and burped. Mr. Acevedo looked around for someplace to put the glass. On the wall in front of the sofa was a picture of the Last Supper. "That's a nice picture," he said. "Is it new?"

"It's been there for many years," she said. Mr. Lucas and Mr. Acevedo had visited Papa countless times before and had sat on the very sofa where they were now sitting, but she knew they were just trying to make conversation until Kate arrived. "Papa hung it on the wall the first day we moved to the house.

Mama told me about it. She said it was a wedding gift from Grandpa, Papa's father, who was also a minister."

Mr. Lucas and Mr. Acevedo began to squirm as if a couple of worms had crawled in their pants. Mary glanced at the door, but there was no Kate, and she resigned herself to dealing with their business. She sat down in the armchair and said with as much calm as she could muster, "I guess Kate may not be coming home straight from church. She might have gone out to lunch with Simon."

Mr. Acevedo cupped the lemonade glass with both hands. "I s-s-see," he stuttered. He looked at Mr. Lucas for guidance. Mr. Lucas shrugged his shoulders. Mr. Acevedo frowned, then cleared his throat and began to speak.

"We" — he made a gesture with his hand to include both himself and Mr. Lucas — "I mean, the church council and the deacons wanted us to talk to you and your sister." He paused, clearly hoping that Mr. Lucas would continue, but Mr. Lucas chose that moment to gulp down half his glass of lemonade. Mr. Acevedo had no choice but to go on. "Well, I guess, first I want to tell you that the church is going to pay for your father's funeral expenses. That came to about four thousand dollars. You decided on a burial rather than cremation, but that was okay with the church."

"Cremation is a lot cheaper," Mr. Lucas piped in.

Mary wondered why he was bringing up the fact the church would pay for Papa's funeral. It had never occurred to her or Kate, she was sure, that they wouldn't. Maybe it was a mistake for them to think that way and they just didn't know any better. But it made her sad that the church found it necessary to tell them about it. Papa's life and death felt cheapened by talk of the cost of funerals and money.

"We have also collected a special offering for you and your sister from all the church members. The members of our church are poor, you know that, but somehow they dug deep and sacrificed, and we took money from a reserve fund, and all told we collected ten thousand dollars." He paused for Mary to react.

"Thank you," she said. It would take a lot of money from each of the two hundred members to make up ten thousand dollars.

"There's also a pension plan that the church contributed to," Mr. Lucas said. "It had built up to about sixty thousand dollars before the market came crashing down, and now it's about a third less than that, but it will help."

"The church also paid for seventy-five percent of your father's health insurance," Mr. Acevedo added, "and correct me if I'm wrong" — here he turned to Mr. Lucas — "but you two girls should be covered perhaps until you graduate from college. Coverage for your mother, of course, ran out a long time ago."

"That's correct," said Mr. Lucas. "But you'll need to check up on the coverage because the law has changed."

Mary nodded that she understood, but she was beginning to lose grasp of what they were saying. She wished with all her heart for Kate to be sitting next to her. Kate would bring a chair from the dining room, place it in front of the two men, and pepper them with questions. Mary took a deep breath, because from the look on their faces, it appeared as if Mr. Acevedo and Mr. Lucas were about to deliver the bad news.

Mr. Acevedo spoke. "You know that the church misses your father very much. We appreciate all that he did for it." He swallowed. "But . . . we need to move on. The church council and the deacons have a responsibility to find a new minister. I mean, it will be hard to fill your father's shoes, but we need to."

"We have to do it as soon as possible, otherwise we're going to lose members. They'll go to another church." Mr. Lucas moved to the edge of the sofa. His right eye began to twitch.

"The Protestant churches here in El Paso are so small. You know, everyone is Catholic. We're very, very fortunate to have as many members as we have. But we've been losing them by the dozen. In the past two years alone, we've lost over fifty people."

They seemed to be attributing the loss to Papa, and Mary prepared herself to defend him, the way Kate would if she were there.

"We set up a search committee right away," Mr. Acevedo said.

"But then an opportunity came up that we're all excited about." Mr. Lucas finished Mr. Acevedo's sentence. Mr. Acevedo glanced at him, annoyed.

"Reverend Soto, you know, you saw him today. He's agreed to be with us until we find a permanent minister. Many members are already saying that even though he's young, he'd be the perfect replacement. They want someone more vibrant like him, who will attract young families with children. Young families are what keep churches going."

"More vibrant?" Mary said. How could these people possibly think that Papa was not vibrant? Papa was dynamic in the way that mattered most. His sermons made souls vibrate with warmth and praise and, yes, sometimes, sorrow and shame. How could they think that the preaching of Reverend Soto was better?

"We don't mean any disrespect to your father," Mr. Acevedo said apologetically. "What we mean to say is that the direction of the church is different from when your father was leading it. Actually, the direction has been different for quite a while."

She looked at them, perplexed. Father was leading people to God. What other direction was there?

"You saw how people were this morning at church. They were inspired. The Holy Spirit filled them up and they expressed that. There was so much emotion. That's what people are looking for in a church these days."

It almost seemed as if they had fired Papa a long time before and now they were telling her why they had done it. Okay, maybe Papa wasn't giving the church what the church was looking for, and maybe the Reverend Soto was God's special gift come to save it, but Papa was dead now. Why tell her all of this? "So?" She sounded rude, but she didn't care.

"We're very lucky to have Reverend Soto," Mr. Lucas said. "There are churches all over that are eager to get him. And if we grab him now, we might be able to keep him permanently.

He's indicated his willingness to be our permanent minister. It's such a blessing for a church to find someone so young who is willing to stay with us forever."

"Good," she said. It was as cold and distant as she could be.

"But . . ." Mr. Lucas started to say. He turned to Mr. Acevedo.

"There's a . . . I guess you can say a small problem."

"Reverend Soto already has an offer from a church in Lubbock as an assistant pastor," Mr. Lucas said. "A church offering him better pay, better living expenses." He looked around the room, and Mary followed his eyes. Their living room suddenly felt very shabby to her. "He has to let them know yes or no on the offer by next week."

She was feeling dizzy. They were trying to tell her something, but she wasn't catching on. "So?" she repeated.

"The problem is that we need the parsonage right away." Mr. Acevedo seemed relieved to finally get the words out, the same words that had probably been stuck in his throat since he came in.

Mary breathed in. Mr. Acevedo's announcement was harsh, but its harshness did not affect her. Instead she felt strong, the kind of strength she had always admired in Kate. "What is 'right away'?" she asked.

"The thing is," Mr. Acevedo said. He was looking at his brown, pointed shoes. "Reverend Soto needs to have a place for the summer . . . say, by the first day of June."

Mary laughed. She couldn't help herself. "It's the beginning of April. That's not possible."

"I know it's short notice," Mr. Acevedo began to say.

"There's nothing we can do about it. If we don't agree, we'll lose him," Mr. Lucas added.

"Does he know it's just Kate and me and Mama? Can't he at least wait until the end of summer? Can't he find a place to live for a few months? Where are we going to go?"

"It's not that he doesn't understand your plight," Mr. Acevedo said. "He's a very kind man. But he's not from El Paso, as you know. He needs a permanent place to live. He's made having the parsonage by June first a condition of staying with us. He knows your circumstances, and he thinks it's best for you if you don't stay in this house past June."

"Best for us?" She felt disgusted. "But where will we go?"

"We heard you have an aunt," Mr. Lucas said tentatively.

"Aunt Julia." She was beginning to look more and more like their best hope. Mary took another deep breath. There was no reason why she should be upset. It was something everyone knew was coming. But June first? She looked at them. "Papa served in your church for twenty years and you want us to move out in two months?"

Her words rattled Mr. Lucas. "Look," he said, "if you want to know the truth, the council has been considering letting your father go for a number of years now." Mr. Acevedo elbowed Mr. Lucas, but he went on. "We weren't attracting any young members, members with children. And then there was the matter of your father not having a car. How can you be an effective minister unless you can drive to visit people?"

She bit her lip. There was no way she was going to let these men see her cry. All these years, Papa was consuming himself slowly for the church, and this is what people were thinking of him.

"All that doesn't really matter," Mr. Acevedo said. "We're very sorry about your father and we want what is best for you. We'll do everything to help you. We'll help you move to wherever you go. Most of all, we hope you can stay and be part of the church."

Mary stood up as soon as he finished speaking. Everything he said seemed like an insult, as if he'd spat in her face and then said he did it to wipe a speck of dirt off her cheek. The men stood as well, looking confused. She walked to the door and opened it. They moved toward her, guilt on their faces. As soon as she opened the door, she saw Simon's car stop in front of the house.

"So can we count on you to leave by the end of May?" Mr. Lucas asked as he passed Mary.

She imagined what would happen if they didn't leave. Would a group of people from the church come and throw them out? They would lift Mama up and dump her in the back of a truck.

"I'll need to talk to Kate," she said. Kate was out of the car by now and looking at Mr. Lucas and Mr. Acevedo with curiosity. "Or you can talk to her yourself. Here she is."

"That's all right," said Mr. Acevedo. "You can convey to her what we said." He seemed afraid of Kate. They probably thought they got off easy when they found out they only had to talk to Mary.

They all walked past one another on the path to the house.

Mary stayed in front of the door, watching the pair of men leave.

"What did they want?" Kate asked.

"They came to tell us we have to move by the end of May."

"What?" Kate almost yelled. Mr. Acevedo and Mr. Lucas were still within hearing distance. They picked up their pace.

"Reverend Soto needs the house by then."

"That's ridiculous," Kate said. Mary saw her breath quicken and her fists tighten. She opened the door and touched Kate's back, gently pushing her inside.

"We knew it would happen," Mary said once the door was closed again.

"Did you tell them it was impossible? We can't leave by then! We're in April. We'll barely be out of school by then. Did you ask for more time?"

At that moment, Mary didn't remember exactly what she had said to Mr. Lucas and Mr. Acevedo. "I let them know it wasn't right."

Kate looked at her like she didn't believe her. "I wish I'd been here," she said.

"I wish you had been here too. Where were you?"

"I went with Simon to get an ice-cream cone." Kate looked sheepish for a second or two. "What else did they say?"

They sat down on the edge of the sofa facing each other, and Mary recounted the conversation as best as she could. She started with the part about the money the church was giving them and slowly worked her way to how the church had wanted to fire Papa for a long time. Kate listened in silence, her face turning pale and red in turn. When Mary told her about

Reverend Soto and how he thought it would be best for them if they left by June first, Kate sprang up from the sofa and headed for the door. "I'll be back," she said.

"Where are you going?"

"To talk to the mighty reverend," she said.

17

Kate almost ran to the church. She didn't truly believe that Reverend Soto would still be there, but she needed to search for him anyway, as if the act itself would vent her feelings. She'd go to church, not find him, and somehow she would feel better returning home. And if he was there, that was all right too. She'd tell him — what? What a jerk he was? He couldn't possibly be the one pushing the June first move, not with the way he spoke that morning about love. And why would he want to meet with her if he was the one who was kicking them out? Wouldn't he want to avoid her at all costs? Most likely it was Mr. Lucas and Mr. Acevedo and all the rest of them, the church council and the deacons. They were blaming it on Reverend Soto because they were cowards. How she wished she had been there when they came over.

Going to get an ice-cream cone with Simon had been a big mistake. They had sat stiffly in the car, each waiting for the other to say something about the proposal, neither one of them brave enough to bring up the subject. Nor did she tell him about Stanford, although it was the perfect opportunity. Now all that had been unsaid was weighing on her, a load too heavy to carry anymore. She needed to let things out, and Reverend Soto might be just the right person to receive all her pent-up frustration.

She slowed down as she approached the church. If Reverend Soto was there, she didn't want to be all sweaty and out of breath. She wanted to be able to reason. She wouldn't beg; she would reason. Would it be begging to tell him about Stanford and how they needed time to find the right place for Mary and Mother? Would that be playing on his feelings? Well, he was a minister, a man of God; shouldn't his feelings be attuned to the hardship of others?

She stopped for a few moments when she saw the church. There were people lingering in front who had probably stayed behind to talk to Reverend Soto. She didn't want to be seen by them. It felt almost as if she were doing something shameful, as if her meeting with Reverend Soto needed to be kept secret. But there was nothing shameful in standing up against unfairness. He needed to see whom he was up against.

The two ladies in the front of the church finally went their separate ways, and Kate headed through the children's playground to the back door of the church. The minister's office was located on the bottom floor near the back entrance. She entered the building and saw the office door standing open. She hesitated for another moment, realizing she was afraid after all. She felt sorry for accusing Mary of not pushing back.

Kate stepped forward into the doorway. Reverend Soto was putting books into a box. She waited for him to lift his head and notice her. Finally, he did.

"Hello," he said, jumping back. "I wasn't expecting to see *you*." She had surprised him, and that made her less nervous. He smiled. "Come in, come in."

He offered her a chair and then closed the door. She sat down, and he pulled the chair from the desk and sat in front of her. She noticed the pile of books on the floor and recognized them as her father's. He was replacing her father's books with his.

He followed her gaze. "I was going to take these to you."

"We don't need them," she said. "They can stay here."

"All right. I'm sure we can find a place for them here, in one of the classrooms perhaps. Books like your father's will always come in handy." He sounded eager to please.

"Reverend, I wanted —"

"Please. Stop right there. If we're going to talk, you have to call me Andy."

She looked at him quizzically.

"My real name is Andrés Soto, but some people call me Andy."

She noticed he didn't say that people called him Andy. He said that *some* people called him Andy. Was she being singled out? She tried the name to see how it sounded. "Andy." She blushed. She was not used to blushing.

"What?"

"It feels strange to call you that."

"I know, I know. It's this." He touched the white collar around his neck. "I can take it off if it'll make you more comfortable."

"That's all right," she said quickly.

"Okay, I'll leave it on. But please call me Andy."

She was aware that he was looking at her with the same intensity she had felt when she shook his hand in the greeting line. He seemed to be probing inside of her, looking for an answer to a question. Did he look at everyone that way, or was it just her? "I wanted to talk to you," she said softly, her eyes lowered. She caught herself immediately and raised her eyes to meet his. "About the time that the church is giving us to move out of the parsonage."

"Ahh. I see the deacons paid their visit. I wasn't expecting them to talk to you until later this week. I wanted to talk to you first."

So he *was* the one pushing this. "That's why you wanted to come on Wednesday? You wanted to give us the good news yourself." It felt good to be sarcastic.

"I thought I could probably put the request in a, how shall I say it, a more spiritual context."

Kate didn't mean to laugh. It was a short little laugh that almost sounded like a snort. When she was a believer, "spiritual" to her meant believing in things that couldn't be seen. But booting them out was something you could see and hear and feel and touch. There was nothing spiritual about that.

"Surely you knew it would happen, sooner or later," he said quietly, gently, as if he was trying to console her.

"Not *that* soon." She expected to see some recognition of how ridiculous that deadline was, but his face was blank. "We'll be barely out of school."

He shifted in his chair. "The church plans to do everything it can to help you."

"Help us do what?"

He didn't answer, perhaps because the answer was too obvious. The church was going to do everything it could to get rid of them by June first. She remembered suddenly that the deadline for responding to Stanford was May first. She felt her stomach turn. She was being eaten away by deadlines.

"Will you let me tell you something?" He moved his chair closer to her, their knees almost touching. She pulled in her legs. "It's what I wanted to tell you before the deacons came to see you, before you formed an idea of me as some kind of monster. But they beat me to it, and now you probably think I'm unfeeling."

"This is the spiritual part." Kate grinned bitterly.

"Believe it or not, it is. There are good reasons for having you move by that deadline, which I know is short. Yes, they are spiritual reasons." She had noticed before the spark in his eyes, a spark he could dim or brighten at will. Now the spark was dimmed, the voice shifted down into an intimate tone. "I confess that when I saw you in church this morning, and as I talk to you face-to-face, talking about the deadline is harder than I imagined."

He leaned back in the chair and made himself comfortable, as if he were preparing to tell a story. "A couple of years ago, my *abuelita* fell and broke her hip. She was eighty-five and lived by herself. She lived in the same home she'd lived in all her life and never wanted to move anyplace else. My mother and the grandchildren paid for someone to come in every day to take care of her. We knew that even with this arrangement, she was too old to live in her house by herself, but we didn't want to accept the fact that she needed to be placed in a nursing home. Probably we also felt guilty that neither Mom nor the grandchildren wanted to take her into their homes. Among other things, Abuelita was a very difficult woman to get along with. She really was not the sweet Mexican grandmother we all imagine when we hear the word *abuelita*.

"Anyway, when she broke her hip and she was in the hospital, there was this Indian doctor who was treating her. They had put restraints on Abuelita because she wanted to yank her IV out and go back home. So this doctor, he took me aside and very harshly asked me what our plans for her were. 'What arrangements have you made for her?' he said. At first I thought he was talking about the arrangements we'd made in case she died, but then I realized he was talking about Abuelita's future living situation. I stuttered something about how we hadn't made any arrangements yet. So he yelled at me, 'She's out of here in two days. You need to have arrangements made by then.' Then he walked off, leaving me stunned there in the hallway."

Kate narrowed her eyes. What did this story have to do with her?

He went on. "What that doctor did was hit us, all my family, with the truth, with the fact that something needed to be done about Abuelita. We had to admit that none of us were capable of taking her into our homes. And even harder, we were forced to admit that we didn't want her in our homes." He paused. He seemed to be expecting a lightbulb to click on in her head. "The point is," he continued, teacherlike, "the doctor gave us a deadline that was way too short, but it was that ridiculous deadline that made us decide to place Abuelita in a nursing home. Without the shock of that deadline, it would have taken us a long time to come to that realization because of how guilty we all felt about it. And more significantly, we would probably never have been honest with ourselves. Do you see?"

"Actually, I don't," Kate said. "We know we have to leave the parsonage. We expected it. It's not like we have to be 'shocked' into admitting it." She made quotation marks in the air.

He smiled, then his countenance went serious. "I wasn't really referring to your decision to move. There are other decisions you need to make."

Did he somehow know about Stanford? Was he telling her to have Mary and her mother settled before she left in September? "Like what kind of decisions?" she asked.

"You need to do something about your mother."

"Excuse me?" For an instant she thought she imagined what he said and hadn't actually heard it.

"You need to make some decisions about your mother. There are things you need to accept about her, just like there were things we had to accept about Abuelita. I know you may not like me for it, but I'm doing you and your sister a favor, just like that Indian doctor did for my family."

"Thanks a big bunch," she said. It was a childish thing to say, but she couldn't think of anything else. She blinked a few times. The anger she felt at that moment was keeping her from seeing straight. She shook her head, almost amused.

"What's so funny?" he asked.

"Nothing, *Andy*."

"You don't think I'm old enough to counsel you on this?"

"Counsel?"

"Yes, counsel. Give you advice about what is best for you."

It was too bad that Mary wasn't here. As bad as Kate imagined the meeting with Mr. Lucas and Mr. Acevedo to have been, there was no way it was as terrible as this "counseling" session was turning out to be. "What do you know about my mother?" she demanded.

"I know," he said, as if he really did know everything there was to know. He took a deep breath and then spoke with an authority and gravity Kate had not heard in him before. "I know she's no longer alive. Not in a way that we determine human life. She's a body that breathes."

Kate caught her breath. She had been ready to yell at him, to shout about his ignorance and injustice, but what would she yell? He was telling the truth. Someone had finally said, "She's not alive." She was used to telling Mary that Mother was not conscious, but she had never said that she was not alive, and now she realized that those were the words she had wanted to say all along.

"What kind of decisions?" She was breathing heavily, but she was calm.

"Pardon?"

"You said there were decisions that I needed to make. That *we* needed to make. Mary and me. Before June first." There was a quiet anger in her voice.

"You need to consider all your options," he said.

"What kind of options?"

"Options," he repeated. "Options that you need to consider, pray about, ask the Lord for discernment."

She searched through her mind for any options with respect to Mother that she had missed, that she hadn't thought about since Father died. The only option that came to mind was finding someone to help Mary. Maybe he was referring to putting Mother in a hospital of some sort, but that was so expensive it was unfeasible. She shrugged her shoulders. She didn't understand what he was driving at.

"There are options with respect to your mother, for someone in her condition, that are moral and legal, that may be what are best for you and your sister and even for your mother herself."

She felt a burning blast explode in her head as the significance of his words dawned on her. "No," she gasped. She almost jumped out of the chair. The room, the man in front of her, they were all asphyxiating her. "I have to go now." She tried to step over his leg but he stood up and took her arm.

"Wait, Kate, please."

"You'll have your house whenever." She had forgotten the exact date.

"I know that sounded harsh, even shocking. But I meant what I said this morning at the pulpit. The truth sometimes hurts. What I'm asking is for you to face the truth. The truth will set you free. You need to be free to grow, to express God's love inside you. You need to make a decision based on the truth, on love, on what is best for you and your sister, not on guilt or cheap sentimentality. Love has to do with growth and life and it requires courageous decisions."

He was still holding on to her. She did not try to move away. "I have to go now."

"Don't shut me out. Let's talk. Promise me we will continue to talk. You can call me day or night."

"Counseling?"

"No, not counseling."

"What will it be, then?"

"Two people searching for the truth together."

She shook her arm loose and went out the door.

18

Mary saw the letter as soon as she opened the door. Aunt Julia had placed it right in the middle of the coffee table, leaning on the plastic flower arrangement, so that Mary or Kate, whoever came home from school first, would see it.

"It's from the insurance company," Aunt Julia said.

"Oh." Mary didn't mean to sound uninterested, but she had forgotten that they were waiting for it. She dropped her backpack on the floor and started to walk toward her mother's bedroom.

"Aren't you going to open it?" Aunt Julia asked.

"I'm going to check on Mama," Mary said. She didn't mean to be rude, but she knew that Aunt Julia never looked in on Mama. Every day when she came home, Mary had to change Mama's diaper as soon as she arrived.

When she returned to the living room, Aunt Julia was holding the letter up to the light streaming in from the window. "I'm trying to see if there's a check in there," she explained.

"Do you see one?"

"I can't tell, but it feels heavy. Here, open it." She thrust the envelope at Mary. Mary weighed the envelope in her palm before quickly placing it on the coffee table.

"What is it?" Aunt Julia sounded worried.

"Nothing. I think we should let Kate open it."

"Nonsense. You can open it as well. You're part of this household."

Mary shook her head. "We need to wait until Kate gets here. It's addressed to her. Also, she'd be disappointed if we opened it without her." Mary made it sound as if she didn't want to take the joy of opening it from Kate, but inside she was afraid of what the letter might say.

Aunt Julia dropped herself on the sofa. "I will never in a million years understand how you girls think. That man sure did a number on you." Mary could tell she was about to start on Papa. "Oh, relax," Aunt Julia said, pointing for her to sit down in the armchair. "I'll keep quiet. I know you don't like me to criticize your father. I sit here all day long without anyone to talk to except the TV and that Talita woman, who's as quiet as a rock, and you can't keep me company for a few minutes? What I'd really like to do is give a piece of my mind to those people at your church, telling you to get out in two months and then wiping their consciences with some measly dollars."

"We can find someplace else to live," Mary said weakly. She didn't want to defend them. She just didn't want to hear any more of Aunt Julia's raving.

"Don't get me started," Aunt Julia huffed. "My blood pressure shoots up just thinking about how they're treating you."

Mary sat down. She wanted to change her clothes and go out to the backyard to try her hand at painting once again, but she felt sorry for Aunt Julia. She knew it was hard for her to be quiet most of the day. Talking was her favorite kind of entertainment, and even when Kate and Mary were home, there wasn't a lot of conversing going on. Mary wasn't much of a talker, and Kate . . .

Something had been happening to Kate ever since Simon sort of proposed to her. She was happy when she got the letter from Stanford, but then she had been sulkier and more irritable than ever after talking to Reverend Soto three days before. It was as if a cloud of gunpowder hovered over her, ready to ignite. When Mary asked about her conversation with the minister, she mumbled something about how it made sense for them to move out of the parsonage as soon as possible anyway. Mary hoped that the insurance letter brought good news. Maybe then the dark mood that enveloped Kate would disappear for good.

Aunt Julia and Mary sat looking at each other. She was probably waiting for Mary to speak first. She had told Mary on numerous occasions that she hated to be the one who always asked the questions. "Well," Aunt Julia said at last, "what are you thinking of doing with the money?" She glanced at the envelope. "I guess the first thing you have to do is deposit the check. You should put a little in that credit union account of your father's and then you should invest the rest in some CDs." Aunt Julia must have seen the blank look on Mary's face. "Certificates of Deposit," she explained. "They pay more interest than a savings account."

"Oh."

"You know what interest is, don't you?" She examined Mary closely.

"Yes, even I know that," she said.

"I don't know how you girls are going to do it. I can't imagine."

Mary decided to ask Aunt Julia the question that had been burning in her mind ever since Kate got her acceptance letter from Stanford. "Why don't you stay with us?" she said quickly.

"What do you mean?" Aunt Julia perked up.

Mary could tell she understood very well what she was asking, and even that she was glad to be asked. Mary didn't know what her answer would be, but she knew Aunt Julia would have been deeply hurt if they hadn't brought it up. "I mean live with us here, or wherever we are," she said.

By "us" Mary meant Mama and herself. Aunt Julia didn't know about Stanford. Mary thought that maybe what was weighing Kate down was guilt at leaving Mama and Mary alone, and if Aunt Julia stayed with them, Kate wouldn't feel so bad leaving. And it was all right to ask Aunt Julia without consulting Kate because, even though Kate never mentioned it, it was the best solution. Kate didn't get along with Aunt Julia, but that wouldn't affect her since she wouldn't be around.

"Gosh, child. My job, all my friends, my cats, my home is in San Jose."

It made Mary happy that she did not say no outright. "You can help us find a nice apartment with your own bedroom, and you can bring your cats, and maybe we can find a place close to St. John's. Papa was friends with Father Hogan, and he would tell us about all the activities St. John's has for seniors. They even have bingo every week. You'll make new friends in no time."

Aunt Julia hung her head down for a second. Her nose made a funny little twitch, as if she smelled something bad. "Don't think I haven't thought about it. That's my sister in there," she pointed to Mama's bedroom with her chin, "and I'm the only living family you have."

Mary smiled. She always smiled when people said *living* family. It meant that people didn't stop being family when they died; they just turned into your *dead* family.

"I don't know," Aunt Julia continued. "I need to do some more thinking about that. I think you would be okay without me. You can hire someone with the money." She glanced down at the insurance envelope. "Your sister will be down the street going to college and you'll still be able to get home early."

"I don't know if we can live by ourselves. Don't we need an adult living with us?"

"I guess your sister will need to be declared your guardian. She's an adult. You're not *legally* an adult, but you're old enough to take care of yourself, or you should be, anyhow." That was Aunt Julia's way of joking.

"Promise me you'll think real hard about staying with us." Mary looked at the envelope on the table. "We can live off the insurance money and maybe even pay you for taking care of Mama while we're away."

Aunt Julia's eyes lit up for a brief second. "Oh no," she said quickly, "I wouldn't do it for any money."

"But you promise me you'll think about it. Really consider it."

"I promise. But maybe you should have asked your sister first. I'm not so sure she would like the idea of living with me on a permanent basis."

"Kate likes you, Aunt Julia. She has a lot of pressure on her right now, with school and everything. And . . . our papa just died. People mourn in different ways. Kate may seem distant and even angry sometimes, but that's just her way of dealing with sadness."

"I guess you're right. And who can blame her for being gloomy when the church where your father worked for twenty years is putting you out on the street?"

Mary looked at Aunt Julia without any expression on her face.

"Oh, go on, change and go paint. My favorite show is coming on."

Mary put on an old T-shirt and her painting overalls and then went to check on Mama one more time. She reminded herself to move and massage her legs in an hour or so.

Out in the backyard, Mary stared hopelessly at her painting of the irises. A sinking feeling came over her every time she looked at it. Where did the pleasure of painting go? Who took it away? It made her angry to feel that way about painting. She wished she could feel excited about painting, the way she used to feel.

She had just begun to listlessly mix colors on the palette when she heard a whistle from the Domínguezes' house. She took a deep breath. She wasn't in the mood to make conversation with anyone, much less with nosy Mr. Domínguez. But when she turned around, she saw Marcos instead. "What are you doing there?" she asked.

"I saw you from the street."

"You saw me from the street? You can't see my backyard from the street."

"Yeah, you can. If you drive real slow and lean your head way out of the car, you can. I saw you coming out of the shed." He grinned. "I was driving by to see a friend who lives over on Dale."

"You don't have to come through my street to get to Dale."

"Your street?"

"That street." Mary pointed toward the front of the house. But he stood there very sure of himself, as if he was waiting for Mary to realize that he had come looking for her. "And why are you in Mr. Domínguez's yard? Do you just walk into people's yards whenever you want?"

"I'm not hurting anything. I'm just standing here talking to you."

"What if Mr. Domínguez comes out?"

"If he comes out, he comes out. He's not going to shoot me, is he?"

She reached down to the ground and picked up the wooden box with her paint tubes and brushes. Then she stood there not knowing what to do. She looked at the painting and realized she was not going to paint. "You just — shouldn't do that," she managed to say.

"Can I come over?"

"Where?"

"There." He pointed to where she was standing.

"Here?" She looked down at her feet. She could hear her heart thump. "Why?"

"Just in case the guy that lives here decides to shoot me." He sounded as if he was teasing her.

"Why did you come here? Really." She lowered the paint box to the ground.

"Okay, so I wasn't on my way to see my friend. I need to ask you something. But I don't want to talk to you from someone else's backyard. What I need to say won't take long." He sounded sincere.

"Ask me what?" Was he going to ask her to go out with him?

She must have had a very scared look on her face, for he said, smiling as if he had read her mind, "Don't worry. It's business."

"Business?"

"It has to do with painting," he said.

She hesitated and then gave in to a new and unaccustomed impulse. "Okay."

She started walking toward the gate to the backyard, but he took a few steps back and then leapt over the fence. "*Ay!*" he said as he landed in front of her. There was a mixture of self-satisfaction and pain on his face.

She stepped away from him. "That was silly," she said, even though she was amazed by his feat. The fence stood as high as his chest.

"Is there a place we can sit down? I think I just twisted something."

She pointed to the wooden chairs under the willow tree. He limped toward them and sat down. He took off his black shoes. "Look," he said, pulling down his sock, "the ankle's starting to swell. Would you get me a bag of ice?"

"I don't think so," she said.

"Oh. Okay." He rubbed the ankle.

"What is it you wanted to ask me?"

"You seemed nicer that day when I drove you home."

She remembered that day and that ride with him. "I didn't mean to be," she said.

He tried to stand up, grimaced with pain, and sat back down. "I can't believe I landed crooked. Usually I clear fences without any problem."

"When you're running from the police?"

"You're funny," he said, grinning. "And strange."

"Strange?"

"I mean you talk strange. Most people would say 'cops,' but you say 'police.' You don't use words like other kids."

She stayed quiet. She always stayed quiet when people called her strange. Kate thought they were weird too, because they didn't talk like anyone else. But what was strange about saying *police* instead of *cops*?

"I didn't mean to offend," he said. He stood up. He had left his shoe off and was now holding it in his hand.

"I don't hear you using the words kids use either, whatever those are."

"That's cause I try to clean up my act when I'm around you." He took a step on the bad foot. "Ouch!"

"I'll get you some ice," she said.

"No, really. I'll drive home. It's my left ankle, so I can still push the accelerator and the brake with my right foot."

He began to hop to the gate. Mary blurted, "You didn't say why you were here. You said you had something to ask me."

"Oh yeah. To be honest, part of the reason I came was because I wanted to see you, you know, kind of get to know you."

She tried to hide any expression that she was flattered. "And the other part?"

"The other part is kind of hard to explain." He was having trouble keeping his balance on one foot. "Mind if I sit down again for a second?" He hopped back to the chair, sat down, and looked up at her. "It's real hard to talk to you when you're way up there." He reached out and moved the other chair toward her.

She looked at the painting of the irises on the easel, then walked over slowly and sat down. He was looking at the space between his feet, and he began slowly, like he was embarrassed about what he had to say. "Turns out that I was told I have to do a mural on one of the outside walls of this community center over in Socorro." He waited for her to ask him a question, but she didn't. "Anyway, I never done a mural before. All I've done is these drawings and some . . . you know, signs and stuff on walls."

"You mean graffiti."

"Yeah. Anyway, the reason I came, part of the reason I came" — he smiled — "was to see if you could help me with the mural, you know, give me some pointers. I'll do it. I mean, I got to. But I don't even know where to start."

Mary could see Aunt Julia standing behind the screen door, snooping. From the expression on Aunt Julia's face, she wasn't sure what to make of Mary talking to a boy, especially a boy with only one shoe. Mary stared at her until she disappeared into the house. "Why do you have to paint a mural?"

Marcos turned to follow Mary's gaze, but Aunt Julia was no longer there. He sniffed and then cracked his right index finger with his left hand. "This judge told me I had to."

"A judge? So it's like a sentence," she said.

"You mean instead of like going to jail? Kind of. I guess I could have gone to jail. Turns out graffiti is a felony in Texas. The judge gave me a break."

She paused to look at him closely, perhaps more closely than she had ever looked at him before. He was a weird mixture of childlike interior and tough-looking exterior, and all the pieces fit together and contradicted one another at the same time. "That's so bad." Her voice trembled a bit.

He must have noticed the flash of fear in her eyes. He said, "Don't worry, it wasn't anything obscene or violent."

"What difference does it make what you sprayed?"

His ankle was slowly turning purple. "It was the name of a friend of mine. His name was Carlos."

"Why did you do that?"

"He was killed a month ago by the Calle Cuatros." Marcos grabbed the bottom of the chair with both hands. "I — You probably won't understand this, but marking that bus was something I needed to do."

"Why?"

"I owed it to my friend. I wanted him to be remembered somehow. It's the only way I knew how. Do you understand?"

She thought about the portrait of Mama she had painted before Mama's accident. "Why are you painting that? I'm so ugly," Mama had said after Mary had finally gotten her to pose.

"You're beautiful, Mama, and I want to always remember you that way."

"Do you think I'm going to turn ugly?" Mama had objected, laughing.

Mary turned to Marcos and answered his question. "Yes, I understand," she said softly.

"Even if I didn't want to do it, I'd have to."

"Last time you said you had no choice about being in a gang. Now you have no choice about spraying buses. Do you get to choose anything for yourself?"

"You wouldn't say that if you understood."

"I guess I don't understand, then."

"Being in a gang is the best way some of us have to survive. You don't know," he said quietly. "There's not a whole bunch of choices where I live."

"I know there's always a choice," she said.

"Yeah, you're right." There was regret in his voice. "It was a mistake for someone like me to come here." He started to lift himself out of the chair, but he stumbled and grabbed on to her.

She held on to his arm for a few moments until he steadied himself, her heart suddenly thumping again. Then she let go of him. She stood up and walked to the gate with him, far enough away that he wouldn't think she was encouraging him to lean on her. When they got there, she opened the gate. He stepped through and then she asked, "What kind of help were you looking for? For the mural?"

He stopped hobbling. His eyes lit up for an instant. "I was hoping you'd take a ride with me to Socorro some day after school or a Saturday and give me some pointers. I'm good with spray cans, but I don't know anything about brush painting. I think the mural needs to be done with brushes because the wall is big and we'd need about a zillion spray cans to spray-paint it."

"Did they tell you what to paint?"

"The guy who runs the community center says it's up to me, so long as it's clean and I tell him what I'm going to do beforehand."

"Well, what are you thinking of doing?"

"I don't have the slightest. I'm not good at drawing people. I like to draw the kind of designs I showed you back in school. I'm going to stay away from people if I can ... and horses." He grinned. "Maybe some mountains with a lake and some boats."

"Are you sure that's appropriate for El Paso?" she said. "It's all desert around here, remember."

"See, that's why I need someone like you, to help me come up with some ideas and then tell me how to do it."

She started walking again and he followed. "You're the one that got sentenced."

"I'll put in the sweat labor. All I need is a little help."

They stepped onto the driveway. "Shit," he said, when he realized he had left his shoe by the chair.

Mary was a hundred percent sure that it was the first time anyone had uttered the word *shit* in their house. "That must be a kid's word," she told him with a smile. She had never made fun of anyone as much as she was making fun of him. She walked back and grabbed his shoe by the shoelaces, then brought it to him as if she were carrying a dead mouse by the tail.

"Thanks," he said. He took his shoe and resumed walking to his car.

"Looks like your ankle is getting better already," she said.

"I need to have good feet to climb the ladder and paint that wall. It's a monster. It's going to take a couple of months." He gazed into her eyes, a serious look on his face. "I'd like to do a good job on it. It's a nice community center. That wall's going to be up there for a long time and it'd be good if it was nice, you know."

She nodded. She knew how it felt to want to create a work of beauty that was lasting. He opened the door to his car. "All right," she said softly, almost hoping he wouldn't hear it.

But he did. He turned to face her. "You'll help me?"

"I'll help," she said. She felt excited for some strange reason.

"All right! How about tomorrow after school?"

"Do you even go to school? I haven't seen you since that other day."

"So you've been looking for me, huh? I go to school now and then. Tomorrow after school?"

"I can't after school." There was no need to tell him why her afternoons were taken.

"Saturday?"

"Maybe. I'll have to check."

"That's cool. I'll call you. What's your cell?"

"I don't have a cell."

"That's all right. I'll find you."

She stood by the gate and watched him settle in the driver's seat. The engine started with a roar. "I'm not getting in that car unless you put in a seat belt for me," she yelled at him.

He gave her a thumbs-up. Then he waved and drove away slowly.

God, what did I just get myself into? Mary said to herself.

19

Kate had to take the bus after school to the Red Sombrero, since neither Simon nor Bonnie could give her a ride. It was just as well. She needed time to think, to relive the conversation she had with Reverend Soto yet again. He had said the truth required that she consider all the options, that she look at all of them squarely. She leaned her head against the window of the bus and tried to do just that. She went to Stanford, and Mary and Mama stayed with someone. That was the top option, the only one she had considered so far. Who would Mary and Mama stay with? Aunt Julia would be best, but her aunt had never given any indication that she would be willing to take on that responsibility. Besides, it would be cruel to saddle Mary with Aunt Julia. Finding someone to live with Mary and Mama and paying that someone with the insurance money was a better solution. But was it realistic to have someone take care of Mama for four years or maybe longer while she went away first to college and then to medical school?

The bus stopped and a lady with a canvas bag full of groceries started to get on. She had trouble making it up the steps of the bus. She ambled slowly to an empty seat, and as she passed by, Kate saw her thin brown legs. Every night, before Kate went to sleep, she poured rubbing alcohol on her palms and massaged Mama's legs so they would not atrophy. When she first started doing it, she kept expecting Mama to open her eyes, to sit up, say thank you, hug her. But as time went on, the nightly hope gave way to a sense that the limbs she was touching were devoid of energy, that life would never come back to them.

The bus passed a sign pointing toward Ascarate Park and she remembered suddenly her mother playing volleyball during a picnic game. It was a school outing, and Mother had volunteered to serve as chaperone. The rest of the mothers sat together talking, but not Mama. She saw that players were needed for a volleyball game and she jumped in uninvited. Kate remembered her bare feet and how she ran to get the ball, laughing with all the joy of an eight-year-old lost at play.

"Mama, we need to let you go," she whispered.

But the thought that she wanted to let Mama go for her own convenience stuck in her head like a painful splinter she could not remove. *She's no longer alive.* Reverend Soto's words kept coming back to her. *Andy's* words. The images of her mother's limp legs as she massaged them and of her chasing a volleyball, full of life, whirled together in her head one after another. And she saw Andy's soft hands, his fiery eyes and thick black hair. She tried to shake the feelings that came with the thought of him, but then she remembered his sermon and the way he gave it, the emphasis he placed on certain words. *This is crazy*, Kate kept telling herself, hoping she could regain her senses. But it was no use. She felt like a rock hit by a sledge-hammer and now there were pieces of her scattered all over the place.

When she got to the Red Sombrero, she was distracted for the first time since she began waitressing. She took food to the wrong tables. She spilled water on a customer's lap. She wrote down the wrong orders. The other waitresses, Simon's father, and even José, the cook, asked her if she was okay. She smiled and nodded that she was fine. She tried to regain her focus, but the efforts lasted only a moment. Then the thoughts, the images would come back like angry bees.

Her shift at the Red Sombrero ended at eight P.M., but sometimes, when the restaurant was crowded, she would stay longer to help out. Tonight it was almost nine when she got in the car with Simon to go home. She was feeling slightly drowsy, but the drowsiness felt good. Work hadn't made the thoughts disappear, but it had slowed them down to a manageable speed. Now she could see them float before her without menace, as options rather than threats.

"Are you all right?" Simon asked as soon as they were out of the restaurant's parking lot.

"Sure." She reminded herself to be careful. She didn't want Simon to know her thoughts, especially about Andy. And yet a part of her did want him to know she had been thinking of someone else.

"I've never seen you like this."

"Like how?" She slouched in the car seat.

"You're drunk, aren't you?"

"No."

"Are you sure?"

"I'm carrying a bottle in my purse."

"What?" Simon's head snapped in her direction.

"I'm kidding."

He slowed down, maybe so he could focus on the conversation. Kate saw a small bubble of peace in her brain about to be disturbed. "What's happening to you?"

"What *is* happening to me? I'm not sure I know."

They drove in silence for a couple of blocks. Simon tapped the steering wheel with his fist a few times. She could tell he was trying to decide whether he should hold in what he wanted to say or let it out. Finally, he said, "Ever since we talked that day in your backyard, you've been different. I thought you'd be happy that I talked to you about us getting married, and instead it seems like it's one more thing for you to worry about."

"All I said was that I needed more time." She didn't understand why she felt suddenly angry.

"All right. You can have more time, but you don't have to push me away in the meantime."

"You're the one who's been acting strange, like your manhood was humiliated because I didn't jump at your offer."

"I've been acting strange because you've been strange," he said defensively. Then he spoke in a different tone, as if he'd just understood what she said. "My offer? You say it like I made you some kind of business deal."

For a moment she was surprised at Simon's sensitivity. She

hadn't thought he could perceive the nuances hidden in her words. "Wasn't that what it was? You were offering to take care of us. The only thing I wasn't clear about was in return for what."

She realized the cruelty of her words too late. Simon pushed down on the accelerator and the car sped down the empty street. "Simon, be careful," she pleaded. He slammed on the brakes and then resumed speed at a crawl. Kate felt her anger turning to deep sadness. She opened the glove compartment and took out a package of tissues. She used one to wipe her tears. "Honestly, I didn't have anything to drink," she said.

"I believe you," he said.

She looked at the tissues. "Remember these?"

Simon nodded and then his face contorted as if he was about to cry. They were both silent. About a year after they started dating, they had gone to Ascarate Park one Saturday evening after a football game. They kissed and fondled each other for a long time and then Simon insisted on revealing himself to her. She touched him and he immediately exploded in her hand. The package of tissues she held now was the same kind she took out of her purse then.

"You made sure that never happened again, didn't you?" She heard the resentment in his voice. But it was true. They had kissed and touched many times since then, but Kate had never again let them be as intimate as that.

She reached over and touched his hand. He jerked it away. Perhaps he sensed that the sentiment behind her touch was similar to pity.

It was only half a mile to her house. When they arrived, he parked in front of the house and turned off first the head-lights and then the motor. There was a look of steely determination on Simon's face. He held the steering wheel and looked ahead as if he were driving on a straight road some-where in the middle of the desert. Then he turned to face her, his back to the door. "I guess I need to know if you love me or not."

"That sounds almost like a threat." She said this with humor in her voice, but the question troubled her.

"It's no threat. I just need to know. I can wait if you love me, but if you don't . . ."

"Can't we talk about this some other day? I'm not feeling all that well."

"Tell me. Why is it so hard?"

"I've told you many times that I do."

"But you never meant it. Tell me only if you mean it. If you don't mean it, just say so."

"Why don't you think I meant it?"

"I don't know." He let his head fall on his chest for a sec-ond. "You were always cold. I thought it was just the way you were. I guess I never really felt you liked me as a man. That you liked being with me."

"I liked you as a man."

"Liked?"

"Like. Like you," she corrected herself.

He shook his head. "Sometimes it felt as if I was someone you needed to get you out of the house." He looked at her and she could tell he was asking that she deny what he had just said. But she couldn't. He took a deep breath and said with finality, "I need to know if you really love me."

She rubbed her eyes. All the emotions, the thoughts, the images and memories had made her sick with confusion. She needed to clear the cobwebs so she could figure out how best to respond, calculate the best way to proceed. She needed to buy time before responding to his question, the vital question of love's meaning. "Why now? What set you off like this?"

Simon tilted his head back and stared at the roof of the car. "How can you not tell me that you were thinking of going to college at this place in California? How can you not even tell me when you got accepted?"

"Bonnie," Kate said.

"She didn't mean to tell me. She just assumed you told me. It's normal for a girlfriend to tell her boyfriend, don't you think?"

"I wasn't sure I was going. I'm still not sure."

"But you want to go."

She thought for a few moments. She had come to a place where there were two paths and she needed to choose one of them. She pushed through the haziness and saw the one that had to be taken. She was tired of hiding what she wanted from her father, from Simon, from Mary. She was plain tired of pretending. *The truth will set you free*, Andy had said.

"Yes. I want to go to away to Stanford more than any-thing else."

She could feel Simon stare at her in disbelief, shock, hurt, anger, she didn't know what. He swallowed. "I need to know if you love me. If you love me, I can wait for you."

She looked at him tenderly, gratefully. "Simon, you don't want to do that."

"I would. I would wait if . . ."

"If. That's just it. You want me to promise you that in four years, I'll come back to you and marry you. Isn't that what you want? But after college comes med school and I don't know where I'll be. There are so many years. I can't make any promises. You can understand that, can't you? I can't make any promises."

He shrugged his shoulders. "Yeah. I guess you can't. You make it seem like I'm asking for too much. It's not too much to ask if you love someone."

"Simon . . ." She saw him close his eyes. He seemed to know what was coming. He opened them again and looked at her. He was ready for whatever she was going to tell him. "I'm having a hard time figuring out what love is."

"Oh, come on!" he said, exasperated.

"Obviously, I care for you. It's just that going to Stanford means so much to me. It's part of who I am, of who I want to be."

"But I told you I would wait."

"And this caring for you, maybe it is love, but it's not strong enough to give you any guarantees about what will happen when I'm away or when I graduate."

Simon nodded. "Fine. Whatever you say," he said.

"It doesn't mean what we have has to be over. Can't we just see what happens?" She owed it to him to say that. She owed it to his kindness and his patience.

"No, we *can't just see* what happens. You think I'm stupid or someone you can step on? You want me to stay and wait for you for four years even if you don't feel anything for me? I always knew you had a selfish side, but I didn't know how bad it was. It's not just me. You're going to go away and leave your sister with your mother? You don't think that's selfish? Why this place Stanford? You can pursue your dream of being a doctor here. Do you give a damn about anybody other than yourself?"

Kate listened to Simon without responding. He wasn't telling her anything new. She had questioned herself endlessly about whether her desire to go to Stanford was selfish and she had never been able to resolve the question. Every time she thought about it, she became more confused. But right now she wanted him to have the last word. Her silence was her last gift to him.

When he saw that she was not going to say anything more, he said, "I guess this is what they call breaking up."

"Yeah," she said. She was still holding the package of tissues in her hand. She placed it on the dashboard. She looked at Simon one last time and then opened the door.

"Kate," Simon called when she was about to close the car door.

She leaned down to look in at him. She thought maybe he was going to ask her to reconsider, to say he was willing to leave things as they were. She wished he would say that. What she would be stepping into without him was new and it frightened her. She wanted him there and yet she didn't.

"I don't think it's a good idea for you to work at the restaurant anymore," he said. "It'd be too hard. I have to tell my folks that we're not together and they're not going to want you around either."

Kate laughed a short, disbelieving laugh. "You're firing me."

"Yeah." She saw a sad grin on his face, and then he started the car.

The house was dark except for a yellow outdoor light. Father claimed that yellow lightbulbs lasted longer than white ones of similar wattage. It was a ridiculous notion, but Father had been full of unscientific ideas. When she was younger, Kate tried to persuade him of his many errors, but she gave up because she never won a single argument, no matter the evidence and no matter how hard she tried. The longest and most bitter argument had been about evolution. She once brought home a book that traced in pictures the development of humans from ape to man, and Father almost burned the book on top of the stove as blasphemy. Andy would laugh if she ever told him that story.

She stood outside the house and watched Simon speed away. It was funny. Here she just broke up with her boyfriend and she was thinking about how different Andy was from both Simon and her father. Andy had given her permission to think about what was right for everyone even if it went against some people's beliefs. It was right for her to go to the best college she could get into, and as hard as it still was to consider, it was right to see the truth about Mother.

She opened the screen door carefully and then the wooden door. Aunt Julia was snoring on the pullout sofa bed. Kate gently placed her backpack on the floor and headed for the bathroom. When she turned on the light, she saw a white envelope propped against the mirror of the medicine cabinet. She moved closer and read the return address, then smiled and pressed the envelope to her chest. Her first impulse was to wake Mary up so they could open it together, but she ignored it. She grabbed a nail file and carefully slit the envelope, then she took out the single sheet of paper and unfolded it. There was no check. She began to read, her eyes widening, her chest constricting as she went. Words dripped into her consciousness like acid.

Claim denied
misrepresentation
false statements
medical records
preexisting cardiac condition
not disclosed at time of application
Fraud

She dropped the letter in the sink, closed the lid to the toilet, and sat down. She tried to get her brain to function. There must be a way out, a way to fix this terrible mistake. Father lied in an application for insurance? Father did not disclose that he had a preexisting condition? It wasn't possible. There must be a way around, a way to get to where she wanted to go.

She pushed her mind to strategize, but her mind could not generate the necessary voltage. It was like one of Father's yellow lightbulbs.

She heard her mother groan. She opened the door to the bathroom and walked to her mother's bedroom. There was a lamp next to her bed that Mary kept lit during the night. Mother's sleep cycles usually coincided with the sleep cycles of normal people, but tonight her eyes were open. Kate fingered the feeding tube that connected to her stomach. "What should I do?" she whispered. Then her mother's face turned toward her, and in her eyes was an urgent message she couldn't decipher.

She went to her bedroom, feeling her way with her hand against the wall. She had left the bathroom light on and so she saw that Mary had fallen asleep with her overalls still on. She must have stayed up waiting for Kate to get home so they could open the envelope together.

Kate stopped at the door. There were many times in the past year when her room had been a friendly space filled with her hopes for the future. Tonight it was dark and solid and closing in on her like a vault. She needed air. She needed the light of truth and the warm unencumbered sky of freedom. There was only one place she could think of where these might be found.

20

When Mary woke up the following morning, she saw that Kate's bed was empty. The bed was made, but Kate always made her bed as soon as she awoke. Mary thought she must have left early for school. The library opened early and Kate went there often, especially when she worked late the night before.

Mary found the letter from the insurance company on top of the sink. Her heart sank when she read that Papa had made false statements, and she couldn't believe it could ever be true. But what bothered her most was what she imagined Kate must have felt when she read the letter. Kate had counted on that money to pay for Mama's care, to pay for someone to live with them when she went to college. The letter must have devastated her.

Mary could hear Aunt Julia in the kitchen boiling water for her instant coffee and her daily bowl of oatmeal. She wished she had woken up when Kate came in. She could have stayed up with her and comforted her, listened to her vent her anger about Papa if need be. It hurt to think that Kate didn't feel like talking to her, but maybe she felt it was too hard to talk about Papa's deception, if that's what it was.

Mary put the letter in the back pocket of her pants and then went to see Mama. Her eyes were still closed. She checked her diaper to make sure it was okay and checked that the liquid mixture of food and water flowed at the same rate that Talita set it every day. She turned off the bedside lamp and opened the curtains so light would brighten the room. She lifted Mama's head and fluffed her pillow, then took a hairbrush from the drawer in the bedside table and brushed her hair.

It always made her sad to brush Mama's hair. Touching Mama always brought the realization that Mama had gone to a different, inaccessible place. She felt lonely. Mama used to have beautiful black hair that came to the middle of her back. After the accident, her head was shaved so the doctors could go into her brain to stop the internal bleeding. Now her hair was no longer black but a lush silver-gray that gave Mama a distinguished look. When people entered the room, Mary saw them turn solemn and reverent, as if they were in the presence of royalty.

"Where's your sister?" Aunt Julia asked Mary when she came out of Mama's room. Aunt Julia was in the bathroom. She had a habit of leaving the door open when she was in there.

"She went to school early," Mary said. She hurried to the

living room before Aunt Julia could ask any more questions. As she started to put away the sofa bed, she saw Kate's backpack. Kate never went to school without her backpack. It was so unlike her to leave the insurance letter in the bathroom, to go to school without her backpack. And now that she thought of it, Kate's teddy bear was in the same position on the bed as it had been the night before. Had Kate not come home the night before?

Mary looked at her watch. She figured Simon or Bonnie was awake by now. She went back to her room and found Kate's address book. She called Simon first. His mother answered, sounding upset that Mary had called so early. After a couple minutes, Simon came to the phone.

"Simon, is Kate there?" There was a long pause. Maybe he had just woken up and he hadn't understood what she said. "Is she there with you?" Mary repeated.

"Why would she be here?" His voice sounded strange, irritable.

"I thought she might be. Did she . . . did you drop her off last night?"

"Yeah, I dropped her off," he said coldly. Part of Mary wanted to pursue why he was using that tone of voice, but more than that, she wanted to find out where Kate was.

"Did she call you or anything after you dropped her off?"

"Nope. Did something happen?"

Mary heard concern in his voice, and for the first time he sounded like the Simon she always knew. "She's not here."

"Maybe she went to school."

"No, she left her backpack here. She never goes to school without her backpack." Then, out of the blue, it occurred to her to ask, "Did you guys have a fight or something?"

"We broke up," he said. He sounded like he didn't want to elaborate.

"What?"

"She broke up with me or I broke up with her. We broke up together. I don't even know what happened. All I know is it's over. I can't talk right now. I didn't get any sleep. I might skip school today." He was mumbling. "Maybe she went over to Bonnie's."

Mary hoped Simon would offer to help her find Kate, but he sounded as if he had all the hurt he could take for a while. "I'll try Bonnie," Mary said, and hung up.

Mary called Bonnie, but Bonnie's brother told her she was in the shower and Kate was not there. She asked him if he could have Bonnie call her before she went to school.

Aunt Julia had been hovering while she was on the phone.

"Something happened to Kate, didn't it?" Aunt Julia finally asked.

Mary tried to sound calm. "I don't think anything happened. It's just that she left so early and she didn't take her backpack." She decided not to mention that Kate's bed hadn't been slept in.

Aunt Julia dismissed her concerns with a wave of her hand. "Oh, she just forgot. Or maybe she has all the books she needs at school."

"She always takes her backpack to school. It has her calculator and everything she needs for her classes." Mary went over to the backpack and lifted it. It was heavy. Mary could never understand how Kate could carry such a heavy load without being permanently hunched over. Her own backpack was light by comparison.

"I heard you on the phone with Simon just now. She got here safely last night, and then she left early to go someplace. Why are you so worried all of a sudden? Have you ever known Kate to not take care of herself?"

Mary picked up the cushions from the floor and placed them on the sofa. In those few seconds, she struggled with herself whether to tell Aunt Julia about the insurance letter. She remembered the conversation they had the day before and Aunt Julia's response when she asked her about coming to live with them. She took the letter out of her back pocket and handed it to her.

In the kitchen, the kettle began to whistle. Mary went to turn off the stove while Aunt Julia read. When she came back, she found her slumped on the armchair, shaking her head. Mary could see that she was reading the letter for the second or third time. Aunt Julia dropped it on her lap.

"That no-good son of a —"

"Aunt Julia!" Mary stopped her.

"I'm sorry, but how could he do that? How could he lie on an application and take a chance that he would leave you without any money?"

"Maybe he didn't know he had a heart problem when he applied."

"That's not what the letter says. It says right here: 'Fraud. Misrepresentation.' That means 'lying' in my dictionary, and lying means he knew. Oh, God, I knew it! I knew that man was no good. He was a big phony, that's what he was." Then she looked at Mary and saw what her words were doing. "Oh, honey, come here." She pulled Mary over to sit on the sofa and put her arm around her shoulder. "I'm sorry. I didn't mean to upset you. It's very hard for me to keep my mouth shut, you know that. Here." She took a balled-up tissue from the pocket of her bathrobe and handed it to Mary. "I've got to calm down here," Aunt Julia said to herself. "Let me get a cup of coffee. I don't think I can eat anything right now. I'll settle down after a cup of coffee. I'll have decaf this morning. I'm already too riled up. Regular coffee will put me over the edge." She stood up, began to walk into the kitchen, then stopped. "Oh, that's why you're worried about Kate. She came home last night and read the letter, and you think she got upset and took off. Oh no. Kate wouldn't do that." Aunt Julia disappeared into the kitchen, still mumbling.

Mary sat there, paralyzed. For something to do, she went to look for Kate in the backyard and, ridiculously, in the shed. All along she was overcome with a feeling, a certainty almost, that something bad had happened to her. As soon as she reentered the house, the phone rang and a wave of hope and relief traveled through her body. "That must be Kate," she said as she ran to the phone. Aunt Julia popped out of the kitchen, a look of curiosity on her face. "Hello," Mary said, out of breath.

"Hey!" It was only Bonnie.

"Have you seen Kate?" Mary asked.

"My brother told me you called asking for her and then Simon called a little while ago. Is it true they broke up?" Bonnie sounded eager, excited, as if she were wishing the answer was yes. Mary always suspected Bonnie had a secret crush on Simon. Maybe that's why she was so glad Kate was going away to college.

"If Simon told you they broke up, it must be true."

"I couldn't get a sense from Simon whether it was a major breakup or not. He sounded sort of shaken up. I wonder . . ."

"What?"

"Nothing."

"Bonnie, if you know anything, please tell me. It's not like Kate to disappear like this. She's not at school, because she didn't take her backpack. It doesn't even look like she slept here last night. Her bed is still made." She wondered whether that was something she should have said. But surely she could trust Bonnie, Kate's best friend. "You know something," Mary said.

Bonnie exhaled on the other end. "I was just thinking that maybe Kate told Simon about her acceptance to Stanford and that's why they broke up."

"Forget about the stupid breakup and help me think where she might have gone," Mary said, annoyed.

"I don't have the slightest. Have you looked around the house?"

"She's not here," Mary said.

"Listen, I got to go to school. I'm sure she'll turn up. She's probably at school already. You said she didn't sleep at home? That's super weird. I wonder where she could have gone?"

"Bonnie," Mary said quickly, thinking that she was about to hang up. "I'm pretty sure she's not at school, but if for some reason I'm wrong, can you ask her to give me a call?"

"You're not coming to school?"

"No, I'm going to stay here in case she comes home."

"Okay, but you're overreacting." Bonnie's usual sweetness had disappeared. She hung up when Mary didn't respond.

Mary held the receiver against her ear until she heard a dial tone. It could be that she was overreacting, as Bonnie said, but dread lodged in the pit of her stomach. She had never felt that kind of premonition before and it was impossible to ignore it. She placed the receiver back on the phone and stood in the hall, waiting for someone to tell her what to do. She barely noticed Aunt Julia offering her a glass of juice.

"Nothing?" Aunt Julia asked.

Mary shook her head and took the glass with both hands. She let Aunt Julia lead her by the elbow back to the living room. She sat Mary down on the armchair. Mary tried to think of the places Kate could have gone. She had other friends, but none she confided in, none whom she would go to in the middle of the night or the early morning. There was no one from church. . . .

And then it hit her. Church. She put the glass down and rushed into Papa's study. She opened the top drawer of his desk and saw the empty space where he kept his keys. The keys to the church were gone. They had never bothered to return them after Papa died and now they were gone. Kate had taken them, Mary was certain. Kate was at the church. She hurried out of Papa's study, stumbling over herself. She went to her room, put her sneakers on, and ran past Aunt Julia. "Where are you going?" she heard Aunt Julia call as the screen door slammed behind her.

"I'm going to check at church," she said.

"Why on earth would she go there?"

Aunt Julia was right. Why on earth would Kate go there? Mary herself might go there if she had some terrible news. The silence of the empty sanctuary would bring her peace, would put her mind in the right place once again. But Kate? Then again, nothing about Kate was predictable any longer. Something new and complicated was emerging.

She jogged the two blocks to the church. The windows were dark and there was an air of abandonment to the building. The church could have been an empty warehouse with a cross on top of it. She opened the main door, hoping that Kate was sitting quietly in the sanctuary, reflecting, praying, but the sanctuary was empty and dark. She walked through and felt the somber quiet of the place invite her to sit and rest, to accept whatever the day was going to bring. She pushed on. She needed to be strong for Kate.

There was no one in any of the Sunday school rooms. All the doors were locked except for the door to the minister's office, Papa's old office. Papa always kept that door locked and she couldn't imagine Reverend Soto leaving it open. She remembered that the office had a couch and once again she was filled with hope that Kate was there. Perhaps she had come to be in the place where Papa spent so much time, where she would be surrounded by his books and his lingering presence.

She opened the door slowly so she would not startle Kate from sleep. But Kate was not there.

For a few moments she felt the anguish of what it would be like to lose her sister forever. "Kate," she said. She sat down on the couch and covered her eyes with her hands. She could feel tears rising, but she shook them off. She needed to think clearly. She looked around and saw the boxes full of Papa's books and the decorations and knickknacks that people had given him over the years. Reverend Soto was clearing away Papa's things.

She walked over to Papa's oak desk. His calendar was gone. The top of the desk was empty except for a Rolodex and a set of golden pens that protruded from both sides of a brass clock. She ran her hand over the desk's surface but it no longer felt like Papa. He always kept the desk cluttered with papers and magazines. Beside the desk sat a table with a laptop and a printer. Mary was looking at these when something shiny on the floor caught her eye. She bent closer and saw Papa's keys.

She picked them up and sat on the desk chair, her head reeling. Kate had been there. But where was she now? Maybe Mary missed her in one of the classrooms. She decided to look through the church one more time, but then, with her head at this level, she could see the card where the Rolodex was opened.

Rev. Andrés Soto
El Camino Hotel and Apartments, Room 157
6781 Alameda
El Paso, TX 79915
(915) 859-1104

"Oh, Kate," Mary said quietly.

21

Kate found the keys in Father's desk where they always were and then she headed for the front door of the house. She made no effort to be quiet. She was not going to tiptoe out of the house or act as if she was sneaking out. The discussion with Simon, the letter from the insurance company, had both drained her and strangely exhilarated her. She felt both exhausted and unable to be still.

The night was full of electricity. Her nerves tingled as she walked the two blocks to the church, the keys dangling in her hand. Now and then a whispering voice told her to stop, to consider what she was about to do, but she pushed through it. The warnings sounded like Father. Whenever she heard them, she remembered the words in the insurance letter: *misrepresentation, fraud*. Who was he to warn anyone? She felt as if she were being honest for the first time in her life.

Kate was certain she would find his name and telephone number somewhere in the office. It was in the Rolodex on his desk under A. *For Andy*, she thought with a smile.

The voice on the other end of the line sounded fully awake. It was eleven.

"Hello? Hello?"

Kate hesitated. She could hang up now and go back home. Home. Home was a mother who was dying but never died, a sister who couldn't live alone. Home was the place that gripped you by the ankles whenever you tried to make something of yourself. "Hello," she said tentatively. There was something about taking that first step that gave her strength. She was on her own now.

"Who's this?"

"It's me."

"Kate?"

It was a relief to be recognized. "Yes."

"Is everything okay?"

"Remember when you told me I could call you day or night?"

"You sound like you're in trouble. Where are you?"

She took a deep breath. She knew what she was doing and had no doubts. She wanted to make sure she didn't sound as if she did. "Did you mean it?"

She heard silence on the other end of the phone. "Where are you?"

"I'm at the church."

Silence again and then, "I'll be there in a few minutes."

She was sitting on the steps by the side of the church when he drove up. He got out of the car and walked toward her. It was a warm night and he was wearing a polo shirt, blue shorts, and flip-flops. "I'm glad you're dressed like that," she said. She tried to sound cheerful.

"Why?"

"You look more like an Andy than a Reverend Soto."

He sat down next to her on the steps. Moths flitted around the lightbulb above them. They stared silently at a row of garbage cans that lined the edge of the church's property. Andy leaned back on his elbows and stretched his legs. He acted as if she had called him to have a pleasant chat. After a while, he said, "Do you want to go inside and talk?"

She shook her head. "There are too many memories in there."

He sat up. She was aware that he was looking at her as if trying to figure out the real reason for her call. It occurred to her that she herself did not know the real reason. Was she there for Andy or for Reverend Soto? She became aware of a nervous hope that he would ask her to go someplace quiet, but the idea that he would decide where they would go or what would happen next made her feel weak and helpless. The day had battered her with too many instances of her own powerlessness. She couldn't afford one more. He was about to speak when she preempted him.

"I know a place where we can get a Coke and talk." He probably thought she was a child for suggesting a Coke. A cup of coffee would have sounded more mature.

"That sounds good to me," he said.

They went to a place called Menudo 24, the only place she knew that was open twenty-four hours. She and Simon used to go there occasionally and sit in a back booth. They ordered a Coke for Kate and a cup of coffee for Andy. As she sipped the Coke through a straw, she tried to figure out where to start. All her thoughts and feelings were like a ball of yarn that had lost its beginning and its end.

"So . . ." he started to say.

She cut him off. "I wanted to talk to you about the options you mentioned the other day." It was the first thing that came to mind. She added quickly to soften her harsh tone, "It's so hard to discuss."

"It is hard," he acknowledged.

She took a deep breath. "How does one go about removing a feeding tube from someone who is in a vegetative state?" There. The words were out. They were real now.

He lifted the cup of coffee to his lips and blew on it. There was not the slightest sign on his face that her words had shocked him. He took a sip, then put the cup down and looked at her. "How you go about it is not as important as the decision itself."

"I don't understand," she said.

"You're not a horrible human being for considering it." She shrugged, though it was reassuring to hear his words. He went on, "What happened tonight? Did something trigger you wanting to talk about this?"

"Not really," she said. But she was not sure her response was honest. Was she talking about disconnecting her mother's feeding tube because she broke up with Simon, because the insurance was denied? Was she thinking about this because all other options had run out? "I don't know."

"Something must have happened. I can tell. The last time I talked to you, you seemed upset about even thinking about it."

She twirled her hair for a few seconds, reflecting, and then she spoke. "About a year after the accident, one of the doctors told Father that the law would allow him to take Mother off life support, and Father went crazy. I've never seen him so angry. Father thought that ending Mother's life, I mean, her vegetative life, I don't know what to call it really —"

"Vegetative life is okay."

"He thought ending Mother's vegetative life was a sin. We had no right to end human life under any circumstances."

"And what do you think?"

"I never believed there was any hope of Mother coming back to real life. I always saw her as being gone to the world, to us. After I talked to you, I don't know, it seemed like we were keeping Mother alive for our sake, like we weren't being honest with ourselves." She pushed the half-empty glass of Coke away from her. "I thought that underneath church doctrine and following God's will and everything, Father was really keeping her alive because of his own guilt." She stopped. She felt as if she had just betrayed her father. "He was driving when they had the accident. It was his fault. He went through a yellow light, thinking he could make it, but he didn't."

"Ahh."

She pulled the glass back toward her and stirred the liquid with the straw. Andy was looking at her as if he could see what she was hiding. "Things are different now."

"How?"

"Without Father, it will be hard to take care of Mother."

"Hard, but not impossible," he said.

"We were expecting money from Father's insurance policy, but that's not coming," she blurted out.

He leaned forward and waited for her eyes to meet his. "If you wanted to keep your mother alive, there would be some way to do it. We'd have to investigate."

He said we, she said to herself. The magnetic force she had felt last time came back stronger than before. She ran her hand over her hair and turned her head away to break their gaze. The man flipping hamburgers behind the counter had a white net over his hair, and an apron grimy with black grease and a brown smear that looked like dried blood. He pressed each hamburger with a spatula and the meat sizzled and smoked.

"It's hard to talk about this," Kate said. "It seems so cold and calculating. . . . I loved my mother."

"Loved?"

"Love."

"The thing is, the past tense, *loved* is also the right word. The person with a feeding tube in your house is not your mother. Love implies that there's another person to love you back. It's a two-way street."

His words made her think of Simon. Was their relationship ever a two-way street?

"Your views are so different from Father's, but you're both ministers."

He furrowed his forehead. "Different churches have differ-ent views on this. The Church of God doesn't have one set doctrine on end-of-life decisions. It's possible for your father to think one way and for me to think another. Anyway, it's you and not I who will make the decision. What does your faith tell you?"

Faith? She hadn't heard that word since her father used it the Sunday when he died. "You mean like 'What would Jesus do?'" She wondered for a second what his faith was telling him about the way he was looking at her now. The tension made her laugh, and he laughed with her.

"In some ways it's as simple as that and in others it's extremely complicated," he said, still smiling. He gestured to the waitress for a refill of coffee.

"You won't be able to sleep," she said.

"That's all right. I don't much feel like sleeping tonight," he answered, looking at her, and she found it hard to breathe. She tried to refocus on his question.

"I'm not sure what happened to my faith," she said. There was almost sadness in her voice.

"You don't believe?"

"Believe? I don't even know what the word *faith* means anymore."

"What do you hope for, then?" he asked.

She thought of Mary. Mary hoped that Mother would wake up one morning, really wake up, and take up where she had left off. She'd walk to the kitchen and start making flour tortillas. Kate's own hopes seemed small in comparison, more like wants and wishes.

"We can live without faith," Andy continued quietly, "but not without hope, not without some kind of hope that we can make our lives mean something. Without hope we are empty."

"I want to be a doctor," she said. "I was accepted by Stanford. That's a university in California."

"I know where Stanford is," he said. He sounded impressed. When she didn't elaborate, he went on, "That's your hope — to be a doctor." He said this as if it was the explanation for many things. "When did you decide you wanted to be a doctor?"

"I must have been about eight. My father was in the hospital, and while he was there, my mother asked one of the nurses to give me a tour. I met this little girl, her name was Patty, who had cancer. We became pen pals. A year later she died." Kate paused. Her eyes reddened. "That's when I decided I wanted to be a doctor, to work with children like her."

"You see, that's your hope."

"It kept me going," she confessed.

"And now?"

Kate looked at her hands. Then, raising her eyes, she said, "Am I selfish for wanting to go to Stanford?"

"I don't know. Are you?"

"I promised Mother that I would be a doctor. I even promised her that I would go to Stanford. She wanted me to go there."

"You know" — he stopped to swallow — "I hope you don't take this the wrong way, but I have a good idea of how your father was with you. I've seen it many times before. Fathers like yours want a household where everyone is a saint, and a saint always sacrifices her interests for others. Saints are taught to think that wanting to go to the best college or wanting to have a high-paying job is a kind of ambition that God forbids. You're not selfish because you want to go away to Stanford. When I was telling you that there were probably ways to keep your mother like she is, it was because I wanted to make sure that if you disconnect her feeding tube, you'll be doing it without guilt, without the sense that you're being selfish. If you do it, it's because it's in everyone's best interests, including your mother's."

"You think letting my mother go is best for my mother? Why? You think she's being kept from going to heaven?" She was not being cynical.

He puffed out his cheeks as if he were blowing a high note on a trumpet. "Your mother is already in heaven. Her soul is already there."

"You should talk to my sister, Mary, someday," she said, drinking the last of her Coke from the bottom of her glass.

"Why?" He finished his coffee. She hoped he would ask for more, but he simply wrapped his hands around the cup.

"She talks to Mother as if Mother can hear her. She'll tell you that Mother's soul is still with her, that God has kept her alive for a purpose."

"I see."

"That will make it harder, won't it? I mean if I decided to . . . I would need to get Mary to agree."

"I don't know. Maybe not. You're an adult and she's not. You asked me how you would go about it. I suppose you would need to go before a judge with a doctor's affidavits and so on. That shouldn't be too hard. Texas law permits the stopping of life-support systems in cases like your mother's. Maybe your sister could fight you if she didn't agree with you. It would certainly be better if she agreed with you. Do you think you can convince her?"

"I'm not sure," Kate said, her voice weighed down with a sudden realization. What would happen to Mary if she went through with it?

"There's a lot to think about. You need to keep your sister's welfare in mind. What is ultimately best for her?" There was a moment of silence as Andy waited for Kate to respond, but she didn't. "What will you do?"

"I don't know. I don't know. I needed to talk about it, that's all."

"At 12:30 A.M.?" he joked.

She smiled back at him. "I'm sorry. It was a rough day and I needed someone to talk to. I broke up with my boyfriend tonight, Simon, then I got home and saw the letter that said we weren't going to get any insurance. I couldn't talk about this with Mary. She would worry. I know how she is. And I kept going over and over what you said to me in Father's . . . in your office the other day. I couldn't stop thinking about all you said. I'm sorry." Kate stopped abruptly.

"I'm glad you called me. Does it look like I'm regretting this?"

She took a deep breath and looked at him directly, in a way that let him know she saw him as a man. She wanted to be equal to him in all respects when she spoke.

"You said we could be two people searching for the truth together. What did you mean by that?"

He squirmed in his seat. It was exactly what she wanted him to do. She waited for his answer while carefully observing the expression on his face. Had she been too forward? He bit his lip and tried to find a place to put his hands. She grinned.

"I meant that . . ." he stuttered, "I am willing . . . to do . . . whatever you feel comfortable . . . whatever your heart tells you is all right to do."

"Are you attracted to me?"

He chuckled. "You noticed."

She studied his face. He looked older than Simon, but only in the way maturity makes a person look older. Simon. He seemed just then like someone she knew a long time ago. Andy had a slight wrinkle in his forehead, between the eyes, the same wrinkle her father had — the scar that came from reading. She may have felt comfortable with Simon, but with Andy she knew what it meant to be attracted. What she was feeling was not ignited just by his good looks, but by his words, intelligence, and something she couldn't fully understand — something like the desire to have him surrender.

"What's going on in that head of yours?" he asked.

She picked up her glass and looked at its empty bottom. "I'm trying to understand what's happening here." She thought as soon as she said this that it was a lie. She understood what was happening.

"There seem to be a lot of things happening here," he said with a smile. "Where do we go now?"

She felt a rush of fear and started to stand up. Then she pushed the fear away. As far back as she could remember, what she wanted had been labeled wrong by the voice of her father or of God. For too long she had been afraid, tentative with the expectation that punishment would follow when she pursued what she wanted. She sat down again.

"I don't want to be alone tonight," she said.

"Do you want to go back to the church?" he asked.

"No."

They stared at each other. There weren't many options left.

"Do you have a couch at your place where I could spend the night?" She didn't want to let him know she was afraid.

"Yes, if that's what you would like." He glanced around. "We need to be careful," he said. "I don't know how it would look if someone from the congregation saw us."

A bubble of hurt rose within her. "Why? Are you embarrassed to be seen with me?" Hurt was not something she had ever felt with Simon. *Maybe hurt is a part of love*, she thought, *and this is how I know I love him.*

"No, of course not. I meant . . . that . . . I don't think you coming to my place is wrong, but there may be people in the church who might not agree with me."

"Even if we just talk?"

"It doesn't look good."

"You don't have to worry about anyone finding out from me. If you want, you can just drop me at home."

"No," he said quickly. He reached over and placed his hand on top of hers. "I didn't mean to imply that *I* think it's wrong, or that I don't trust you."

He was right. Of course it looked bad. What was she thinking? She tried to think things through, to work it out until she saw the consequences of all that was happening, but she was tired of thinking and planning. She couldn't remember a time when she had not been consumed by tomorrow. Tomorrow was a prison. Today she was free.

"Let's go," she said.

22

Mary left the church dazed. Part of her said that Kate was old enough to make her own decisions, and part of her thought she needed to stop her from making a huge mistake. It was a terrible idea for Kate to get involved with the minister of what used to be Papa's church. Mary remembered what he had said in his sermon about Papa. There was something mean about Reverend Soto.

She was halfway home when she felt Papa's keys in her pocket. If she put the keys back in Papa's desk, Kate would know for sure that she knew where she had been. Mary hoped Kate would talk to her about whatever happened, but she didn't want her to feel that she had to explain herself. She decided to go back to the church and leave Papa's keys where she found them.

When Mary finally got home, Kate still had not returned. She checked on Mama and then she went to the backyard, where Aunt Julia was watering the willow tree. "These kinds of trees need lots of water." Aunt Julia spoke without looking at Mary. "They usually grow near creeks and rivers. They're not desert trees."

"Papa said that when we first moved into the house, there was an irrigation ditch that brought water to all these yards. Back then, people had fields where they grew corn and vegetables and stuff," Mary said.

"You need to dig around the tree so the water stays." She pulled on the hose and went over to the back fence to water the roses. "I guess you didn't find Kate."

"Sometimes she stays with this other waitress who works with her," Mary said quickly. Now if she could just remember the name of one of the waitresses in case Aunt Julia asked. But Aunt Julia didn't ask. She had this tiny smirk on her face as if she knew that Mary was lying.

Aunt Julia shook her head and sighed. "I don't know what I'm going to do. I really should go back home pretty soon. I don't think I can stay like you asked me."

"Is it because of the insurance?"

A guilty look came over Aunt Julia's face. "Who planted those petunias?" she asked.

"I did," Mary said.

"They're nice. You're a nice girl."

"We can figure something out about the money."

"I can be more help to you in San Jose than I can here. I have my job and I can send you a little money now and then. I can't give you any of my savings because it's not all that much, and I need it for when I can't work anymore."

"Can't you get a job here? There are beauty salons all over. I can help you find one."

"Look at me." Aunt Julia stretched out her wrinkled arm. It trembled like a leaf in a breeze. "Who's going to want to let me cut her hair with these hands? Over there I cut the hair of old ladies who've been coming to me for years and who wear their hair all puffed up and sprayed so no one can see my mistakes. You mind turning off the hose?" Mary went to the faucet, and when she came back, Aunt Julia was sitting on one of the wooden chairs. She always sat with her back very straight, like a queen on her throne. Mary sat down in the chair next to her.

Aunt Julia went on, "The one thing that always gave me comfort about you girls was that you were so responsible. Don't get me wrong. I thought your father was way too strict with you. He took away your opportunity to just be kids, ordinary kids. But I'll say this for him; he sure got you ready for when he wasn't around. Maybe that's what he was doing all along. I've been thinking about it ever since I read that insurance letter this morning and while you were away looking for Kate. What if he knew he had this heart that wasn't working all that good and he set out to prepare you for when he was gone? He knew you were going to be alone."

"But we're not alone. We've got you."

Aunt Julia ignored what Mary said. "I know Kate and I butt heads. She doesn't like me, I can tell." Mary started to interrupt her to tell her that, deep down, Kate was grateful for all she was doing, but she didn't let Mary speak. "We're both proud and stubborn. Not a good combination." She slapped the side of her neck. "Are there mosquitoes during daytime?"

"They're supposed to go away when the sun is up." They both looked up at the same time. The sun was hidden by gray clouds.

"It never rains in El Paso except when I'm here," Aunt Julia said. She was looking straight ahead, as if she were talking to someone only she could see. "I always felt it would be okay to go home and leave you girls alone because Kate was capable of taking care of you, of herself and you."

"And Mama," Mary added.

"Yes, Catalina also. But now I have my doubts about Kate."

"I'm sure she's okay. She didn't do anything for you to doubt her. She's still the same Kate. That letter just really upset her. She . . . we were all counting on that money." Mary tried to sound convincing, when the truth was that she probably had more doubts about Kate than Aunt Julia did. "She broke up with Simon."

She blurted this out, thinking it might make Kate's disappearance more excusable, but she could see by the expression on Aunt Julia's face that it only made matters worse.

"What is that girl thinking? Has she gone crazy? That boy was the one good thing the two of you had going. He's the only way I can see you two survive. I hate to say it to you, but your sister's just downright selfish. Just like her father."

Mary wanted to remind her that just a few seconds before, she had thought Kate "capable," but maybe you could be capable and selfish at the same time. She remembered all the moments when she thought Kate was selfish: when she told Mary she had to give up her hour of studio after school, or when Mary found out she was going away to college. Now that feeling came to her again, but more confusingly: Was Kate selfish, or was it Mary who was being selfish, wanting Kate to give up what she cherished most? And Aunt Julia? Was she the one who was selfish, wanting Kate to marry Simon so that they'd be off of her hands? This selfishness thing was very hard to figure out.

"Maybe it was just a lover's quarrel with Simon. It happens," Mary said, as if she were the world's expert on love.

"It's too much to ask!" Aunt Julia said loudly, almost shrieking. A sparrow that was hopping on the grass flew away. "You girls can't ask me to do this. You can't ask me to give up my whole life. That's just too much to ask of somebody. I feel sorry for you and you're my sister's daughters, but I have to live my life." She looked straight at Mary.

"So you're not staying?" Her voice quivered.

"I'm staying until Saturday and then I'm leaving." There was anger in her words, but it wasn't directed at Mary. Mary realized Aunt Julia needed strength to get the words out. Then her face softened and she said, "I'm not leaving you alone. I'll come for a few weeks every year to give you girls a break, and I'll send you what little money I can. What else can I do?"

"You've been really helpful," Mary said, but she probably didn't sound too sincere. Aunt Julia was Mama's sister. Aren't sisters supposed to do everything for each other? If Kate were in the same situation as Mama, if Kate were in a vegetative state, her husband dead and two kids on their own without any money, she would do all within her power to help them. Aunt Julia was rubbing her thighs as if all that speaking had cramped her legs.

Then, slowly, another idea began to take life inside of Mary. "Aunt Julia," she said tentatively, "what if I went to live with you?"

Aunt Julia's head snapped around. "What?"

"Mama and I. What if we went to live with you?" Mary said. She didn't want to tell her about Stanford, so she said carefully, "Kate's sure to get a scholarship that pays for everything. She's got the highest SAT scores any student at Riverside has ever gotten. She can live in the college dorms. Then it's just Mama and me. We could move her to San Jose in an ambulance. I would take care of her, Aunt Julia. You wouldn't even know she was there. We can find a nurse with the money the church gave us and Papa's retirement, and I could take high school courses by mail or online. I could keep our computer, and Kate could get a new one. I wouldn't mind staying at home with Mama. All I like to do is paint anyway." She was out of breath by the time she finished speaking.

Aunt Julia shook her head and smiled. That was good, Mary thought. At least she didn't say no immediately. "What about your friends?"

"I really have only one good friend, Renata. I'd keep in touch with her. She could come visit if it's okay with you. We can put Mama in the guest bedroom and we can put a cot in there for me, like we used to do when Kate and I visited you."

"No," Aunt Julia said firmly, with no guilt or regret in her voice.

"No?" Just like that? She wasn't even willing to consider it? Mary knew by the way Aunt Julia said it that any other argument was hopeless. It wasn't a matter of money or of rooms or cots. Mary didn't know what it was.

"I'm sorry," Aunt Julia said, getting up slowly, like her legs were not strong enough to support her. She tottered for a few seconds and then sat down again. "I can't take care of you girls. I'm ill."

"What?"

Aunt Julia brought her arm to her eyes and wiped away the wetness. "I can't take care of you girls. I can't be with Catalina. I'm ill. I've been diagnosed with breast cancer." She began to sob.

"Aunt Julia, I didn't know." A wave of sadness came over Mary.

"I don't want anyone to know. I'm only telling you so you don't think I'm the witch you think I am."

"But you should have told us."

"Maybe I should have from the start. I have a hard time facing up to it. And you girls already have so much on your shoulders."

Mary pulled her chair closer and put her arm around her. "Aunt Julia, now more than ever, we should all be together.

You can't be by yourself in San Jose. We're family. We can take care of each other."

Aunt Julia was dabbing her eyes with a tissue. "Maybe you're right. I've never been much for family. But I tried my best."

"Promise me you'll think about us staying together."

"I have to go home and start with the chemo."

"Just promise me that you'll think about it, all of us being together." Mary felt like telling her about Stanford. Stanford was close to San Jose. Kate could go to Stanford, and Mama and Mary could live with Aunt Julia, and they could all take care of one another.

"I think I'm going to make me a cup of tea. You want some?"

Mary looked at her watch. It was almost eleven. Talita would arrive in a few minutes to see Mama. "No, thank you," Mary said. "I think I'll go to school. Maybe I can find Kate there."

"Okay," Aunt Julia said.

"Aunt Julia. Can you promise me?"

"What?"

"What I asked you. That you would think about us being together."

"I promise you. I'll think about it. There," Aunt Julia said, mustering a smile, "does that make you happy?"

"Yes, it does."

Mary's lunch period was at noon, so as soon as she got to school she went directly to the cafeteria and found Renata sitting with Evangelina. Fortunately, Evangelina stood up as soon as Mary sat down. "I have to finish my algie," Evangelina said.

"She's not leaving because of you," Renata explained after she left. "She really does have to catch up on her algebra. She's flunking out in just about all her classes. She wants me to tutor her, but it'd be like dumb and dumber. Hey, you weren't in history this morning. What happened to you? And where's your baggie lunch?"

Mary wanted to tell Renata about Kate. How odd that she had never before felt the need to share what she was going through. But she decided to hold back for the moment. "Aunt Julia and I had a long conversation this morning."

"And?"

"She's not staying with us. We were counting on Papa's insurance money, and yesterday we found out we were denied, and now Aunt Julia says she's going back home."

"Tell me exactly what happened."

"I asked Aunt Julia if she could stay with us or if Mama and I could go live with her, but she didn't want us to. It turns out that she has cancer."

"Wait, you're going way too fast for me. Start at the beginning. I'm missing something here. Why would you ask her to live with you?"

Mary took a deep breath. She could feel her eyes redden. "It's a long story."

"Well . . ." Renata moved closer to her. She was willing to listen.

Words came out fast. "Kate got accepted into Stanford. A school in California. She really wants to go. It's her dream. So I thought one solution was for Aunt Julia to live with Mama and me while Kate was away, or Mama and I could move to San Jose where Aunt Julia lives. I thought we could use the insurance money, but then it turns out that we were rejected because the insurance company claims Papa committed some kind of fraud. He didn't tell them he had a heart condition." She stopped to breathe briefly. "But even if we had the insurance money, Aunt Julia said no."

"She said no?"

"When she first said no, I thought it was because she was selfish, but it turns out she's ill. She has cancer. I feel terrible for doubting her."

"Wow. I don't know what to say. Where to start? Kate is actually thinking of going away to college? Are you kidding me?"

"It's her dream. Don't hold it against her."

"I'm not holding it against her, it's just that dreams have to adjust to reality. The reality is that she can't leave you and your mother alone. Talk about being selfish."

"Do you think so?"

"Well, what do you think? What would *you* do? Would you go away and leave her and your mother alone? Tell the truth."

"But it's not the same. I would never be able to get into a place like Stanford."

"But you have your own dreams. You want to be a great painter. Remember that school fair when you donated one of your paintings? And remember what the man who bought it said, that he would buy paintings like that anytime. You're a great painter already. My point is that you wouldn't hesitate to sacrifice your dream for the sake of your mama and your sister if it ever came to that."

"I don't know," Mary said. Tears welled up in her eyes.

"Listen to me," Renata said. "Guess what."

Mary took a napkin from Renata's tray and wiped her cheeks. "What?"

Renata put an arm around Mary, took an orange that she had already peeled, and offered her half. Mary contemplated it for a few seconds and then placed it on the table in front of her.

"My mother has this friend who's a social worker. She called her — you know Mom, she really gets into these things. Mom told this Mrs. Fresquez, that's the name of the social worker, all about you and your sister and your mother, and Mrs. Fresquez says there are definitely programs that can help with medical care for your mom and help for you and your sister."

"Yeah?" Renata's words made the tears come even more abundantly, but for a different reason. It felt good to have someone worry about her.

"I got Mrs. Fresquez's number. We can go tomorrow after school. Kate could come if she wants to. You think Kate would want to?"

Mary sniffed. Kate. She looked around the cafeteria for her. "Maybe."

"Knowing Kate, she's probably too proud to accept help. But what else are you going to do? You're running out of options." When she saw that Mary had stopped crying, Renata moved closer and whispered, "What happened between Kate and Simon?"

"How'd you know?" Mary asked, raising her head.

"Are you kidding me? Bonnie's cell phone has been burning up telling people the news. Even us puny sophomores knew all about it by second period."

"But it only happened last night."

"What did Kate tell you? Tell me, tell me, don't hold back a single dirty detail." Renata was pretending to be gossipy, but she was also truly itching to know, Mary could tell. But how could she say anything without divulging that Kate hadn't come home?

"I was asleep when she came in last night," Mary said.

Renata cocked her head. "How about this morning?"

"She told me she broke up with Simon. You know Kate. If she doesn't feel like talking, she won't."

"She wasn't upset? When you saw her this *morning*, I mean?" The two girls stared at each other — a friendly stare, a who-will-blink-first kind of stare. Mary had a feeling Renata knew Kate hadn't come home. "Kate's not in school this morning," Renata continued. "Everyone knows everything around here. This is big, Mary, huge. Bonnie's walking around drooling and fawning over Simon."

"Stop," Mary said gently.

"Okay. But where's Kate? Think carefully about the lie you're about to tell me. You already said she didn't say anything to you before she left this morning, so you can't say she's at home. She didn't come home last night, did she?"

"She came home." Mary was glad that she could be truthful about something.

"You're utterly hopeless. That's all right. I'll get my information elsewhere." Renata stuck her tongue out at Mary. "She was out with another guy."

"No way!" Mary tried to make it sound as if that was absolutely impossible.

"That's what Bonnie's saying. She's saying it was Simon who broke up with Kate. Is it true?"

Mary could not believe all the rumors that had spread in the four hours since she spoke to Bonnie. "Did she happen to say why?" She tried to sound annoyed, but she was actually more concerned that people might know about Kate and Reverend Soto.

"No. You know, Simon's not a bad guy. Girls like Bonnie would not hesitate to snatch him."

"She's Kate's best friend."

"Bonnie's her own best friend, trust me. She's been eyeing Simon all along. He's just her type too. You know all she wants is to get married and have babies, and Simon with his restaurants fits the bill just perfectly."

"How do you know all this?"

"Cause I'm an observer of human nature, girl! Personally, I never liked Simon that much. He's a little too goody-goody. You and I need someone wild and dangerous, like him."

Mary followed Renata's hot gaze to the front of the cafeteria and her heart leapt. Marcos was standing with a tray in his hand, looking around for a place to sit. "Look at that body, those eyes," Renata said. "If he ever even smiled at me, I'd melt. Oh. Oh. He's looking straight at us." Mary looked down and covered her face with her hand. "Mary, Mary." Renata was shaking her arm, whispering. "He's walking. Here. He's, like, going to sit with us." She stopped talking and proceeded to nervously dismember her half of the orange.

"Hey," Marcos said. He was standing at their table.

"Hey," Mary said. Renata shot Mary a shocked look.

He sat down without asking if he could. "I had this great idea for the mural I wanted to show you."

"Renata, this is Marcos. Marcos, this is Renata." Someone had to be polite.

"Hey," he said, smiling at Renata. Renata was totally mute.

"She actually can talk," Mary said. "Ouch." She experienced a sharp pain in her foot, the kind that comes when the person sitting next to you stomps on it.

"You're a junior, aren't you?" Renata had found her tongue again.

"Sort of," Marcos said. "I've missed so many classes they're threatening to make me come back another year."

"Why do you miss so many classes?" Renata asked.

"Renata!" Mary said.

Marcos shrugged. "I had to take care of business." He scrunched his eyebrows to make himself look scary. Renata gulped. He turned to Mary with a grin. "Want to know what I'm thinking . . . for the mural?"

"I guess," Mary said.

"Wait, are you guys in art class together or something?" Renata said.

"Or something," Marcos answered. "I have to do this mural as a community service thing, and I think I got Mary here to help me."

"Oh." Mary could see that Renata was torn between wild curiosity and her desire to give them privacy. Curiosity won out, and she stayed put.

"Well," Mary said to Marcos, "what's your idea?"

He opened the spout of his milk carton. "This mural I'm supposed to do. It's for this center where they teach English as a second language and they also have these programs where they try to make Chicano kids learn about their culture in Mexico. It's like they want kids and even old people to make it here in the U.S. but not forget where they came from, you know what I mean?"

"Yes," Mary said.

"Which center are you talking about?" Renata asked.

"The one in Socorro."

"I know that one. You're going to paint something on that?"

"On one of the outside walls."

"Cool. What you gonna paint?"

A strange feeling came over Mary as she listened to Renata and Marcos. Renata and Mary had grown up together; they were in many ways closer than she and Kate. But just then, as Renata talked to Marcos, Mary wanted Marcos to be talking only to her. "Wow," Mary said, amazed at what she was feeling.

"What?" Marcos asked.

"Nothing. I was just remembering something." Mary felt she had probably done more lying that morning than she had in her entire life.

Marcos took a folded piece of paper from his back pocket. He turned it toward Renata and Mary and spread it on the table.

"What is that?" Renata asked, squinting.

"Two eagles," Marcos said.

"Oh!" Mary exclaimed. One of the eagles was exactly like the one in the drawing she had given Papa.

"Is it that bad?" Marcos asked.

"No," Mary said. She was unable to say anything else.

Marcos looked somewhat confused, but he went on, "This one's an American bald eagle and this one's the Mexican golden eagle — you know, like the kind on the Mexican flag, only here I have it flying. I didn't do a very good job at showing the two eagles with their wings spread." He stopped and looked into Mary's eyes, waiting for her reaction.

Mary felt pride, as if she herself had done the drawing. "It's great," she finally said.

"Really?" Marcos asked, excited.

Renata clapped as if something wonderful had just happened. Mary could tell by the way she looked at her that there was no jealousy or envy in her heart. *She's a better person than I am*, she said to herself.

"I didn't say the drawing was great," Mary said. "I meant the idea is great. You don't have any perspective on the wings, and the eagles look like skinny chickens, but the idea is good."

Renata elbowed Mary. "She's kidding, she's kidding. The eagles are awesome, just fab!"

"It's a start," Mary said, trying not to show any more emotion.

"We're still on for Saturday morning, right?"

"I never told you I could go."

"That's right. You said you were going to check. I'll call you on Friday." A few boys at a nearby table were staring at Marcos. He nodded in their direction as if telling them that he'd be right there. Then he pushed himself off the bench and picked up his tray.

Mary didn't want him to leave. "Work on the drawing," she said quickly. "You'll need to have a detailed sketch before you start painting."

"Yeah. I'll work on it." He smiled at Mary and winked at Renata, then went to the table with the boys.

When he was out of earshot, Renata said, "Oh. My. God. What was that all about? You have A LOT of explaining to do."

"There's nothing to explain. Mr. Gomez asked me to help him with some drawing, and then he asked me to help him with that mural."

"You're in love with him."

"Pleeease! Don't be silly. I don't even know him. Besides, he's in a gang."

"I saw you light up like a Christmas tree when he was talking to you. You'll have to work out this gang thing, but you're in love with him. You don't even know it yet, but you are."

"I have to go to my locker. You coming?" Mary picked up

the uneaten half of the orange. Suddenly she thought of Kate. She searched for her one last time around the cafeteria, but Kate was nowhere to be seen.

Her heart, the same one that had just soared, plummeted to the ground.

23

They pulled into the El Camino Hotel and parked in front of number 157. She could see a light in the room through a crack in the curtains. *Nothing's going to happen*, she told herself. *I just need a place to rest.*

"Are you sure you're all right with this?" Andy asked. There was something that made her feel safe in the way he said that. "I can drive you home if you want."

For some reason his words reminded her of Simon. She and Simon had gone out for three months before they kissed in his car, and when they kissed, she felt Simon's lips tremble as if he were afraid she was a mirage too beautiful and good to be true.

"What was your boyfriend's name?" Andy asked.

"Simon."

"You were thinking of him just then, weren't you?"

"Yes. How did you know?"

"You said earlier that you broke up with him. It doesn't take a genius to figure out that right about now, you'd probably be thinking about him. What's he like, Simon?"

"Simon is your standard nice guy," Kate said. "He's hard-working, dependable, steady." She let go of the door handle and leaned back in the car seat.

"Why'd you break up with him?"

"I'm not sure what happened." She ran her fingers through her hair. "I think he broke up with me. He wanted to get married. He wanted to take care of me and Mary and Mother."

"And . . ."

"I asked for more time, but I guess he could tell that I was really saying no." Kate exhaled. "Maybe there's something seriously wrong with me. I don't know. I've had this stupid dream about going to Stanford for so long that I've never let anything or anyone interfere with it, not a nice guy like Simon, not my little sister, not anything. If Father hadn't died, I would have ended up fighting him to keep that dream."

He turned the ignition switch on for a moment and opened both of the front windows. Immediately a cool breeze blew through the car. She heard the roar of noise from Interstate 10 and imagined each truck that went by as a wave crashing on a beach.

"Don't be so hard on yourself," he said. He reached over and gave her hand a tiny squeeze. "Do you love Simon?" He didn't take his hand away.

She closed her eyes and concentrated on the warmth of his hand. *More.* What she felt asked for more. With Simon, she was content, full, at peace. With Andy she felt the need for more conversation, more emotion, more touch. Which of the two feelings was love? She opened her eyes and remembered that he had asked a question.

"I'm sorry, what did you ask me?"

He chuckled. "Do you love him? Do you love Simon?"

She shook her head. "Mary has never dated anyone and she knows more about love than I do. She says that when she paints, she sees this light in whatever she's painting, and this light is the same as a light she recognizes inside of her. This recognition of lights is what she calls love. It's all very joyful, but it involves hard work at the same time to keep them together. I think that something along those lines is probably what it means to truly love another person."

"Wow," he said.

"What?"

"I was just thinking about your sister's love. That's beautiful, but unreal, not human. Most of us have to settle for the regular human kind of love. Regular human love is all we've got."

"And what's regular human love?"

"Wanting the other person physically and emotionally, hurting with their absence, needing them, that's part of it."

She closed her eyes again as she spoke. "I've always felt that my dream to go to Stanford, to be a doctor, is similar to how you defined love. It's wanting something very badly, searching for it at all costs, needing it. I always felt ashamed when Father used to preach against ambition, because I knew I had it in me in the worst possible way. And now I don't know whether I've been blinded by it so I can't see what is really good for me — like Simon."

"Or it could be that Simon is not the right person for you. You can't really force yourself to want someone. You do or you don't."

"I thought I wanted Simon."

"Is he like you? Is he ambitious?"

"No, not in the sense of wanting what he doesn't have. He's happy already. He's going to run one of his father's restaurants. He's content with that."

"Maybe you need someone more like you, someone who believes there's nothing wrong with ambition. It's how God gets things done in the world."

"Like you? You're ambitious too?"

"Sure, why not? You seem surprised."

"It's just that I never imagined the Church of God attracting someone ambitious."

"There are different kinds of ambitions. The saints were ambitious."

"Are you a saint?" She pretended to be shocked.

"Hardly." He let go of her hand and gently stroked her cheek.

She smiled. "How are you ambitious?"

"I guess it started when I was a small boy. My mother used to watch these mega evangelists on TV. You know, the ones who preach to auditoriums and stadiums full of people, with choirs larger than most churches. I'd watch them with her, and then I'd stand in front of the mirror with a Bible in one hand and preach. I was pretty good at it too."

"You are good at it," Kate acknowledged.

"Thank you. So that's how it started. I love to preach. I love the energy that you feel when a room full of people is silent, waiting on every word you say. I was called to it. I wanted to be like those preachers whose words moved people to tears. So I looked for opportunities to speak in public. I joined the speech club in high school. I got super involved with our church youth group. I couldn't wait to have my own church. I went to college, got a master's degree in four years when it usually takes six. Now I'm twenty-two and my dream of being pastor of my own church has been realized. These are things that I've wanted desperately, just like you want to go to Stanford. God works through our ambitions. He puts them there for a purpose, so we can do His will."

"Will you be happy at a place like the Church of God?"

"For a while," he said, looking at her. "You have to start someplace."

"Then after a while you'll want a bigger church."

"Yes."

"That's part of your ambition, to move on to a bigger church?"

"Yes. For me, it's a question of finding a place where all of my potential is fulfilled, where all of my talent is tapped."

"And the Church of God doesn't do that?"

"It's a beginning. But I wouldn't be true to myself if I said that it's enough. After a year or two, I'll move on. We need to find the place where we can have the greatest impact. There's nothing wrong with that."

"Do the deacons know?"

"Know what?"

"That you plan to move on in a year or two?"

"No. You need to keep that confidential, okay?"

She thought of Mrs. Alvarado and her electric organ. The image made her sad.

"In a way, me wanting to move on to a bigger church eventually is like you and Stanford," he went on. "Why Stanford and not UTEP? You can study to be a doctor at UTEP. Why go all the way to California? The quality of the school, sure, but also the prestige, the status. I've come to terms with the side of myself that wants those things. They offer the opportunity to reach more people. People in a big church need a good pastor as well. That's my calling. Some people are called to work with the poor, others are called to work with the rich. Am I shocking you?"

"No." He was not shocking her, but he was unsettling her somehow. His words were breaking through an inner shell, revealing an image of herself she had never known was there. To have something to say, she said, "It's hot in here."

"Do you want to go inside? It's not much of an apartment, but the air conditioner works really well."

"In a little while," she said. "I like listening to the waves."

"What waves?"

She cupped her ear to the sound of a semitruck speeding by on the interstate. He chuckled. She turned so that her back was leaning against the car door, and shook her head.

"What?"

"Nothing."

"Tell me what you were thinking," he insisted.

"I was just thinking that for someone who wants to work with the rich, you picked a bad place."

"It's a start. I had an offer to be an assistant pastor at a church in Lubbock, but then this opportunity came up. It's better to be a big fish in a small pond." He stopped suddenly.

"My father's death was the opportunity," she said.

"I'm sorry."

"It's all right. It *was* an opportunity for you." There was a pause, then she continued, slowly, "His death was also an opportunity for me." It made her sad to say the words out loud.

"You and I are very much alike," he said after a few moments of silence.

She reflected and then said, "How?"

"In so many ways. I'm an only child — my father died when I was twelve — and when the opportunity came to go to a good school in Dallas or stay in Lubbock, I chose Dallas even though I had to leave my mother alone. I didn't think twice about it. We really are called to develop ourselves to our fullest potential, and that includes taking advantage of the opportunities that are offered to us, even if it's not what others want. I went to Dallas even though it meant hardship for my mother. You need to go to Stanford even if it means it will be harder for your sister. So you see, you and I are not so different."

There was a long pause and then she said, "Maybe we are different."

"How do you think we're different?"

"I don't know. I don't understand how, but we are. Maybe

it's that you have faith in God and I seem to have lost it. At least you can say that your ambitions are part of His will. Maybe you thought you were following God's will when you left your mother alone. I won't be able to say that if I leave Mary. What can I say about my ambitions? Right now they seem so . . . selfish, so ugly."

"I'm like you, Kate. I'm groping in the dark when it comes to detecting God's will. Maybe there are people like your sister who see God's light. The rest of us live in darkness or in shadows, doing what we can. I give people hope through a body of scripture. But I have to be true to myself. I can't pretend I'm someone I'm not." She looked at him steadily. "Am I disappointing you?" he asked.

"No." She was not lying. *Disappointment* did not describe what she was feeling. *Emptiness*, a cold and new desolation, was more accurate.

"We should go inside," he said, looking around.

She opened the door to the car and stepped outside. She waited for him to come to the front of the car and then they climbed the three front steps to the apartment. He held the door open for her as she went in. She saw the bed, unmade, and next to it a nightstand full of books. Near the door was a beige sofa and an old-looking television set. At the far end of the apartment stood a small Formica table with two chairs, a stove, and a refrigerator.

"Can I get you some juice, soda, water?" he asked once he had closed and locked the door behind him.

"No, thanks." She took off her shoes and sat down on the sofa.

"Will you excuse me for a second?"

"No," she teased.

"I'll be right back."

She stretched her legs in front of her. She had a feeling of being in the wrong place, like an uninvited guest in a room full of people who had known each other since childhood. If they had come into the apartment as soon as they arrived, who knew what would have happened? But some new realization had taken place in the car that she couldn't quite put her finger on, some revelation about him and about her that made her feel ashamed. She had no words for it.

"Hi," he said, sitting next to her. He held her hand, his eyes fixed on hers, and then he reached over and gently turned her face toward him. Their kiss was soft and tentative at first and only gradually yielded to hunger. When she started to let go, he held her tighter against himself. There was something that held her back, she realized. Some uneasiness, some lack of trust that kept her from being totally absorbed in his embrace.

"This is probably not a good idea," she whispered when they finally caught their breath. "All that happened today. I'm not really thinking straight."

He sat up on the sofa. "I thought . . . I must have misunderstood . . ."

"You didn't misunderstand. I wanted to kiss you. I wanted to be kissed by you. I'm sorry."

He slapped both of his cheeks as if to wake up. "I'm the one that's sorry. What was I thinking? You were vulnerable and I took advantage of that."

"You didn't take that much advantage," she said, joking. "I held on to my virtue. Most of it."

"But I should have known better. You came to me for advice."

"And I gave you different signals. Besides, you did give me advice. I'm really glad we talked."

"Do you want to go home?"

She thought about it. "Can I rest here? It's almost morning, I think. Do you have a pillow? I really need tomorrow to get here."

He brought her a pillow and the bedcover from his own bed.

"Sweet dreams," he said.

"Good night, Andy. Thank you."

He turned off all the lights in the apartment and she heard him undress in the darkness. The air conditioner made a whirring sound and blew cold air directly on her feet. She lay down, covered herself, and listened to his movements across the room. He seemed as restless as she was. She could hear him turn one way in the bed and exhale and then turn the other way and do the same. The more he turned and tossed, the calmer she became. There was nothing to stop her from getting up, undressing, and sliding into bed next to him, flesh against flesh. She knew from their kiss that he would not reject her if she did.

She waited for him to fall asleep and then she sat up on the sofa. She sat very still, thinking, remembering, feeling. Images whirled inside her head: Andy telling her that he planned to stay only a couple of years with the Church of God. Mrs.

Alvarado playing the organ. Mr. Cisneros with his hand out-stretched. Andy's mother in a house all alone, watching television in a dark room. Then she suddenly turned into Mother, and Mother was telling her no one could keep her from her dream unless she let them. And why would she let them? "For love," said Mother. There was Father saying that love made all burdens light, and Simon appeared to ask her if she loved him. Kate had the sensation that she was falling into an endless, dark pit and there was nothing to hold on to. She thought she was alone in the darkness. But she wasn't. She heard a voice and it was Mary's, calling *Kate* . . .

Kate . . .

Kate.

Kate opened her eyes, surprised that she had fallen asleep. She sat up and willed herself to be fully awake. Around the edge of the curtain, there were streaks of rose and vermilion in the sky.

Mary would like those colors, she thought. Of all of Mary's paintings, the one Kate liked the most was her painting of the Sangre de Cristo Mountains, which she had done a few months before Mother's accident. The mountains were painted from the perspective of someone looking up as if about to start the climb. When she first saw the painting, Kate thought it captured life: We could either live in shadow or climb to the sun-filled summit. Now she remembered the different shades of white and gray and black that made up the shadows in the painting. It must have taken Mary hours and hours to capture the subtle interplay of light and dark. Kate's heart suddenly filled with love and pride. Her little sister! Mary's gift to create beauty was as important as Kate's powerful desire to be a doctor. Kate hadn't always honored that, she knew.

But what had Mary said about her painting earlier? *I always imagined love to be like what I felt for painting once* — comparing love to the tangled lights. But then she'd continued, *I haven't seen this light since Mama's accident. The lights I used to see in and around everything are not there anymore.* That was it. How painful it must be for Mary to be without light. How could it be that she hadn't seen the darkness that enveloped Mary? Now she remembered the times she would find Mary alone in their room, a blank piece of drawing paper in front of her, and all the trouble she'd mentioned having with her latest canvas. Even when Mary told her how she felt, she didn't listen. There she was, so consumed by her own ambition, her own dreams, that she had not noticed her sister's pain. Mary needed to see that light again, to shine her own light again. What would bring that joy in painting back for her?

In many ways, that ability to see the light in things and in people, that joy in painting came from Mother. But Mother was neither living nor dead, neither with them nor gone. Because they could not let her go, there was no opportunity to heal. And the need to care for her kept Mary from her painting. As long as Mother remained in a vegetative state, there would be no joy or light for Mary. Mother would not want that, Kate knew.

And Mother wanted Kate herself to go to Stanford. But it couldn't be that Stanford was more important than Mary. Her ambition must be different from Andy's. Dreams must yield to love. She had an irresistible urge to cry, and so she did, softly at first and then biting her arm so her sobs would not wake Andy.

When the tears ended, she felt exhausted. She swung her legs off the couch and cringed a little. The digital alarm clock blinked that it was 9:00 A.M. It was too late to make it home, jump in bed, and pretend that she'd spent the night there. All of her acts of carelessness came back to her. She'd left the letter from the insurance company in the bathroom. Mary would find it and worry that her absence was caused by desperation. She would no doubt call Bonnie and Simon. Kate needed to come up with a story — or she could just tell Mary what happened. And Aunt Julia? The last thing she felt like doing was lying. She was too tired to lie.

She stood up slowly and went to the bathroom, wet the soap, and then scrubbed her face and dried it. The towel smelled like him. If she walked to Alameda Avenue, she could catch a bus. She wanted to be gone by the time he woke up. She didn't want to talk to him this morning.

She put her shoes on. Then she stood up and checked the pocket of her jeans to see if she had money for the bus. *Oh, God, the church keys.* She had probably left them at the church. Anyone who saw the keys would recognize her father's key chain, with its medal of St. Christopher, the patron saint of drivers. He had the same key chain when he crashed and Mother . . .

Mother lost her life. Mother was not alive anymore. Mother would want Mary and her to live their lives. She needed to find the way for Mary and her to have their dreams, but it had to be done in a way that Mother would approve, with Mother's blessing. That was the understanding she needed to save above all else.

She decided she would worry about the keys some other day. They were probably in Andy's office and she could get them later. They would need to talk about last night sooner or later anyway. She didn't have any money, so she borrowed a dollar from his wallet. It was a brown wallet made of shiny leather. She dropped it on the floor and walked out of his apartment.

Aunt Julia was waiting by the door ready to pounce. "Where have you been? We've been worried sick!" she exclaimed.

Kate saw her backpack by the door where she had left it the night before. "Where's Mary?" she asked.

"She's in school, where else would she be? She waited for you, called your boyfriend, your friends. No one knew where you were."

"I was out with someone from work. We had a few drinks. I stayed with her."

"Who? What friend?"

"You're not my mother!" Kate said forcefully. Her anger had nothing to do with Aunt Julia except that Aunt Julia was there.

Aunt Julia took a step back, a shocked expression on her face. "Don't talk to me that way. I'm here to help you and you talk to me that way? I don't have to be here, you know."

"I'm sorry. I'm very tired." Kate reached out to touch Aunt Julia's hand.

"All I wanted to know was where you were. We were worried." Aunt Julia's voice quivered and her right eye twitched. She seemed suddenly very old and fragile.

"I'm sorry," Kate said again. "I'm tired. You saw the letter?"

"Yes."

"I was upset, that's all. I went out. I . . . I really need to go to the bathroom."

"Kate." Aunt Julia sat down. It didn't look like her shaking legs would hold her up. "I talked to Mary this morning. I don't think I can stay here any longer. I need to go back home. There are . . . things I need to do."

"Oh?" Kate said. At that moment, there was nothing anyone could say that could make her feel worse.

"I was going to leave at the end of the week."

"Whenever you think is right." She saw Aunt Julia's eyes redden. "Thank you for coming."

She walked into the bathroom, closed the door, and began to fill the tub with hot water. This state she was in, she was not going to let it last long. She would go out after the bath and hug Aunt Julia and apologize for her bad mood, and then she would go about trying to make things right for Mary. She undressed and eased herself into the cleansing water.

After her bath, she slipped into her blue terry-cloth bathrobe. It sounded like Aunt Julia was doing something with her things, like she was packing. Kate had a choice when she left the bathroom: to turn right and talk to Aunt Julia or turn left to her room. She turned left. It would be better to talk to Aunt Julia when she was dressed. She sat on the bed and then she lay down on it. She needed to close her eyes for just one minute. Only one minute to subdue the anger and sadness and whatever else was in there.

She woke up three hours later.

24

H i," Mary said when Kate opened her eyes. "Are you all right?" She was sitting on the edge of Kate's bed.

"Yes." Kate shook her head slightly. "Sorry to make you worry."

"I'm just glad you're okay."

Kate sat up on the bed and propped a pillow behind her back. Mary waited for her to speak. "I had a terrible night. First Simon and I broke up, and then I read the insurance letter. I . . . needed to go out," Kate said without looking at Mary.

"I told people that you probably stayed with Stephanie," Mary said.

"How's Aunt Julia doing?" Kate asked, changing the subject.

Mary bit her lips. "Aunt Julia left."

"She *left*?"

"She wrote a letter."

"What did she say?"

"She was leaving because she needed to get back to work. She said she would send us a little money now and then and come visit us as often as she could. She didn't write down the real reason."

"What's that?"

"She's very ill, Kate. She has cancer. She needed to go back to start the chemo treatments."

"She has what?"

"Breast cancer, I think she said."

"Oh, God!"

"It explains a lot," Mary said.

"Why didn't she tell us?"

"She didn't want to worry us with one more thing. She said she had trouble accepting it. Kate, I think that's why she didn't want to sleep in Mama's room. Mama reminded her that she was ill."

"And all along I thought she was just mean."

They were quiet. Mary was aware they were both silently asking the same question: *What are we going to do?* The question had plagued them since the first night Father died, only now it was louder and seemed to have fewer answers.

"There's still hope," Mary said. "Renata's mother talked to a social worker who said there are programs to help us. Maybe we can get someone to come in and watch Mama while we're in school."

"We'll work it out," Kate said. She seemed distracted.

"Kate, we can't do it alone." Mary could feel a newfound strength in her voice. "I think we should talk to the social worker."

"We need to figure out this week first."

"I already called Talita and Mrs. Guerney. Talita can come a couple of extra hours in the morning, and Mrs. Guerney can stay with Mama until I get home from school."

Kate tilted the alarm clock next to her bed. She didn't look to Mary like the usual focused Kate. The Kate in front of her seemed disoriented, like she had woken up from a long dream she could not shake off.

"I called the insurance company," Mary continued. "The lady who answered told me we could appeal the decision. She said we could write and ask them to explain their reasons for not giving us the insurance. We should write to them, Kate. Maybe they got it wrong. Papa made all those payments all those years. It just doesn't seem fair."

"You called them?" Kate seemed surprised at Mary's initiative.

"We can even go talk to them in person. They're right on Mesa Street. We can take the morning off from school tomorrow and go together."

Kate shook her head. "We'd be wasting our time. The medical records showed Father had a congenital heart defect. That means he had it since birth."

"But what if Papa never knew about it? If he didn't know about it, he didn't lie to the insurance company."

"Think about it. How could that be? All those years of going to the doctor. And why was he rejected by the army when he was young? He never told us."

"You make it sound as if he lied to us too."

"He knew, Mary. The heart condition was noted in Father's

records. How many years had Dr. Rulfo been seeing Father? Can you imagine Dr. Rulfo not telling him? Father went out and found a rinky-dink insurance company that didn't require a medical exam, and he bought a policy. Or maybe he got Dr. Rulfo to say there was nothing wrong with him. You know what great friends they were. What was Father thinking? Didn't he think the insurance company would check before they paid? He wasted all that money on insurance premiums that we could have used for other things."

"We should at least get the medical records from Dr. Rulfo. Suppose they show that Papa and Dr. Rulfo discovered the genital condition after Papa bought the insurance policy."

"Genital?" Kate laughed and then Mary followed. For a few moments they were two sisters again, laughing together. Then Kate stopped laughing.

"I don't know if there's anything more we can do."

Mary looked at Kate. "Why are you giving up so easily?"

"Mary, he didn't tell the truth when he filled out the application."

"We should take a look at the application. Suppose the insurance company is lying just so they don't have to pay."

"Okay, we'll write to them or go to their office on Mesa Street and talk to them," Kate said. She sounded exhausted. She started to lift herself out of the bed again, but Mary wasn't budging.

"What's going on with you anyway? Tell me. Are you worried about not going to Stanford?"

Kate looked as if she wanted to tell Mary something and then changed her mind. "I'm not worried," she said, looking away.

"You haven't given up on it, have you? When do you have to let them know?"

"May first."

"So there's still time. Maybe we can still convince Aunt Julia to let Mama and me live with her. It would be perfect, wouldn't it? You could go to Stanford and we would be close by. Aunt Julia needs us and we need her. Maybe when she's had time to think, she'll change her mind."

"You asked if you and Mother could go live with her?"

"She said no. But I made her promise that she would think about it. I don't think it was an it's-out-of-the-question no."

"You shouldn't have asked her."

"Why?"

"It's an incredible burden to ask of someone, especially someone with cancer. To take Mother on? And what about you? You'd be taking care of Mama and Aunt Julia both. You need to start thinking about yourself." Kate's eyes lingered on Mary. "We all need to start thinking about you."

"But Mama is her sister. Mama is her family. We're her family. People in a family carry burdens for each other. Besides, Mama's not much of a bother."

"Well, I'm glad she said no, for your sake. It would be too much for you."

"We need to find a place for me and Mama to stay so you can go to Stanford. They won't let me live alone with Mama."

"Who won't let you?"

"Social Services, I don't know who else. I'm underage. I don't know how it all works. That's why we need to talk to that social worker. Can we do that? Promise me we'll do that?"

"Mary, we need to talk. But not now. I want to make sure that what I say to you comes out right. Let me get up and get dressed."

Mary didn't move. "Kate." There was a pause. "I know who you were with last night. I went looking for you this morning. I saw Papa's keys were missing from his desk, so I thought you might have gone to church to . . . pray. I found the keys in his . . . in Reverend Soto's office." Kate stared at her as if waiting for Mary to get it all out. "I know it's none of my business, but . . ."

"Mary, don't. There's no need to bring this up right now." Kate's voice was almost a whisper.

"I care about you. I'm your sister."

"I know. But I'm all right. There's nothing really to talk about. Nothing happened."

"I don't think it's right for you to go out with him."

"I'm not going out with him. Trust me."

"I trust you, but . . ."

"Mary, thanks for telling me how you feel. I don't think you need to worry about it." There was exhaustion in Kate's voice.

"I'm your sister. I wouldn't be a good sister if I didn't tell you what I thought."

"I know, I know. I don't know what's come over me lately, but I'm all right now. I haven't been a good sister to you. I know. I promise you that's going to change. But now I have to get up. There are some things I need to do."

Later that afternoon, Mary was lying next to Mama, listening to Mexican soap operas on the radio. Kate was out in the hall making a telephone call. She heard the word *postpone* and she understood that Kate was calling the Stanford admissions office to postpone the deadline for accepting their offer. Mary saw the call as a good sign. It meant that Kate had not given up on her dream.

The next day, Renata persuaded her brother Jaime to drive them downtown to see the social worker. Jaime seemed happy to take them, probably because he was skipping school. Mary didn't want to get Renata into trouble, but she needed her help and she had no one else. Kate had said she had something else to do that day.

Jaime drove a truck that had an extended cab with cramped foldout seats. He insisted the girls sit back there. He was a big senior on campus, the star football player, and he didn't want anyone to see him with two insignificant sophomores. As they squashed next to each other with their knees to their chests, Renata wanted to talk about Kate.

"I still can't believe it about Stanford," Renata said. "She can attend UTEP right here, and she's making you do all this because she wants to go *away*? And you *want* her to go?"

The radio was so loud Mary could hardly hear Renata. She shouted, "I keep thinking of what it would be like for me if I couldn't paint. Going to Stanford is like that for Kate."

"It's not even close." Renata reached over and tapped Jaime on the shoulder. "Could you turn that down? We're trying to have a conversation back here."

Jaime turned it down a notch. "Don't push it," he said, "or I'll drop you right here in the middle of the street."

"You do that, and I'll tell Gracie you-know-what," Renata said. Gracie was Jaime's girlfriend. Now Mary understood why Jaime had agreed to drive them. "And don't listen, either. This is private."

"Like I care," Jaime responded.

Renata continued where she had left off. "She can go to college here and take premed and become a highfalutin doctor or whatever. It's not like she'd be giving up *that*."

"You should have seen her when she heard she was accepted. Going to Stanford and being a doctor are part of the same dream. I've never seen her so happy as when she got that letter."

"Yeah, well, we don't always get what we want. I'd like to get that hunk Marcos interested in me instead of you, but instead I'm going to prom with Lalo and his dumbo ears."

"Will you stop it with Marcos?" Mary elbowed her.

"Yeah, I know you. Little Miss Spiritual. I bet you'd like to paint *him*, wouldn't you? Maybe you can get him to model naked for you and you can invite me to the session."

"Who's getting naked?" Jaime asked, and Renata and Mary laughed.

The social worker's office was in a five-story building that looked like a cinder block with windows. Jaime dropped them off in front and told them he'd pick them up in an hour. Renata reminded him about Gracie.

They told the receptionist who they were, and soon the social worker, Mrs. Fresquez, came out to greet them. She led them up an elevator to the third floor and then through a maze of cubicles overflowing with different-colored folders. Mary got the impression that thousands of people were drowning with problems and there were only a couple of life jackets. The lone visitor's chair in Mrs. Fresquez's cubicle was full of black plastic binders. She put them on the floor and then went next door to borrow another chair.

Mrs. Fresquez was a heavy woman whose legs made a scratchy sound when she walked. Mary couldn't tell whether she was wearing a red wig or her own hair had been overly dyed. Every few seconds her tongue would come out and lick her upper lip. Renata and Mary looked at each other, and each knew what the other was thinking: *This was a big mistake.* There was no way this woman was capable of helping anyone.

But Mary soon realized her initial impression was wrong. As soon as they were all seated and Mrs. Fresquez had asked Renata about her mother, she turned and looked at Mary in a way that made her feel as if she were the only person who mattered in the whole world.

"Lucy told me about you. I'm very glad you came to see me. I heard about your dad. I'm sorry."

"Thank you."

"I know about your mother and I know you and your sister are all alone. You don't have any family?"

"We have an aunt in San Jose, California."

Mrs. Fresquez scribbled something on a pad of paper. "And your sister, how old is she?"

Mary had a feeling that she already knew everything she was asking, but needed to hear it from her. "She turned eighteen in February."

"You're sixteen, right?"

"Yes." Renata was looking around the cubicle with a bored look on her face. Mary saw her zero in on the picture on the desk. It showed a teenage boy next to a woman dressed in white. Mrs. Fresquez recognized the object of Renata's attention.

"That's my cousin Aurora and my son Albert. She's a nurse in Las Cruces. He's a good-looking boy, huh?" She smiled at Renata.

"Nice," Renata answered. "How come Mom never told me about him?"

"She probably wanted to protect him." Mrs. Fresquez winked at Mary.

"Ha-ha," Renata muttered.

Mrs. Fresquez grinned and then got serious. "Tell me in your own words," she said, looking at Mary, "how I can help you."

Mary told her about the deacons asking them to leave, about the insurance money falling through, about Aunt Julia's cancer and her not wanting to stay with them or have Mary and Mama live with her. She hesitated to tell her about Kate wanting to go to Stanford because she didn't want to lump that in with all the bad things, but Renata poked her in the arm and told her to tell Mrs. Fresquez everything.

"My sister got accepted to Stanford. She really wants to go there."

Mrs. Fresquez sat back in her chair and seemed to be trying not to look surprised. "She's going to go?"

"Yes. I want her to go too." Renata frowned, and Mrs. Fresquez rubbed her forehead with her hand as if she had just been presented with a puzzle she couldn't solve. But then she snapped her head upright, and Mary saw that she knew exactly what needed to be done.

"Okay. Let's look at what we have here. The best option is for you and your mama to live with your aunt, but I understand why that's not possible at this moment. The second-best option is for you and your sister to stay here in El Paso. I think I would be able to get you into affordable housing, get help for your mom and money and food stamps for you to live on. We'd have to make your sister your legal guardian, but that's not hard. If your sister goes away, we would need to get you a guardian appointed. If we can't find anyone, I could be your guardian." Mary smiled at the prospect of having Mrs. Fresquez be her guardian. She'd be a kind of earthly guardian angel — though never in a million years would she have imagined her guardian angel to look like Mrs. Fresquez. The social worker went on, "You say your sister wants to go away to college, so let's assume we don't have that second option. Where does that leave us? I think we'd have to place you in a foster home and find a facility for your mother."

Mary let the words sink as far as they would go. *Foster home. Facility.*

"She could come live with us," Renata said. "We could be her foster family, couldn't we?"

Mary asked nervously, "What kind of facility?"

"It would have to be a nursing home or a facility that accepts people in a vegetative state. Finding one wouldn't be easy. Probably a home with a religious affiliation. Those are the only ones that take someone in her . . . condition."

Mary was having difficulty understanding what was being said. It was like being on the verge of remembering a dream. "Why?" she asked.

"Pardon?"

"Why would some facilities not want to take Mama?"

Mrs. Fresquez attempted to inhale deeply. This time she put her hand on her chest. Maybe all of the problems she listened to and all the painful news she had to convey had broken her heart, and now she had trouble breathing. "Well, most hospitals and facilities don't take people like your mom, people being kept alive through a feeding tube." She hesitated. "They feel they need to save their space and resources for people for whom there is still hope of living."

"Mama's still alive. Maybe someday she'll wake up. We don't know for sure that she won't."

Mrs. Fresquez nodded and put her hand up, signaling there was no need to discuss the issue. "If we go with the foster care option, I will find you a place that takes your mama."

It was the first time since Papa died that Mary heard anyone outside her family call her mother "mama." It made her feel that Mrs. Fresquez really cared.

"Honestly, Mary, you can come live with us," Renata said again. "My mom and dad would love it. It's only Jaime and me at home right now and Jaime is joining the army this summer. You can even set up a studio outside, next to Dad's carpentry shop."

Renata had an enormous, shady backyard full of flowering trees, and for a moment Mary imagined herself sitting back there painting. But then she thought of Mama. After the accident, Mama had stayed in the hospital until the doctors declared she was in a persistent vegetative state. Then she was taken to a kind of nursing home where she stayed until Papa was allowed to bring her home. Mary remembered visiting her in the nursing home. Mama was in a room with four other people. Sometimes the halls were lined with stretchers because all the rooms were full. Mama developed bedsores because no one moved her, and rashes because no one changed her diaper. It was almost as if they were trying to let her die.

"I can't leave Mama alone," Mary said. Renata parted her lips, and Mary could almost hear her start to say that maybe Mama could come and live with her family as well, but then Renata stopped herself. Mary wished she could somehow let her know that it was all right, that no matter how much she thought Mama was no bother, she understood it was beyond anyone else's ability to take her on.

"Why don't you think about all the options we discussed?" Mrs. Fresquez said. "We can talk more later. In the meantime, let's see what we can do."

Mrs. Fresquez filled out some forms with financial information. She promised to try to find a way to pay Talita and get someone to watch Mamá while Mary and Kate finished the school year. Then she said that she would personally contact the insurance company and ask to see all the records used in the denial of the claim. "Don't worry," she said, "I'll take one of our lawyers. One of the reasons these small companies don't require medical exams is so they can later claim the least little thing was a misrepresentation. I know one company tried to deny benefits because the insured didn't inform them she'd had her wisdom teeth pulled! Don't worry, we'll get something out of them. We'll at least get back all the premiums your dad paid. You can count on that."

Mary liked the way she sounded. She had a lot of fight in her, just like Kate.

Jaime was late. Renata and Mary sat outside on a concrete bench next to a group of smokers huddled around a metal ashtray. Renata was unusually quiet. "What are you thinking?" Mary asked her.

Renata made this little pucker expression that she liked to do whenever something was bothering her. "I was thinking that you're up you-know-what without a paddle."

"I'm between a rock and a hard place," Mary added, trying to get her to smile.

"Out of the frying pan into the fire," Renata said.

"I'm not sure that one applies."

"Whatever." Renata took a deep breath and coughed. "You ever smoked?"

"What do you think?"

"I smoked a couple of my dad's Salems once. I thought the menthol would taste good. Yuck! Maybe smoking helps people with their worries, and that's why so many smoke."

"You think I should take up smoking?"

"You got a load of worries, girl. What the heck is keeping Jaime? I bet you he went to some bar to play pool. Let's go sit over there." She pointed to another bench farther away from the smokers. They escaped the fumes, but now they were directly in the sun. Renata lifted her hand to shield her eyes. "You've got to talk to Kate. She needs to stay here with you. You got no choice."

"There's always a choice," Mary said.

Jaime's truck turned the corner. They stood up at the same time. "Whatcha going to do?" Renata asked.

"I don't know."

As they climbed into the truck, Mary tried to remember the last time she painted. For a moment she wondered if she would ever do it again. She had told Renata her wanting to paint was like Kate wanting to go to Stanford, but it was not a good comparison. She didn't want to paint. She felt empty. Blank. The world was as drab as the building they had just left. Then she remembered that hidden in the drabness, buried in its midst, there were sparks of light, like Mrs. Fresquez. It wasn't much to go on, but it was something.

25

That same morning, Kate couldn't sleep, so she left the house before Mary woke up. She wrote a note to let Mary know she had gone to school early. She had two hours before her first class, so she decided to walk the three miles to school.

Kate walked to the football field and sat on the top rung of the aluminum bleachers, leaning back against the railing. She took out the book that she needed to read for her English class — *Madame Bovary* by Gustave Flaubert. It was about a woman who, bored with married life, decides to be unfaithful to her husband. She read a few pages and then stopped. When she first started the novel, she had empathized with Madame Bovary: Her domestic life was oppressive. But today she felt annoyed with her. There was something selfish and self-indulgent about the character that she had never seen before. Kate flipped to the end of the book to see how it would end. That and what she had already read would be enough to answer any essay question that might come up in an exam.

She closed her eyes and massaged her temples. Even as she felt more certain about what they should do for her mother, another stream of memories, thoughts, and images had kept her up all night. There was Mary, her mother, the insurance, Aunt Julia. And there was Andy. A voice inside told her that what he said in the pulpit and his ambition were at odds, contradictory. But she couldn't exactly say how. He had spoken about truth, and he had been truthful in confessing his ambition to her. But accepting and confessing her own ambition would not set her free to pursue it. Her ambition had been good. It was just that there were goods more important than her ambition. *Jesus's love is sacrifice*, he had also said.

Students began to arrive around seven. At seven thirty she walked to the parking lot. Classes started at eight, and though Bonnie usually arrived about five minutes before class started, Kate wanted to be there just in case she happened to arrive early. Simon also had an eight o'clock class. What would she say to him if she saw him? Did she have any regrets about the breakup? With Simon she hadn't felt what she thought was love. With Andy she had felt something, but it wasn't what she anticipated love to feel like. She anticipated love to be both wanting and safety, Andy and Simon rolled into one, but in Andy she had found only Andy.

"Bonnie!" she yelled as soon as she saw Bonnie step out of her car. Bonnie saw her but continued walking. Kate hurried to catch up to her. "Bonnie, what's the matter?"

"I have to finish my homework," Bonnie said brusquely.

"Stop." Kate grabbed her arm, but Bonnie shook her loose. "What's wrong?"

"What's wrong? You don't know what's wrong?"

"No."

Bonnie put her backpack on the ground and turned to face her. She spoke with the anger of a bad actor. "You disappear God knows where and you don't even call. You don't care if people are worried about you. You break up with Simon and don't even tell me. Best friends don't do that, Kate."

"I'm sorry, Bonnie. I couldn't call you, honestly. There's so much going on in my life right now, I wouldn't even know where to begin."

"You know what? I don't care. What you did to Simon is so unfair I can't even believe it. And I'm not talking about where or who you spent the night with. You don't have that many *girl* friends that you can spend the night with, Kate."

"After Simon and I broke up, I found out that we weren't getting any insurance money. I called Stephanie, you know, she works with me, and I went to her house. I stayed over with her." Kate spoke calmly, her eyes fixed on a silver gum wrapper balled up at her feet.

Bonnie laughed. "You actually expect me to believe that? Don't you think Simon already asked Stephanie? And guess what Stephanie said. God, I don't care what you do. You can literally do whatever. You're a mean person, Kate. You don't care about Simon and never did, obviously. And I was never your true friend because you never trusted me."

"That's not true. I told you about Stanford. I didn't tell anyone else."

"Well, big doo-dah! When have you ever told me how you *felt*? When have you ever shared with me? You think you're so above us poor peons with your grades and fancy colleges and all. People like me and Simon are nobody to you. You needed a boyfriend and you needed a girl friend for I don't know what, so you wouldn't be called a geek, I don't know."

"That's not true," Kate objected weakly.

"Whatever. I don't have time for this. Shit! I have exactly fifteen minutes to finish a paper." She picked up her backpack and strutted away.

Kate stood motionless until she saw Bonnie enter the school. *What was that all about?* Bonnie's reaction did not seem proportionate to — what? What had she done to Bonnie? Bonnie was mad because of the way she treated Simon. But that showed more loyalty to Simon than to her.

She forced herself to slip her backpack on her shoulder and then began to walk. It felt as if the backpack weighed a thousand pounds. Maybe what bothered Bonnie was not the way Kate had treated Simon, but the way she had treated Bonnie all along. She hadn't come to Bonnie this morning to share how she was feeling with her best friend. She had come to get a ride from Bonnie, to use her. Bonnie was right. When had she ever shared her feelings with her, or with anyone, for that matter? And how ashamed she felt that she had lied again about where she spent the night. She walked quickly out of the parking lot. She didn't want to run into Simon.

It took her two buses to get to the law offices of Ernesto Ortega. He was the only lawyer she knew. He had come to the Red Sombrero a year before to talk with Simon's father and had given her his card. "Call me if you ever need anything," he told her. He seemed professional and he didn't flirt like all the other men who gave her cards, which she threw in the garbage as soon as they left. She had kept his card, and now she wondered what had made her think back then that someday she would need a lawyer.

She took the elevator to the third floor of his building and found his office at the end of the hall. There was a black plaque with his name in golden letters next to the door. When she opened the door, she saw an elegant-looking woman behind a large cherrywood table that served as a desk. The only items on the desk were the flat-screen monitor of a computer and a cream-colored telephone. Kate stepped in timidly and closed the door behind her. She felt out of place in the lush space with its burgundy carpet and leather chairs.

"Can I help you?" the woman behind the desk asked, looking up slowly from the screen. She sounded annoyed by the interruption.

Kate moved closer to the desk. She wished she'd left the backpack someplace. It made her look like a schoolgirl. "I came to see Mr. Ortega," she said.

"Do you have an appointment?"

"No." There was nothing apologetic in Kate's voice. She stood firm and unwavering.

"Your name, please."

"Kate Romero."

The woman began to type on a keyboard hidden beneath the desktop. "The purpose of your visit?" She didn't take her eyes from the computer.

"It's personal," Kate responded. She was almost grateful for the woman's rudeness. It was stirring up her gumption.

"Just a second," the woman said. She rose from her chair and disappeared through the door behind her desk.

"Have a seat," she ordered when she came out. "Mr. Ortega will try to squeeze you in after a conference call."

Kate sank into the soft leather of the sofa. Six magazines were carefully fanned across the coffee table in front of her, and she was tempted to take one, but she decided instead to gather her thoughts and think about what she was going to say. She rested for a few moments in the conviction that she was not there to take any action or make any decision. She would get the information she needed and then act when it was best for Mary.

She expected the wait to be hours, but ten minutes after she sat down, the door opened and Mr. Ortega emerged. He wore a blue long-sleeved shirt with a white collar and gold cuff links the size of quarters. Kate immediately thought that she could not afford someone like him.

He squinted at her, trying to remember who she was. Then his face lit up. "The Red Sombrero."

Kate stood up, nodded, and shook his outstretched hand. "Come in, come in," he said. He was as friendly and welcoming as the receptionist had been rude and inhospitable. She was tempted to stick her tongue out at her as they passed her desk.

Kate sat down in a red leather chair in front of a spotless glass desk. Mr. Ortega sat down in a matching chair, except his had a high back. He reclined in it now, smiling at her, and folded his hands across his chest. "What brings you here?" His voice was inviting.

She started from the beginning: the accident, her mother's condition, Mary, her father's death, Aunt Julia, the money the church was giving them, the need to move out of their house, the lack of insurance. She even told him about Stanford. The only part she left out was Andy, the push that set her moving toward where she was.

After she finished speaking, she waited for him to ask again why she was there — *So what do you want from me?* or something to that effect. She tried to swallow, but there was no saliva. She was all dried up. He walked over to a credenza, filled a glass with water from a silver pitcher, and handed it to her. She drank. He leaned on the edge of the desk.

"So tell me, how can I help you?"

It's what's best for Mary, so she can see the light, so her own light will shine. Those were the words she had been repeating to herself. "I wanted to find out what steps would need to be taken in order to end my mother's life support."

There was no expression on his face. He walked around the desk and sat on his chair. "You've given this a lot of thought."

"Yes, but right now I'm only looking for information."

"You've talked about this with someone else, someone you trust?"

"The minister at my church," she said. Was that a lie? She trusted him, didn't she?

"And doctors have determined that her condition is permanent."

"It's been over two years. Even before my father brought her home, the doctors told him that taking her off life support was considered ethical. I remember how angry he got at them. I think that's why he wanted her home. He was convinced they would let her die in the hospital or a nursing home, since they already thought it was okay for her to die."

"You disagree with your father."

She wasn't sure that was a question. "There were MRIs and CAT scans done on her brain. There's no evidence of consciousness. The only parts of her brain that work are the parts that control the involuntary impulses. I've read tons of studies on the persistent vegetative state. After one year, it is extremely rare for a person to regain consciousness. After two years, I guess you can say it's almost impossible."

She could feel him studying her. Then he said, "What you are considering will be very emotional, very stressful. I want to make sure you've thought this through. I'm not judging you here, I just want to make sure you're ready. It's important that you can articulate the reasons behind your decision, if that's the way you decide to go. So why do you think this is the right thing to do?"

"My sister —"

"Let's start with you."

She deliberated for a few moments. It was so difficult to explain, especially to a stranger. She hoped she would be understood. "My father was a minister, as I mentioned, and we grew up studying the Bible. One of my favorite passages is where Jesus says that He has come to bring life to us and bring it abundantly. I think Mama would agree with Jesus's message.

She was so full of life. She got up in the morning happy, ready for what the day would bring. She'd turn on the radio in the kitchen first thing as she went about making breakfast. There would always be this happy Mexican music playing. She'd keep the music on until Papa came in and then she turned it off. But as soon as he got up from the table, she'd turn the radio on again, and all day long, she would sing as she made the beds and did all the chores around the house. If she wasn't singing, she'd be humming."

She looked at him to see if he was getting impatient with her explanation, but he was not.

"I know that if Mama could speak, she would ask us to not let her live the way she's living. She wouldn't think it was a life worth living. I think Mama would like me to go to Stanford. I know she would. And my sister, Mary, has this wonderful gift for painting. For her to live life abundantly means to paint. But she can't paint like she's able to — she can't express her gift fully while Mama is in the state she's in. Mary needs to be able to pursue her dream. She can't do it and take care of Mama at the same time." Kate stopped suddenly. She felt a peace she hadn't felt in a long time.

"What about your sister? You said she's sixteen, right?" His phone rang. "Excuse me." He picked it up and said, "Hold my calls, please." He was taking her seriously, she realized. "How does she feel about this? Does she agree with you?"

"I'm pretty sure she would be opposed."

"I see." A look of concern came over his face.

"My minister says that without my sister's consent, this will be hard."

"It could be." He tilted his chair forward. He had the air of someone who had obtained all the information he needed to act. "How was your father allowed to bring your mother home?"

"Dr. Rulfo, our family doctor, said that he would take care of her when the hospitals wouldn't do it anymore."

"This Dr. Rulfo takes care of your mother now?"

"He comes every week to check on her. There's really not that much to be done. A nurse changes her nutrition and hydration bag daily. Mary and I clean her, massage her legs, comb her hair, change her diaper. Mary even listens to the radio with her."

"Well, the first thing we need to do is talk to Dr. Rulfo. If he agrees with you and refuses to give your mother further treatment, things will go a lot easier. We'll have to petition the court to make you your sister's legal guardian, or if not you, someone who agrees that the course you want to take is also what's best for her. It sounds like you think it is."

"Yes," she said with conviction. "This is what is best for her." *Thank God*, she said to herself. Thank God for the certainty that this was best for Mary. Maybe there had to be a God just to have someone to thank.

Mr. Ortega continued, "We'd need to go to court to petition for the termination of your mother's life support. I would recommend moving fast, especially if you and your sister disagree. You don't want this to drag on. It could get ugly."

Ugly. She was not prepared to think of what could happen between her and Mary as ugly. Hard, maybe. But ugly? There was nothing ugly about Mary, and here Kate was, about to force her into ugliness. She needed to find a way that wasn't ugly. "How long will it take?" she asked.

"I don't think you can go to Stanford this fall and do this at the same time," he said.

"I'm not worried about Stanford. I've already called them to postpone my entrance for a year. I'm worried about my sister. I want to give her time to . . ."

"You want time to convince your sister?" He finished the sentence for her.

It wasn't time to convince Mary that Kate needed. Mary might never be convinced. She needed time for something more important. "I don't want this to tear us apart. I need to make sure we're not torn apart."

He nodded. "I understand. On the other hand, the sooner we do this, the sooner the healing process between you and your sister can start. It'll take a while, if you're lucky. I've seen brothers and sisters who never manage to reconcile over something like this."

I am doing this for you, Mary, Kate said in her mind. *I'll wait until you understand that and believe it in your heart. I'll take courses at UTEP and then after that, I'll go to Stanford and you can come with me.*

Mr. Ortega was speaking. "I can't guarantee how long this will take. It's a little bit of an unusual situation, your mother being at home, so I'll need to do some research on how best to handle this. I would recommend moving ahead on the legal aspect of it. You can always postpone the actual removal of the feeding tube until you're ready. How have you been paying for your mother's care? I take it your father's medical insurance stopped paying a long time ago."

"We've been paying out of Father's salary. It's expensive."

"Well, you certainly can't afford to pay for those services now." He stood up, and Kate stood up as well. "I'll get going on this. Oh, I'm going to need a five-thousand-dollar retainer from you before I can start working on your case. You can mail me the check, or better yet, drop it off with Linda up front."

"How does a retainer work?" She felt stupid asking, but given the scarcity of funds, she needed to know.

"The retainer is money you give me up front. It means I'm your lawyer. If we spend less, I'll give the rest back to you. If more is needed, I'll ask you for more."

"How much more?" She panicked for a moment as she tried to do the math in her head. They had thirteen thousand dollars, more or less, from what the church gave them and from Father's savings account. There was Father's pension, which was around forty thousand according to what Mr. Lucas had told Mary. How long could they live on that? Not for very long, if the medical bills and legal fees were too high.

"It depends. Five thousand will cover filing the papers and a couple of routine court appearances. Let's start with that." He touched her shoulder as they walked. "I know you have limited funds. I'll keep the costs down. If there are no unanticipated problems, we'll come in around ten thousand or close to it." Once they reached the door, he told Linda to give her the client information sheet. "Give me a call in a couple of days and let me know how you made out with your sister."

"Wait," she said. "I'm not going to make any decisions today. I need time."

"You're not sure about your mother?" he asked pointedly.

"She's not just *my* mother. I need time. I need to talk to my sister and I'm sure she'll need time to take it all in."

"I see."

"Please, I don't want to start this process before I feel she's ready."

"Why don't you go ahead and fill out the form. That way, if you make a decision for me to proceed, you can just call." Then he turned around and marched back into his office.

She took the form from Linda and went to the sofa to fill it out. When she got to the place on the form that asked for immediate family, she wrote down only *Mary Romero (sister).*

26

Mary was in the toolshed, covering her paintings with burlap to protect them from moisture. She held the half-finished painting of the irises before her and couldn't imagine ever finishing it. At that moment, she couldn't see herself painting again.

She and Kate had hardly spoken since their last conversation, the afternoon after she went missing. Even when Mary told Kate about her visit with Mrs. Fresquez, Kate had listened quietly but not said anything. Kate didn't seem angry; she seemed preoccupied. If only Kate would tell her what was worrying her.

Just then she heard Renata's voice. Mary came out of the shed and there she was, with Marcos beside her.

"Look what the cat dragged in," Renata said, proud of herself.

Mary walked toward them. As she got closer, she saw Marcos's face. There were bruises under both his eyes the color and shape of small eggplants, and his lip looked like it was torn in half. "What happened to you?"

"Is a long story."

"He says that it's a long story," Renata interpreted.

"Is Sadurday, 'member?" He took out the sketch of the eagles that he had shown them in the cafeteria.

"I'm sorry. I can't go. I have to take care of my mother." Kate had gone out grocery shopping with Mr. Cisneros, the old gentleman who used to drive Papa around.

"That's why I'm here," Renata piped up. "I can watch your mother while you take a look at this wall."

"I don't think that's a good —"

"Mary!" Renata shot Mary her best *Don't be stupid* expression.

"I vut a sea beld in ma ca," Marcos said.

"He says he put a seat belt in his car. Would you please go now? Go!"

"Eee only dake a secon."

"He says —"

"I know what he said. It's not going to take a second. It will take about an hour. The community center is way over in Socorro. And how did he get you to help him?"

"I vent and god her."

"I couldn't say no to him," Renata said, pretending to flirt. She opened the gate and began to push Mary toward Marcos's car.

"Talita's number is on the wall by the telephone in case something happens," Mary said as she walked. "Kate should be back soon."

"All right already!" Renata shouted.

They drove a block before Mary asked him, "How did you know about my mother?"

"I ast awond about yu."

"Why?"

His eyes were nearly closed and his lip was puffed up, but Mary saw him smile. As far as he was concerned, it was a question that didn't need to be answered.

"What happened to you anyway? Can you see? Are you sure you can drive?" She pulled on the newly installed seat belt to make sure it was tight. "You're doing community service for some crime you committed and you're still getting into fights?"

"I ad to."

"You had to? Here we go again with the I-had-tos."

He gripped the steering wheel with both hands and only nodded. The rest of the trip they drove in silence. It was painful for him to talk, and she didn't feel like asking any questions out loud. Inside she was swarming with them. Why was she with him? She saw his busted face back at the house and still she got into the car with him. Why did she feel he was a good person when all over his face there was evidence that he was bad?

He parked the car directly in front of the community center. She never imagined the wall to be so wide and long. It was going to take him a year of Saturdays to complete. They stepped out of the car and stood in front of the wall. "It's huge," she couldn't help saying.

He made a gesture with his hand as if to say it was no big deal. Then he opened the door to the backseat of the car and took out a large sheet of architectural drawing paper. He signaled for her to follow him to a picnic table, where he unfolded the paper and secured it with bricks and rocks.

She stood back, amazed. The two eagles he had sketched initially now flew inside two circles that overlapped. In the overlap, he had drawn two shaking hands. The perspective of the eagles' outstretched wings was perfect. One was light brown with a white crest and the other was all brown, but both had golden beaks. The circles themselves were blue, but yellow and orange and pink beams shot from their circumferences like bursting sun rays.

"Vat you sink?"

"First you'll need to paint the wall white," Mary said, trying to keep herself from showing admiration.

"Yeah, den?"

"Then you'll have to move what's here to there." She pointed first to the piece of paper and then to the wall.

"Ow?"

"You'll need to draw it on the wall with a thick pencil. First you'll have to locate where the eagles go by putting markers on the wall. Like for this tip of the wing, you draw a spot; for the curve of the wing, you put another spot. Then you connect the dots. You'll need to measure carefully to make sure everything is centered. It's like hanging a picture."

"You elp me."

"No way."

"Vie not?"

"I can't, that's all."

Just then a man came out of the building. "Hey, Marcos!"

he called out. He came over and shook Marcos's hand and waited for Marcos to introduce her, but Marcos suddenly seemed flustered.

"I'm Mary," she said. The man held out his hand and Mary shook it.

"Mary, nice to meet you. I'm Raul Canuto, the director here." He turned to Marcos. "We have that money so you can buy the supplies. Why don't you go in and get it from Betty?"

Marcos limped away. Mary hadn't noticed the limp before. She wondered whether it was from the time he jumped over the fence into her yard.

"So how do you know Marcos?" Mr. Canuto asked.

Mary hesitated and then said, "From school. We met in art studio." It was sort of true.

"You're going to help with the mural?"

"I don't know."

"He could use your help," Mr. Canuto said.

"I can't." Mary said. She thought of Mama and Kate and all that was ahead of her.

"You want to help him but you can't, or you don't want to help him, so you can't?"

It took her a few seconds to understand the difference. She felt herself blushing. She hadn't painted an eagle since . . . since she painted that eagle for Papa.

"You know how he got beat up?" he asked.

"He said he had to get in a fight."

"Yes. That's more or less right. He had to. Only it wasn't a fight. It was a beating. He had to get beat up before he can get out of his gang. Did he tell you he was trying to get out?"

She remembered his first visit to her backyard. "Yes," she answered.

"He's a good kid. He just needs a second chance."

She wanted to tell him that whatever Marcos needed, it wasn't her, but she couldn't. A strange pang of joy kept her from speaking.

Marcos came out with a white envelope in his hand. Mr. Canuto patted him on his shoulder, looked at Mary as if they had just agreed on something, and went back inside.

Marcos stood back to take in the whole wall. Mary could see he was imagining how the mural would look when it was finished. She walked over to stand beside him. The wall was so blank, so open, so ready to be painted. She said, "If you do all the preliminary work, I suppose I could come now and then to make sure you're getting the detail work right."

"Eally? Oo would do dat?"

"Yeah, I suppose."

"Mister Canuto is gonna pay me even dough he doesn ave to. Oo can ave aff of vat I get."

"Half? My part is worth more than that," she said, pretending to be serious.

"Aff and aff," he said firmly.

He offered his hand to seal the deal, and after a moment of deliberation, she took it.

27

Kate needed to talk to Simon and to Andy. She decided to start with Simon. She waited for him by his car after school on Monday and watched him emerge from the building, Bonnie by his side. As soon as they saw her, Simon whispered something to Bonnie and she disappeared back into school.

Simon approached her, a serious look on his face. But she knew him well enough to know he was not angry. It was the kind of focused look he put on when he did the books after the restaurant closed.

"Thank you for letting me talk to you alone," Kate said, looking in Bonnie's direction.

"No problem," Simon said.

She leaned on the hood of his car. "Simon, I owe you an apology."

"Forget it," he said. He didn't sound bitter. He sounded more as if he wished to avoid any discussion of their breakup.

"I don't know what happened."

"You were being honest."

She smiled at him. He was a kind, kind person. "Actually, I need to apologize for my behavior way before that night. I've been a jerk."

"A jerk? How?" He opened the back door of the car and threw his backpack inside.

"It's taken me a while and I still don't have it all figured it out, but I actually don't think I was honest with you —"

"Oh, Jesus! So now you're going to tell me that you never felt anything for me. Is that what you want to get off your chest? Please, I don't need you to be *that* honest right now."

She stopped. Maybe he was right. Maybe what she was doing was more for her own sake. "You're right, you're right," she said quickly. "I don't want to unload my own guilt on you for what I did." She paused and then decided to continue. "But I think you need to know that I took you for granted, that I never appreciated you the way you should be appreciated. You have a good heart, and I didn't deserve you."

He looked at her as if assessing her sincerity and then he offered her his handkerchief. She dabbed her eyes. She hadn't come to cry in front of him.

"That's twice I've seen you cry," he said.

"I wasn't supposed to cry."

"You didn't come here to make up, did you?"

She shook her head. "You'll be happier with someone like Bonnie, trust me."

"So what exactly did we have these past two years? We were friends who made out . . . occasionally?"

She knew he was partly trying to be funny, but she considered only the serious side of what he said. "We were very good friends."

"Being very good friends is not so bad, you know. My mom and dad are very good friends. I think that if you marry your very best friend, you're starting out pretty much where you want to end up. That other stuff, the romance, disappears after a while. That's what everybody says, anyway. We're comfortable with each other, we respect each other. If you wanted to go to Stanford, I wouldn't have stood in your way."

"Simon . . ." She lowered her eyes. "You're a good person."

"But . . ."

"The other night, the morning everyone was looking for me, I ended up spending a very sleepless night thinking about you, among other things. The one thing you need to know is that I *liked* being with you. That wasn't pretend. There may have been reasons I was with you besides the fact that I liked spending time with you, but those other reasons don't take away the fact that I liked spending time with you. Does that make sense?"

"Can I ask you something? Something that's none of my business?"

She knew what he was going to ask. "Sure."

"Where were you that morning we couldn't find you?"

She reached out and touched his arm. "You broke up with me that night, remember?"

"So you *were* with another guy."

"Nothing happened," she said to him. "Trust me."

"It doesn't matter." She detected sadness in his voice. They turned to see Bonnie coming out the front door of the school. Apparently, she had decided that she'd given them enough time.

"I would like it to matter," Kate said. "The next few months will be hard for me and Mary. We could use a friend. And . . . I could use my job back. I'm the best waitress you have. You're not going to fire the most dependable employee you have just because you broke up with her. You're too good a manager to let that happen." She wasn't asking. She was telling him, reminding him.

He tilted his head backward and smiled. "We'll see," he said. "I guess you better go now."

"Do you think Bonnie will ever talk to me again?" she asked.

"Give her time. I'll make sure she comes around," he said.

Andy was sitting at his desk, staring out the window. She looked at him for a few moments before knocking, and in those moments he reminded her of her father. He too used to look blankly ahead as if waiting for the Holy Spirit to drop the right word into his sermon. Andy turned around and sprang to his feet as soon as he heard the knock. "Kate!" he exclaimed.

"Do you have a minute?"

"Yes, come in." He closed the door behind her. She sat on the edge of the sofa and he pulled his desk chair around to sit in front of her. "How've you been? I didn't see you in church yesterday." She could tell he was at a loss as to how to proceed. He hadn't called since the night they spent together. She had told herself she didn't care, but still, the courteous thing would have been to call. Simon would have called.

"I've been more or less okay." She waited.

"I'm sorry I haven't called. You left so . . . abruptly. I wasn't sure . . ."

She waved him off. "I went to see a lawyer last week."

"Oh." It took him a few seconds to understand. "About your mother? You're going to go through with it?"

"Not immediately. When the time is right."

"You're sure about this?"

"I'm sure." She paused. "I have a theological question for you. Is guilt a sign that what we are doing is wrong?"

"That's a difficult one." He shifted in his chair.

"My head tells me that I'm doing the right thing, but my heart is full of guilt."

"Guilt about what?"

"Guilt that I'm ending my mother's existence on earth, that I'm taking away whatever possibility of life she has, however remote. Guilt that I'll be hurting Mary so much. I haven't done anything yet, and I can already tell that I'll feel bad for a long time, maybe forever." She turned to look at the bookcase, which was now filled with his books. "What do your books tell you about guilt?"

"The thing is, sometimes we feel guilt when we shouldn't, and sometimes what we call guilt is simply the pain that comes from doing what's right, even if it hurts others. I'm not sure you'll ever stop feeling that pain in what lies ahead for you. It doesn't matter what you call it. It's going to hurt. . . . But you're smiling. What are you thinking about?"

"Talking about guilt reminded me of the other night at your apartment. Did I make a fool of myself?"

"No, why do you say that?"

"Agreeing to go to your place." She blushed.

"Kate, I'm just as responsible for that as you are. I'm only human, and you are very attractive, as you know."

"I'm grateful that we talked, I really am," Kate said. "I stayed awake after you went to sleep and among many other things, I kept replaying in my mind my mother's words when she took me to Stanford four years ago. She said that God wanted me to be as smart as I could be, to hold nothing back, to become a good doctor so I could help others. And then she said no one should keep me from my dream unless I let them. And I asked her, 'Why would I let them?' and she answered, 'Because you love them.' It's funny that I never focused on the fact that dreams could be abandoned or postponed because of love."

"I think it takes a certain kind of love to make our dreams come true," he said.

"My mother's words reminded me of your sermon, remember? You said that to love is to deny yourself, to put others first. Then I thought about your ambition, about how you wanted to be the pastor of a big church in a rich community."

"And you think there's something wrong with that?"

"It's just that I saw myself in your ambition. At one point I wanted to go to Stanford and be a doctor and I had good reasons for wanting that, but then I lost sight of other good things in my life . . . like Mary. Wanting to go to Stanford is fine, but there are things that are more important. That night, I saw I had lost track of those other things." She looked into his eyes steadily, seriously.

"And you think I have too?" he asked defensively.

She ignored his tone and she went on, "When you told me that you wanted a bigger church, I thought of Father and all the sacrifices he made for his little church. He loved this church. Day by day he picked up his cross and carried it. I thought of all the people who serve the church in their own small way, like Mrs. Alvarado and her electric organ. They deserve a pastor who is committed to them."

"Just because I want to eventually move on, doesn't mean I'm not committed to doing a good job while I'm here."

"I don't mean to judge. I'm doing it, I know, but I don't mean to. What was it that you said in your sermon? 'The truth of love, the truth of sacrifice will set you free.' All I'm trying to say is that love and sacrifice are more important than my ambition."

"You think I don't love or sacrifice?"

She ignored him again. "The one thing that became really clear that night is that there was no way that Mother would want me to leave Mary behind. Dreams need to take into account the present, the circumstances that are handed to us, the people who are given to us to love. So my dream has to include her somehow." She smiled. "I miss the faith that Mary has. You know, Mary's faith is simple and pure. Maybe if I spend more time with her, that faith will come to me."

"So . . ." He looked as if he was wondering what it was she wanted from him or why she had come to see him.

"I could use your help. The church's help as well."

She saw him exhale. "Tell me how I can help you."

"I need you to tell the deacons that Mary and I need more time. We can't move by June first."

"Pardon?"

"We can't move just yet. I don't know when, but it won't be June first."

She saw him cross his right leg first and then his left. "Surely I need to give them a date."

"Tell them I'm willing to pay some reasonable rent, but we need to be in our home for at least a few more months."

"A few more months?" he stammered.

"The church owes that to my father, to my mother, to Mary and me."

They stared at each other for a few seconds and then he smiled. "You're a tough negotiator."

"Please, I need your help with this. It's for Mary. She'll have a better chance at understanding what needs to be done if she doesn't have to worry about moving. If we decide to let Mother go, it would be better if we were all at home."

"Okay," he said, "I think that's reasonable. I can talk to the deacons and let them know we agreed to an extension."

Kate closed her eyes and said a silent thank-you. It was the closest she had come to praying in a very long time.

28

Renata called Mary to tell her she had talked to her mother, and her mother was one hundred percent all right with being Mary's guardian and having Mary live with them. Mary could stay with Renata until Jaime moved out and then she could use his room. Mary told her that she needed to think about it, but she knew that moving in with Renata meant putting Mama in a facility, and she couldn't do that.

After she hung up, Mary went to lie down on Papa's bed. She turned on her side to look at Mama. Sometimes, when Mama had her eyes closed, she looked so peaceful. Mary wished she could feel that peace. What she wanted most of all was to talk to Kate, just talk to her. She wanted Kate to be her older sister, to hold her hand in these hard times. She missed her.

She heard Kate come in, and got up from Papa's bed. Kate was in their bedroom changing her clothes.

"How are you?" Kate asked. There was a concerned tone in her voice.

"How are *you*?" Mary responded.

Kate put on a pair of gray sweatpants and a white T-shirt. "We need to talk." She had the same look Papa used to have whenever he had bad news.

"Okay," Mary said, scared. She started to sit on her bed.

"Not here. Let's go outside."

That worried Mary even more. The only people who ever talked outside were Papa and Kate.

They sat on the wooden chairs. Mary noticed the climbing roses on the chain-link fence. The vines had woven themselves in and out of each link, becoming a permanent part of the fence.

Kate turned her chair toward Mary. "I've been thinking a lot about what you told me the other day, about how you don't enjoy painting anymore." Her words came out slowly, one at a time, like the last, tired drops of a rainstorm. "I should have noticed it before, but ever since Mother . . . became ill, you're different. It's as if the happy, joyful Mary that you were disappeared."

"Oh." It was true, Mary thought. She was different since Mama's accident.

"Remember that time when I sat just about where you're sitting now, and you painted my portrait?"

"Yes. . . ."

"There was something in you then that is no longer there. I can't describe it. The best I can do is to use the same word that you use — *light*. There was a light in you that has gone dark. You yourself said to me how the lights you used to see in and around you were not there anymore. Do you remember telling me that?"

"Yes." Mary was glad that Kate remembered.

"I've never been able to see the light in people, but I *felt* it in you once, and now I don't. When Mama was well I used to see that light in her eyes as well."

"Kate, you're worrying me. What are you trying to tell me?"

"I think that your light and Mama's light are connected somehow, that when hers went dark, so did yours."

"So . . ." Mary's voice trembled.

"So we need to make sure you get that joy back. We need to let your light shine again."

"But how?"

"That light of yours, that joy of yours, came from Mama, but now it must come from you. You need to find it inside of you. That will only happen if you stop grieving for Mama. Right now it's as if you see her die every day. Your grief is with you always. Mary, we need to do what Mama would want us to do."

"Kate . . ."

"She would want us to let her go."

"No!" Mary managed to say. It felt as if somebody had gripped her throat.

"Mary, just hear me out. It's the only way for your light to return, the only way you'll be able to paint again, the only way you'll be the person you're supposed to be."

Mary's heart thumped so loud she could hear it. "No, it's not possible." She began to stand.

Kate stood first, put her hands on Mary's shoulders, and gently pushed her back into the chair. "Think of what Mother would want. She would want us to live our lives, wouldn't she? She's gone, Mary. She needs to be with Father in heaven."

Mary shook her head. "Do you even believe in heaven?"

"It's what Father believed, what Mother believed when she was alive. It's what you believe."

"She's still alive."

"No, she isn't. Not really. Not the way she's supposed to be alive."

"I can feel her love and I give love to her. That's being alive."

"Mary, if she were alive, she'd be aware of the love she gives us and the love we give her."

"Do you really want to go away to Stanford so bad that you're willing to do this?" Mary meant to hurt Kate.

"It's not about that. Yes, I've been ambitious and selfish, but it's different now. *I'm* different now. I've called Stanford and they agreed to postpone my admission for a year. I'm staying here. I'll take courses at UTEP while we work this out. All I'm asking is that you think about this, pray about it. I went to see a lawyer last week to get some information about the process of letting Mother go, but we're not making any decisions until you've had time to think about this. Promise me you'll think about it."

"There's nothing to think about," Mary said softly. She could not imagine a life without Mama in it.

Kate turned to look at the roses. She spoke very quietly, almost in a whisper. "Letting go of her is not going to be easy for either one of us. We both love her so much. But I know she wants us to grow, and we won't be able to grow with her in the state she's in. Right now all our energies, our resources, our hopes go to Mama. But she would want all our energy and resources and hopes to go toward our dreams, the same dreams she had for us. I'm doing this for us, for you, so you can paint again. So you can paint with all your heart and soul like you used to. You're too young to be carrying so many burdens."

What Kate said was true, Mary knew. Her painting had not been the same since Mama's accident, and now there was no painting at all. But she put away that thought and said, "What if I never agree with you?"

"I have faith that with time you will see it's the right decision. There's time. I'll go to Stanford next year, or the year after that. I'm not going anyplace. But letting Mother go is still the right thing to do."

"I can't let go of her," Mary sobbed.

Kate reached over to hold Mary's hands. "Listen to me. I'm bringing this up now because it is something we need to confront. We have time. We can stay in this house. I've talked to Reverend Soto. He agreed."

"It's him, isn't it? This was his idea. He put this in your head," Mary said, shaking her hands loose. "You like him. You're going out with him."

"Yes, I've talked with him. But this is something that I feel is right because it is, not because anyone says it is. And no, there's nothing between us. Even though he's not as bad as you think he is."

Mary spoke between sobs. "Mrs. Fresquez said she could help me, help us. She'll find a place for Mama in a facility. We don't need to let Mama go."

"Putting Mama in a facility will not make things any better." Kate began to cry too. After a while, she said, "Look at us."

"I didn't know you could cry," Mary said sarcastically.

"It's all right, Mary," Kate said. "It's okay to be angry. I'll wait until your anger goes away."

"We're not going to make it, living together," Mary said. She wiped her eyes with the sleeve of her blouse, while Kate lifted the bottom of her T-shirt to her eyes. "You should go live someplace else. Mama and I will manage."

"I'm not going anywhere."

"We're not going to be sisters anymore."

"Yes, we are."

Mary let herself fall back on the chair. Kate tried to take Mary's hand again, but Mary moved it away. There was something new in Kate, a softness that she had never seen before. It was a strange softness that was hard to describe — a softness that would not budge.

"Mary, even though this is hard for us, I know it's the right thing to do. I know it's right to start talking about this. I can't fully explain it. It's like a voice, like Mother's voice, telling me it's okay."

Mary was struck by the fact that Kate *felt* it was the right thing to do, that she heard a voice like Mother's telling her it was okay. She had never heard Kate speak that way before.

After a long time, Mary said, "I'm moving in with Mama. I'll sleep in Papa's bed." She realized that she sounded like a six-year-old, but she didn't care.

"Okay. I'll help you pack," Kate said.

Mary could see that she was trying not to smile. "It's not funny."

Kate shook her head. "I know it's not funny. It's just that, here we are, just the two of us. We're all we have. All this time I've been dreaming of going to Stanford, and now it doesn't seem all that important. I don't want to go there without you. I'm even going to be lonely when you move to Mama's room."

"Why do you want to do this, then?"

"I'm doing it for you, for us. Sooner or later, you'll believe me."

"It's Mama who keeps us together."

"No, it's us that keeps us together, what we do for each other. Our memories of Mother will keep us together, the living Mother we carry inside of us."

"Your problem is that you lost hope. You don't believe in miracles, but miracles happen. Mama could wake up again."

Kate sighed. "Oh, Mary. Maybe I don't believe in miracles as much as you do, but I do have hope. I hope you and I can stay close. I hope I can be the doctor I'm supposed to be. I hope you can continue to paint. I've been trying to look for God's will in all of this, the way you or Father would look for it, and all I can see is that God's will is for the living. God wants us to live. He wants to give us abundant life. He wants to give us light and He wants us to be a light unto others."

Mary shook her head. "The God I know is a god of love and kindness and He loves Mother as much as He loves you or me."

Kate and Mary were silent. Mary listened to Kate's breathing and noticed that the rhythm of each inhalation and exhalation matched her own.

Then, after a while, Kate spoke, her voice trembling. "Remember when Father died or was dying and you didn't call 9-1-1? You said you wanted his soul to leave quietly. You said that's what Father would have wanted. I don't understand. You were willing to let Father's soul go without interference, but you aren't willing to do the same for Mother."

Mary pondered Kate's words. The two situations seemed different, but she couldn't express exactly how. Maybe they weren't different. She needed time to figure it out.

"When Father died you said you saw a light disappear. You said it was his soul. Remember?

Mary nodded.

"What about Mother? Have you seen a light in her since the accident?"

Mary was silent. A small branch fell from the willow tree. She picked it up and caressed its baby green leaves. She felt drained. She wanted to lie down someplace and sleep for a few days. She got up slowly.

"Mary . . ." Kate started to say.

"I need to be alone," Mary said.

"Will you think about this, Mary? Just promise me you'll think about it."

Mary walked away without answering.

29

Kate watched Mary quietly open the gate and walk in the direction of the church. Knowing Mary, she was probably looking for a place to pray, to be alone, in the quiet of the sanctuary.

Kate was about to go inside when she saw that the door to the toolshed stood open slightly. As she went to close it, she noticed Mary's paintings inside. She stepped in, leaving the door open.

The first painting she saw was the unfinished painting of the two irises. She remembered Van Gogh's painting from art history class. It was amazing how close Mary had come to capturing the violet hues, the incandescent light of the Van Gogh. She put the painting to one side and looked at the rest. She was so startled by the last one in the stack that she almost dropped it. It was her portrait, the one that Mary painted before Mama's accident. Her long, dark brown hair flowed over her shoulders; her eyes sparkled with intelligence and kindness. She was glad the eyes in the portrait reflected kindness, for it meant that Mary had seen that in her once. Mary always spoke about the light she saw in others. *There*, Kate thought. *Now I can see the light in me as well.*

She put her portrait back in its place, closed up the shed, and went back inside the house. She wished Father was around. The only decision she or Mary needed to make when he was alive was whether to obey willingly or unwillingly. Now the world seemed to be made of one choice after another, and each choice involved the suffering of someone, somewhere. She remembered Father's words that last morning. *Love makes everything that is heavy light.* Was he wrong? So far, love seemed to be making everything that was heavy heavier. Either that or there was no love in what she was doing.

She entered Mother's room and saw her sleeping peacefully, her eyes closed. Kate lifted the sheet that covered her and lay down next to her. Tears came to her eyes with the realization that what she felt was love, what she was doing was for love and because of love. There was so much love in her and it was uncontainable. She held Mother's hand and let her love flow through.

30

She was about a block from the church when she heard the car honk.

"Hey, Mary!" It was Marcos. "You need a ride?"

"No, thank you." She rubbed her eyes, trying to hide the fact that she was crying. Marcos pulled into the church lot and ran back to her.

"What's the matter? Why are you crying?"

"I'm not crying," she said, turning away from him.

"Yes, you are. Look at you."

She turned back toward him, and the sight of his cut and bruised face only made her feel worse. She buried her face in her hands, sobbing. He reached out for her gently and put his arm around her shoulders. "What's going on? Did someone do something to you? Tell me. I'll beat them up." He was trying to be funny.

"Leave me alone," she said. She shook his arm off.

"I can't leave you alone. I'm going to stay with you. I can

stay without talking, but that's the best I can do." She sniffed. He offered her his red bandanna. "It's clean, honest."

She wiped her eyes and unconsciously blew her nose. She giggled despite herself when she realized what she had done. "I'll wash it for you."

"Yeah, you better. When do you think you'll have it clean? I'll come pick it up."

She wadded the bandanna in her hand. "What are you doing around here anyway?"

"I came looking for you. But first you have to tell me why you were crying."

"I can't." They started walking.

"Well, at least tell me where we're going?"

"I was going to church. I don't know where you're going."

"Okay, I'll go with you."

"Have you ever even stepped in a church?"

"Not actually stepped in. Not lately, anyway. But I take my *jefita* and my sisters to church every Sunday. I wait for them by the park and then pick them up." They stopped in front of the church. "It's closed," he said.

"It stays open until ten P.M. At least it used to when my father was alive. He kept it open in case people wanted to go in and pray."

"Something happened to you that's serious. Tell me."

"It's private."

"Okay. I'll leave you alone," he said reluctantly. "But I wanted to tell you something."

"What?"

"They let me out of the gang. Well, almost. I have to go through a couple more things. Nothing major."

"More beatings?"

"It's just stuff. Nothing I can't handle. And I painted the wall white yesterday. It took only four hours. Do you want to come with me tomorrow and take a look at it? We can start putting up those dots you talked about. You know, the ones we need to connect to make the drawing."

"I don't know if I can help you anymore," she said.

"Let me go inside with you," he said. "I promise I won't say a word. You need to be with someone right now even though you don't realize it. Honest. I can tell."

She wanted to go inside the church to think, to consider all that Kate had said about Mama. Yet there was something about having him next to her that was good, that was needed. He was keeping her from thoughts she couldn't face.

She shrugged and said, "The church is open to all."

The sanctuary was dark and cool except for the evening sunlight coming in through the windows. They sat next to each other in the same place where she and Kate always sat. At first she was conscious that he was sitting next to her, their shoulders almost touching, but then she noticed that she could forget about him if she wanted to.

He seemed to be absorbed in something other than her. Then she saw him take a pencil from his pocket and begin to doodle on the back of the weekly pledge envelope. She watched him for a while and then she spoke.

"What are you making?"

"Oh, nothing really. I like to draw when I'm quiet. It helps me think."

"I do that too." She smiled.

There was silence.

"Was it your mother? Were you crying about your mother?"

"Yes," she said, looking away from him.

"Tell me."

She hesitated. Then she spoke, her eyes fixed on the altar. "My sister thinks we should let her go."

"Let her go?"

"Disconnect her from her feeding tube."

"And you disagree?"

"I don't know what to think." She looked at the cross in the altar.

A ray of sunlight entered through one of the windows. The only sound was the sound of their breathing.

He cleared his throat. "My father was an alcoholic. He died a couple of years ago. His liver was in bad shape. He was also a heavy smoker, so he had emphysema as well. There toward the end, he was home with an oxygen tank. There was really nothing they could do for him at the hospital. You know what he used to ask me whenever he saw me?" She shook her head. "He wanted me to give him some tequila. He used to tell me where he had a bottle hidden in the house. He would beg me for a drink. 'I'm dying,' he'd tell me. 'What difference does it make?'"

"And what did you do?"

"I gave him the tequila. I'd wait until my mother wasn't around and I'd give him a sip. That's all he wanted, a sip now and then. It made him peaceful, just tasting it." Marcos began to doodle on the envelope again. Mary watched. Then he spoke softly. "After about a month of being at home, he died. He and I never got along too well before that. He was mean when he was drunk. He was mean to all of us. I thought I hated him for the way he was with my mother and my sisters. But we got close that last month. Those little sips of tequila that I gave him brought us together. He apologized to me for all his meanness.

"I don't know why I'm telling you all this, except that you telling me about your mother reminded me of him, of that last month of his life. There toward the end, he was ready to go. It was like he lived long enough for us to grow close, and once we were, he felt he could die in peace. I watched him die. He was at peace."

Mary reached over and took the pencil and the envelope from his hand and for a second their eyes met. Underneath where he had drawn what looked like a rose, she began to draw an iris. It felt good to draw again.

She had been wrong about him. Yes, he had been in a gang, but his heart was good. He liked her, she knew, and she was proud of that. She looked inside herself and saw that she liked him too.

Was there light in Mama now? *Have you seen a light in her?* Kate had asked. She hadn't seen it. Even when Mama was in the hospital right after the accident, there had been no light in her. Was Kate then right about Mama? Perhaps she couldn't see Mama's light because it was already gone. A deep sadness came over her at the thought.

Kate was right about her inability to enjoy painting since Mama's illness. But the sadness she was feeling now felt different from what Kate had called her grieving — this was more like what she had felt at Papa's death. She had let Papa's soul depart in peace. Maybe Mama wanted to make sure she and Kate loved each other. Kate seemed different now, more like a sister. That's what Mama would want.

Mary rested in Marcos's presence, in the thought of Mrs. Fresquez and Renata, in knowing she was not alone. And in the midst of that comfort she found a seed of peace. She leaned slightly to her left and her shoulder touched Marcos's shoulder.

Mary began to draw a second iris. Kate was full of feeling toward life, toward the future. It was the way Mary once felt about her painting: an openness, a freedom, the kind of hope she sometimes felt in front of a blank canvas, where everything was possibility. They both wanted to do something with their lives. They both wanted to give. They were sisters. They were their father's daughters. They were their mother's daughters. She was of the same kind as Kate. How close to her she felt just now, now of all times. They were alike and they were different, like the two irises she had just drawn.

She sat like that, next to Marcos, bathed in the quiet of the church until the sun went down.

"I better go home," she said.

Marcos took the drawing of the irises. "It's beautiful," he said.

"Thank you," she answered. She started to get up.

"Can I walk you home?"

She sat down again. It took a long time for her to answer.

"Okay," she said, and then, after a pause, "I want you to meet my sister."

EPILOGUE

Mary sat on a canvas chair, the easel in front of her. She was painting the lemon tree behind Aunt Julia's house. It had rained earlier in the day and the air was cool. The door opened and Kate stepped out.

"Wow! You're almost done," she said.

"Almost." Mary continued painting.

"Can I join you?" Kate asked.

"Sure," Mary answered. Kate brought a green patio chair and sat down next to her.

Sound came from Aunt Julia's bedroom. "Aunt Julia likes to nap with the television on," Kate said.

Mary smiled. "She falls asleep with it at night also."

A yellow finch perched on one of the branches of the lemon tree. Mary and Kate were silent. The finch twisted its head to look at them and then flew away. "It's nice out here, isn't it?" Kate said.

"It reminds me of our yard back home."

"Do you miss El Paso?"

"I miss Renata and . . ."

"Marcos." Kate completed Mary's sentence. Mary blushed and smiled all at once. "Is he still coming to visit?"

"I was waiting to see how Aunt Julia's checkup turned out. He wants to come for Thanksgiving. He'll only stay for two days."

"I'm sure Aunt Julia will be okay with that. You and I can sleep together and he can have the other guest room. Now that I'm more settled in school, I'm going to try to come on weekends."

"You don't have to. I'm sure you have lots of studying to do."

"But I can study here just as easily as I can in my dorm or in the library."

"Aunt Julia's TV doesn't bother you?"

"No, I like a little background noise."

Kate watched Mary paint for a few minutes, then she took a deep breath. She spoke slowly, deliberately. "Today is the anniversary of Mother's death."

Mary put her paintbrush and palette down and stared at her feet. "I know," she said.

"Are you okay?"

There was a pause and then Mary answered. "I'm okay."

Kate leaned forward and took her sister's hand. "This is not the right word, but I'm grateful to you. I don't think I would have gone through with it if you had been against it."

Mary pulled her hand gently away and placed it on her lap. "I'm at peace with everything. It took a long time for me to get to that place, but I did. Thank you for waiting, for giving me that time."

"Sometimes I look at you and you seem so sad."

"I miss Mama. I miss Papa too. I don't feel guilty or have doubts, but I do miss them."

"I miss them too." Kate tucked her hands under her legs.

"Are you okay?" Mary's voice was kind. "You seem worried. Do you have doubts?"

"Not doubts, exactly, but all kinds of images run through my mind. Maybe Mother suffered when we disconnected her from her feeding tube. Maybe, in her own way, she felt hunger and thirst. I guess it's normal to have those thoughts."

"Dr. Rulfo did all he could to make sure Mama wouldn't suffer. He said she didn't. Kate, Mama's in heaven with Papa. I believe she's alive right now in a way she wasn't before. I am certain about it. Aren't you?"

"My faith is not as strong as yours. It never has been."

"Maybe you have faith and you don't even know it. You want to make something good of yourself, you want to be useful. That takes faith. You told me once that it was Mama's dream that you go to Stanford. And now you're going there and you're doing it for Mama. Aren't you?"

"Yes."

"Well, that's faith. You believe she's watching you, and you believe she's with you now, even if you don't say it out loud like I do."

Kate shook her head. "How did you get so smart all of a sudden?"

"What do you mean, all of a sudden?"

They smiled.

"I think I hear Aunt Julia snoring," Kate said. "I better go cover her up. You coming?"

"I'll be right in," Mary said. "I want to work a little longer."

Mary picked up the brush. She gazed at the tree and waited. Then she saw a soft light shine among the leaves. And she painted.

ACKNOWLEDGMENTS

I want to thank my faithful agent, Faye Bender, for all her help throughout these long years. I am grateful to Anna Stork for sharing with me her valuable insights into the minds of young women. Most of all, I am indebted to my editor, Cheryl B. Klein. This is a book that came into being thanks to her loving attention.

ABOUT THE AUTHOR

Francisco X. Stork is the author of five novels, including *Marcelo in the Real World*, which received five starred reviews and the Schneider Family Book Award for Teens, and *The Last Summer of the Death Warriors*, which won ALAN's Amelia Elizabeth Walden Award. He was born in Monterrey, Mexico, and spent his teenage years in El Paso, Texas, where *Irises* is set. He now lives near Boston, Massachusetts, with his wife. Please visit his website at www.franciscostork.com.

THIS BOOK WAS EDITED

BY CHERYL KLEIN

AND DESIGNED BY

CHRISTOPHER STENGEL.

THE TEXT WAS SET IN HOEFLER,

A TYPEFACE DESIGNED BY JONATHAN

HOEFLER IN 1991.

THE BOOK WAS PRINTED AND BOUND AT

R. R. DONNELLEY IN CRAWFORDSVILLE,

INDIANA. THE PRODUCTION WAS SUPERVISED

BY CHERYL WEISMAN. THE MANUFACTURING

WAS SUPERVISED BY ADAM CRUZ.